Albrecht Drue, ghostpuncher.

PAUL D. MILLER

MONTAG

First Montag Press E-Book and Paperback Original Edition January 2021

Copyright © 2021 by Paul D. Miller

As the writer and creator of this story, Paul D. Miller asserts the right to be identified as the author of this book.

Montag Press ISBN: 978-1-940233-86-4
Design © 2020 Amit Dey

Montag Press Team:

Edited: Charlie Franco
Cover: Victor Leza

A Montag Press Book
www.montagpress.com
Montag Press
777 Morton Street, Unit B
San Francisco CA 94129 USA

Montag Press, the burning book with the hatchet cover, the skewed word mark and the portrayal of the long-suffering fireman mascot are trademarks of Montag Press.

Printed & Digitally Originated in the United States of America
10 9 8 7 6 5 4 3 2 1

This book is a work of fiction. Names, characters, places, and incidents are either products of the author's vivid and sometimes disturbing imagination or are used fictitiously without any regards with possible parallel realities. Any resemblance to actual persons, living or dead, events, or locales is entirely coincidental.

Paul D. Miller's *Albrecht Drue, ghostpuncher.*

This spectral, time traversing adventure sucked me in with the wallop of a barroom rabbit punch. In the tradition of John Kennedy Toole and Iceberg Slim, Paul Miller is a keen observer of human nature, in all of its frailty, hilarity, and horror. *Albrecht Drue, ghost puncher.* is a tour de force of dark wit, chock-full of exquisitely macabre imagery that will be with me for many days to come. I can still smell the stale beer and ectoplasm.

—Brian Jacobson,
author of *The Truth About the Moon and the Stars*

If you like plenty of grit in your lit or enjoy excursions into the underotherworld a la *Sin City, Scary Movie,* or *Shaun of the Dead,* you'll love this streetwise tour through Bitburg, full of paranormal shenanigans and boozy brawling.

That said, Paul Miller's writing hits constant high notes of observation and satiric comment that had me laughing out loud.

In *ghostpuncher.* Bukowski meets Bachman. All in all, a fine debut and I look forward to Al's next adventures.

—Pete Peru,
author of *The Reeking Hegs*

When Albrecht Drue finds himself squaring off with the ghost of Silky Cobra, a pimp who was murdered by Junk Mama in the sleazy 1970s, it's hard to not have a rousing good time rooting for Al, who's just another alcoholic trying to find his way in the world after a series of misfortunes. Paul Miller's characters crackle in this satirical supernatural whisky soaked romp. You'll want to hoist one with ghost hunting groups, the Bitburg Supernatural Squad, the TV sensation Ghost Quest, to say nothing of Lilith, Charlene, and the denizens of The Cyclops. Miller's sly prose winks as it wends. From the 17th-century witch hunts to modern times, *Albrecht Drue, ghostpuncher.* delivers action, laughs, with a big boozy grin.

—SS Whitaker,
author of *Mulch*

Paul Miller's *Albrecht Drue, ghostpuncher.* reads like the best kind of pulp. It pulls you in and hits you with paranormal visions with a technicolor punch. From colonial witch hunts to 70's pimps to the dark bars of today, the visions of this story never cease to wonder, and Al, as the washed-up boxer with a heart of gold, is a winning hero for this nightmare tale.

—Gabriel Boyer,
author of *Devil, Everywhere I Look.*

Albrecht Drue, a charming lowlife, foul-mouthed and heavily inebriated, takes us on a wild ride, taking down ghouls, demons, and dead pimps with his signature ghost punch. Ghost punching specters back to hell between benders isn't easy, except if you're Albrecht Drue. No ordinary lowlife, his fists do the talking as he uncovers the mystery behind the haunting of Cardinal's Crest. A bizarro must read!

—James Bodden,
Author of *The Red Light Princess*

Paul Miller has managed to create a saga so drenched in beautiful filth and visceral savagery that the laughs come from a place of fantastic, surreal fatalism -- or just the gallows. A fever-dream of violence and visceral humanity, written masterfully and with an incomparable wit. Macabre, funny, poetic, uncompromising.

—Nicholas Morine,
Author of *Punish the Wicked, Cavern,
Kowloon Walled City 1984,
Fantasy from the Rock,* and *Arcade Rat*

This work is dedicated to Babylon Amadeus Miller, who gave me a reason to stick around long enough to see it published, and to Harmoni deMae Miller, who made me want to.

Framing Device One:Pip

New England, Seventeen-Seventy-Something

Rain like lustful lips fell on the fire, hissing a sizzling scream of flaccid futility ...

Or it would have if some kind of grandeur-deluded teenager were telling this story, but they're not, so conjure yourself a vision of rain coming down like a frat-boy's piss on a fresh snowbank. As in hard, and as ubiquitous as beginning a scary story on a stormy night.

However, the effects of that dangerously cliché weather on the fire were far less immediate than a steaming yellow "Chet" engraved on a luminous sheet of frozen precipitation, since the blaze They'd set wasn't going to be quenched by anything this side of a monsoon, which is something for which New England has never been famous. Now, the "They" in question were the fine folk of a little hamlet that would one day be a major port, then a bustling rail hub, then a *Quiet City* far too given to looking the other way when shit got weird. Whatever it would eventually become, the place had started this particular night as a church-choked Colonial outpost called Bitburg, and whether you know the name or not, it's kept that name and its head down for longer than there've been states to unite around it. For exposition's sake, the reason They'd set the house on fire was that they were damn sick of its resident dandy slaughtering their leadership with the same discretion a fat man shows at an all-you-can-eat buffet, and they figured lighting him on fire would be the most efficacious way of getting him to stop.

Pitchforks gleaming, voices raised in a common chorus of hateful yet tastefully Puritan epithets, torches flickering in defiance of the autumn rain, the Bitburgers had rushed from the public house with one intent: To fuck a mother up.

If they were being honest, after they'd all sodden down a few pints of a lager they hadn't known was brewed with ergot-infested wheat, they'd basically forgotten exactly why they were out to kill Lord Hagenbotham but were fairly sure their cause was a just one.

Regardless of their cause's justness, They were highly liquored up and irate, and when a mob goes to the trouble of convening in the face of spitefully inclement weather, arming itself with farming implements and flaming brands, and getting mother-*fucking*-up shithoused, there's really very little recourse but to follow the momentum until something big is on fire and someone 'bad' is dead. So, like ants up the pantleg of a jungle explorer, they scurried up the side of Fallfallow Hill, aiming their hazy retribution at Cardinal's Crest, which, up until they got there, had been known as one of the finest homes in the New World.

As a fortress, Cardinal's Crest should have been impregnable. Its high walls grew straight from the sides of the tallest hill in the colony, with its back to a sheer cliff and its gates creating a perfect chokepoint on the lone approachable slope. Jarrod Hagenbotham had chosen the site where he built his motte-and-bailey for pre-cisely that reason, and the towers he'd erected two hundred years ago had given him vantage over the entire valley. The additional fortifications his scions had built over the subsequent decades saw the woods recede and the town spring up like sawgrass amidst the bones of the righteously murdered savages who'd had the temerity to live on land attractive to an Englishman. Named for the native avian life, as well as the crimson stone and blood-lacquered timbers of its construction, Cardinal's Crest remains a fine example of Colonial-era fortification, and the Bitburgers should have presented no more trouble than a bunch of drunks banging on a whorehouse door in the middle of the night.

They probably should have asked themselves why the cur-rent Lord Hagenbotham had left the gates wide open, and why he'd set out a number of rather convivial copper braziers replete with cozy fires. The grounds between the massive keep and the smaller homeplace were almost welcoming, as if the horde had been cheerfully expected. Accepting that reasonable, thinking-shit-out mobs are as rare as a New England monsoon, though, it's easy to forgive them for the failure.

As the point man for the mob-- a rabble-rousing acciden-tal ergot farmer called Goodman Ed Lemire-- staggered into the unnaturally cheery enclosure, his buzz mildly abated by the long wet slog up Fallfallow hill, he alone got a distinct impres-sion that something wasn't quite right.

"Summink ain't quite right," he was heard to have said to the oaf beside him.

Oaf may be a harsh word, but Goodman James Thistlewillow shod horses for a living, wrestled burly men and noncey bears for sport, and never understood anything his wife read to him. He was generally well-liked around town, but for all intents and purposes, all of them magnified by the iron-headed maul balanced on his shoulder, he was a fucking oaf.

"Right enough, oi?" said the oaf. With more and more of their Goodfellows joining them, yet so far not committing a single act of arson or anything remotely akin to pillaging, Goodman James looked to Goodman Ed for direction. "Meanin' likes, we're gonna burn this place out and kill the devil-man inside, and all his screaming demon hordes and all, oi?"

That reminded Goodman Ed of something.

"That reminds me of something," he said, holding up his pitchfork for the mob to halt. "Where's that bloody Witchfinder, anyway?"

"Here," said a man from the rear of the mob, most of whose constituents were either wobbling around in a loose pack vaguely focused on Goodman Ed or chasing hallucinatory bobwozzles around the, again, uncharacteristically inviting courtyard. This was obviously the Witchfinder, even if you couldn't see the elaborate gold-and-brass collar emblazoned with whatever the Latin for *Witchfinder* is or the relic-festooned cloak draped over his shoulders. The sword in his hand and the sneer on his face just screamed "religious zealot," while the jutting van dyke beard said, "won't be fashionable again until cronuts are a thing."

One of the drunks slipped in the mud beside him, and well-honed reflexes brought the Witchfinder's blade to bear on him with the kind of speed a viper or a feening crackhead would have envied. Goodman Ed winced, not being accustomed to the sight of unnecessary eviscerations, or even necessary ones. Yet the Witchfinder's command over the saber was so complete that, with a single braking snap, he not only saved the clumsy yokel from impalement but sheathed the shining weapon on his hip.

"I am here," he said again, affecting a much larger presence than his size granted him. He had the attention of the mob and meant to use it. The truth was Goodman Ed wasn't alone in his assessment of the stage on which they played. The Witchfinder didn't like that Lord Hagenbotham seemed to expect them, liked even less that the Lord of Cardinal's Crest seemed the opposite of bothered by the incursion. "Our quarry is indeed inside. His presence tears at my very soul! Be not fooled by the calmness of the eve, for in calmness hides calamity! We must draw the monster from its lair!"

"Not much for calamity, meself," Goodman Ed said to the oaf, then nodded towards a convenient bale of straw. Aside from the braziers, the whole courtyard seemed to suffer from an overabundance of inflammables, from the huddled shacks where the workers of Cardinal's Crest plied their trades to the many barrels of pitch that cluttered up the place. "Let's just set about the creation of general misfortune or disaster in this place of unlikely pleasance."

"Right then," said the oaf, who, lacking a torch, swung his maul at a handy bit of statuary, sundering it in a shower of stone shrapnel.

With a sweep of his arm, Goodman Ed set the mob about its business. Off they shot in all directions, none of them farther from something he could burn than a few staggering steps.

The Witchfinder drew his sword, ready for his moment. The truth was he'd never actually had to fight a witch before. Seven years in the colony and most of the witches he'd found were old women who barely struggled when he tied them to the pyre. Of the nine Bitburg women he'd commanded cleansed with heavenly flame over the last six weeks, only one of them had offered any resistance at all.

She'd been a cutie, too: a little too-well developed at sixteen than the Lord would have allowed. In fact, it was her unbridled femininity that had revealed her as a witch. The Witchfinder trembled at remembering her coal-black hair and sapphire eyes; they were obviously unholy wiles granted by the devil to aid in her seductions, and though he'd failed to withstand the force of her guile, he'd made certain that retribution followed swiftly from the place where he'd valiantly but vainly attempted to fuck the devil from her screaming in the darkness behind the public house. With the full force of the law and all the blessings of God, he'd strung her up in the town square for the requisite three days and nights, Bitburgers of all caste free to level their accusations, or, if they were among her conspirators, beg for her freedom. Sure enough, not a single citizen pleaded for her release. The Witchfinder had known that the revelation of one serpent would draw out more, and the Lord had not disappointed him. Before the bacony smell of stake-burned wife-of-Satan had dissipated from the square, two more lusty maids and a crone had been indicted, and new stocks were thrown up to hold all the condemned.

The killings started before the new stockade could claim even a single victim. Even as the Witchfinder culled one maleficent influence from the flock, another insinuated itself among the sheep. One after another, night after night, the elders and luminaries of Bitburg were found dead or, in one case, not quite dead but in extreme need of a manner of care that would not be available for centuries. Those responsible for the welfare of the townsfolk, the very servants of God who had so bravely named the witches responsible for the evil in their midst, were being murdered by some unspeakable force. The only town father immune to the devil's scythe had been Lord Philip Hagenbotham, and the Witchfinder now cursed himself for so easily believing his ruse.

He remembered well the exchange when Goodman Lemire had brought him before the Lord of Cardinal's Crest just days earlier.

"Pip," Goodman Ed had said to his Lord with a familiarity that should have warned the Witchfinder of Lord Hagenbotham's true nature; no servant of God or true English noble would ever allow himself to be addressed in so casual a fashion by his lessers-- it was positively *American*. In the days that followed, the Witchfinder convinced himself that the comforts of Hagenbotham's estate had woven some kind of spell over him, weakening his mind against Satanic deception: the way Hagenbotham lazed among plush pillows with that immodestly-dressed wife of his, nibbling at fruit and sipping on wine while a half-mongoloid played violin; the way the servants, backs unbent by proper flogging seemed to float about the grounds unhindered by decorum; a dozen cats stalking the house giving no heed at all to the presence of God's witch-killing sword. "Pip, seems summun's goin' about doin' murder to all the town fathers."

Pip had only shaken his head and sat up, shirtless, from his wife and comforts, all but glowering at the intruders. His chest was a topographical map of scars and burns, and the Witchfinder was all but certain he even glimpsed a tattoo before the man had the decency to cover himself.

"Seems senseless murder's a catchy tune, wouldn't you say, Master Witchfinder?" the hedonist Lord had said, stirring with his haphazard nakedness the most vile arousals inside him.

"I would not so sayeth, my Lord," the Witchfinder had said. "I would sayeth that the devil himself has come to defend his brides, and that all Good Men of God must rally to confront him before his evil engulfs this place with the very fires of hell itself!"

In retrospect, the Witchfinder realized that Lord Hagenbotham had derided him with Lucifer's tongue all along. For as long as he'd suffered the New World, he'd felt as if the very land mocked the anointed blade of the crown, and this colonist spoke with its voice.

"Well, you just keep on killing witches, good Master Witchfinder," Pip had said. "And the devil will keep defending the damned. Or quit, and the devil may just go where his business is more pressing."

Pip had only drunk more wine, straight from the bottle, like a damnable common. "Either way, fuck off and be about your own business as I go about mine."

After that, smiling servants had seen them to the door and quickly through the gates. Halfway down the slope of Fallfallow Goodman Lemire had turned in his seat inside the coach, chin-scratching and uncertain, to the Witchfinder, and said, "You think maybe Pip's gone and done all that murderin'? S'not like he's ever been friendliest with the church and wot."

"What do you mean, Goodman?" the Witchfinder had said.

"Well, just last year, when the church stopped its alms-givin', citin' lack of return on investment, ol' Pip done and had all the poor folks come up to the Crest to work for him like. And that time after he come back from Boston with that fancy school-teacher, and the Mayor had her run out for being a harlot, Pip punched him right in the face. Seemed he told the mayor to fuck off about his business too. As what he just did to you."

On this the Witchfinder prayed all through that night and the next, flagellating himself with the sacred scourge, for guidance. On his fifth sleepless day of ergot-ridden-lager-induced prostration, he found himself overwhelmed by a vision of the casually profane Lord Hagenbotham and his lusty wife. Together they writhed and licked and sucked, cast their eyes at him from afar, called to him in ways that caused him to spill his very essence in thick pearlescent puddles on his lap.

It was so clear, what had invited this great evil upon them: Lord Hagenbotham had taken up the cause of the native devil and sought to scour all the good English from the New World. Fueled with holy certainty, the Witchfinder gathered his sword and his faith, flew from his blood-spattered suite, and readied the surviving Goodmen to rain God's wrath upon this devil's henchman.

It came then as no surprise, there in the rain-drenched courtyard of Cardinal's Crest, with the Witchfinder on the precipice of delivering the fire that would purify the affliction gripping Bitburg, that his foe revealed himself.

The minion of the Beast stood there before the doors of his great and ancient house, arrayed in the splendor of the downpour and the finery of the rabid torchlight, a silk-sheathed blade of a man both beautiful and terrible of countenance. Lord Philip Hagenbotham emerged like a feather blown by careful winds, waving assurances to those behind him. Several of his servants had to restrain his young wife, but, even staring down the mob and knowing its sole intent, the lord of Cardinal's Crest betrayed no hint of fear. If anything, he looked annoyed, like a professor drug from his studies to grade underclass research papers.

"Goodman Ed, the fuck's all this?" he said, striding across the mud to confront the leader of the mob. When the oaf inserted himself between the two, Pip cocked an eyebrow at him as if to say, "Really, Oaf?" and the big blacksmith sheepishly drew back. Pip cast a far less friendly glance at the Witchfinder. "Y'all come to burn me out of my home?"

"Well, that's the ken of it, Pip," said Ed. "We're to raze this place and murder you up good, all in the name of the Lord and his appointed Witchfinder."

"This ponce?" Pip indicated the clergyman with as much disdain as he could convey. "Y'all lost yer fuckin' minds?"

By now, the mob had grown far less single-minded. They were wet, the beer was wearing off, and no one had shouted anything incendiary in a good two minutes. They had torches and there was stuff to burn, but Lord Hagenbotham didn't look like any kind of murder-demon they'd ever heard about. The mob was, indeed, showing signs of becoming plural-minded.

The Witchfinder felt them slipping away, lost to the forked tongue and pleasing visage of the demonspawn that stood before him. Without prologue or further provocation, he drew his blade and howled, "In the name of God, I cast thee hence, foul demon!"

The snicker-snap of the Witchfinder's sword carved a silver crescent on the night and a chasm in Pip's chest. A single chrome-bright scar of lightning mirrored the mortal furrow in the sky above.

The arc of red sprouting from the wound hung spotlit by the day-bright sky for the instant it took the blooded lord to crumple on the sodden turf. That instant saw Pip's wife fly to his side. All the movement and the blood must have scared the Oaf, and Goodman Ed couldn't stop him from bringing that crushing maul right down on Lady Hagenbotham's pretty head. Inside the great house, the servants shrieked.

The Witchfinder raised his sword again, brimming with orgasmic triumph. Splayed out in the mud from the shock of the Witchfinder's slash, Pip tried to comprehend the meaning behind the warm corpse spasming in his lap. It had, he was sure, once had a head, and he had loved that head, but his chest was burning and a madman was waving a bloody sword around and a host of soaking, unwashed peasants were gawking about his front lawn.

"Burn it!" howled the Witchfinder. "Let no stone stand! Burn it all, in the name of God!"

That's all it took, really, for the mob to weave itself back together and remember its purpose. All over the courtyard, set against the rising dirge of screaming servants and roaring townsfolk, the flickering face of fire showed itself. All the conspicuous combustibles went up, one pyre after another, and soon the mob, its lust for violence whetted, turned from the burning to the beating. They set themselves on the Hagenbothams' household, killing them in the name of jealousy or over old disputes or just out of the wildness that comes over beasts at the smell of blood. At the center of it all, the Witchfinder gloated over the reeling Lord of Cardinal's Crest.

"See ye now, follower of Satan?" he said, rain and blood dripping from his blade as he posed for the killing blow. "See ye now the glory of Heaven and the foulness of the hell awaiting you?"

Pip did see.

He saw the townsfolk over whom he'd been Lord in name only, guiding but never ruling like the priestly tyrants he abhorred: the people he'd helped in times of sickness and famine; the ones he'd sheltered from war; the men he'd raised houses with; all of them about the bleating business of slaughtering his household and tearing down his house. In particular, he saw Goodmen Lemire and Thistlewillow, men he'd hosted in his own home, as jubilant in their desecration as the rest. He saw men given over to their darkest lusts, all because they'd been offered an excuse by the Witchfinder and the God he represented. He saw the Witchfinder himself, strutting over the desecrated shell of his pretty little wife, and that alone would have been enough for Pip to remember why he'd let these men into his home when he should have burned them on the hillside.

He'd given them a chance, and now all he could do was curse the part of him that had.

Splayed out in the mud, his eyes never leaving those of the one who had cut him down, Pip smiled. Not an evil grin or welcoming one, not a hint of malice or benevolence about it, still it was a smile that chilled the Witchfinder.

"So I do," he said.

The spongy ground beneath him shifted, and the Witch-finder couldn't keep himself upright without turning his blade away from its target.

Pip stood, easing his wife's body, life steaming from it in the cold, oblivious rain, to the ground. "And do you, I wonder, see what your god has wrought here?"

The Witchfinder took in the sights and sounds of the massacre. In a moment of gasping clarity, he found himself struck by the muddy killing field and for once had the decency to question what he saw.

The fact that Pip looked ready to rip his throat out helped, but to his credit, the epiphany owed itself mostly just to what passed for his conscience. He paused a moment, wondering if he still had one of those, or if that too had been left behind on the soggy thighs of the devil-wife succubus who'd stolen his Godly virtue.

The pause lasted long enough for Pip to collect himself a bit. From this vantage, the Witchfinder was just a wet idiot wrapped too tightly in his own world. Pity and anger made fickle dance partners, finally abandoning him altogether as the tune shifted to one of pervasive disappointment.

"I've told you, just stop the killing," Pip said. "Stop the burnings, and the devil would leave."

The fires in the braziers began to pulsate, slowly at first, but ever faster as Pip advanced on the Witchfinder, still scrabbling in the mud.

"But you didn't," Pip said. The gash across his chest howled at him, but the deathscreams of his household rang louder. "You didn't stop, and thus the devil stayed among you."

The Witchfinder's footing left him altogether and he splashed down at Pip's feet. Made mute for a moment by the grime splashed into his mouth he stared blankly at the frightening serenity that had come over the Lord of Cardinal's Crest.

"Well, he didn't really stay," Pip said, casually. Grimacing against the pain in his chest, each movement mingling more of his blood with the storm, he like an artist before a canvas drew with outstretched fingers on the surface of the air. Where he gestured, pale silvery light stained the night: arcane glyphs painted on the fabric of reality. "But he did come back, he came back to give me a gift for dealing with the likes of you.

"Not just you, of course, but for every murdering, raping, horrible thing like you. I will kill you, and I will kill everyone like you, even if it means murdering the earth itself."

The Witchfinder scrambled backward, desperate to bring his sword up, transfixed by Lord Hagenbotham, who was now glowing like the otherworldly runes that hung in the air.

Pip gave a last and fleeting look to his dead wife, the memory of her face forever replaced by the ragged stump that remained of it.

"Now," said Pip. "Burn."

The pulsing fires that surrounded them exploded, a dozen pillars of flame blasting at once from the scattered braziers to a single nexus high above. All around, the bodies of the dead went up like kindling, the wetness of the night be damned. Their killers detonated in one bubonic explosion after another, bodies bursting with a rush of flash-fried meat and gore.

Like ribbons winding 'round an unseen Maypole, the columns of fire twisted and drew in from the braziers, converging high above the spot where Pip held the Witchfinder's eyes in his.

The Witchfinder could hear Hell calling him now, the unmistakable choirs of the damned louder even than the fire gathering above him.

"Lord," he pleaded, realizing at last what he had done, or maybe just with the same desperation as any dying man. "Forgive me my sins, and let me serve you in death as I thought I served you in life. Let not this evil spread beyond this place--"

The swirling vortex boomed and blasted earthward, a lance of flame spiraling down on Pip and the Witchfinder, consuming them both in a slurping swallow.

A final exertion brought the Witchfinder's sword up through Pip's belly into his heart, and the Lord of Cardinal's Crest barely had time to register his own death before every trace of him was smote from existence.

With a contented belch, the fire-- a living thing in a place where life was no longer welcome-- winked out. Not a single body remained as evidence of the blasphemous slaughter that had occurred, nor a single drop of blood or anything that could burn. With the fire went the rain, those redacted lustful lips having spoken enough. Only the bones and viscera of Cardinal's Crest remained, somehow untouched by spark or cinder.

It's still there, actually, right at the top of Fallfallow Hill, just at the edge of modern-day Bitburg. Many think it's strange that such a prime location has remained immune to development for all these years; well, strange if you don't know what went down back in Seventeen-Seventy-Something. There have been a few attempts at reclaiming the grounds since then, but they've all failed, most of them in rather sanguine and spectacular fashion. Because of course they do, people say the place is haunted, but even modern-day enthusiasts of the paranormal have yet to find a reason to get particularly close to the Crest.

And while you can see the defiant old house from nearly everywhere in the city, most folks don't look.

Because they know someone is looking back.

And he's kind of a dick.

Chapter One: The Shitty Life of Albrecht Drue

-Verse 1-

Bitburg, Two-Thousand-Something

Albrecht Drue lived in a hole. Not a nasty, filthy, wet hole, nor a dark, dry, sandy hole. Albrecht Drue lived in a shithole. Not just any shithole, either; Al lived in the kind of shithole only a true drunk can tolerate, abounding with the trappings of loneliness, manic enjoyment, and raging frustration left by years of regular benders.

Overlooking the scenic alley that separated his craptrap apartment building from a sweatshop notorious in its day for the production of sex toys and dead Chinese, his shithole had windows on two sides and seemed to have been designed specifically so that, no matter the time of day, if the sun was up it would bore straight into the occupant's skull. If he'd had the energy to bother or the shits to give, Al could have put up some blinds and maybe avoided the daily battle between the sun and his need to sleep off the previous night, but he didn't have the energy, and he didn't give a shit. He knew that just about every morning he was going to get up, spend around three hours retching bile into the filthiest toilet on the East Coast, then douse his guts in a half a bottle of tonic spiced with a liberal shaking of Angostura bitters. Once that had proven capable of remaining inside him, he'd head on down to the 'Clops for food and whiskey. He might shower at some point, but more than likely he'd just whore-bathe in the sink, change his shirt, and remind himself that he just didn't give a shit. He was, after all, a drunk, and had an image to maintain.

Most days, he also managed to work in a good hour or two of active self-loathing over how he wasn't doing a damned thing with his miserable life, then justify it with recriminations over how the one thing he'd ever been good at-- punching people-- had been taken away from him. He'd lost the limp that kept him out of the ring a long time back, but that didn't much matter anymore.

Today, however, was not most days. It was one of those rare days when the normal comforts of his routine would not be on the agenda. Today was a most magical of days, a day that made all the other drunken, useless days possible, a special day that came just once a quarter and reminded him that he was living the dream: today was Check Day!

Check Day meant that Al had to be Presentable; being Presentable meant that Al had to not only shower but shave and wash his hair; all that mess that he let slide most other days. It also meant that he was going to have to *Talk To People*; and if Al had to Talk To People, he was going to have to make sure that he wasn't so dry that every word came out in a shaking stammer and not so drunk that they all came sloshing out louder and more profanity-riddled than he intended. A certain level of profanity was to be expected, but there's a fine line between calling an acquaintance a "righteous fuckin' dude" and calling a stranger "a cock-gargling rape-shitter," even if that made no fucking sense. So, lying there on the dirty, sheetless queen mattress atop its mismatched twin-sized box-spring that jutted like a Dr. Pepper-stained island out of a sea of laundry he'd neither washed nor worn in months, empty liquor bottles-- most of them plastic handles, because, again, Al really didn't give a shit-- and the tear-off bits of Netflix mailers, Al opened his eyes and stared up at the ceiling in an effort to remember where he was, and to gauge the morning's level of discomfiture. The sun hit him full force and provoked from within him vitriol so blue Gainsborough could have painted a little boy with it.

Like chunks of corn in a puddle of greasy hangover shit, glossy tatters of three-and-half by two-inch cardstock confetti strewn amongst the floor-level jetsam caught the solar light and reflected it against the walls in all the variegated colors of a Pride Parade. Each scrap of embellished seventy-weight high-gloss technochromatic vellum was a slender shining needle in Al's eye, stabbing deeper when he remembered what they were and that-- after last night's hijinks-- he'd have a whole new batch in a couple of days. See, once every couple of months, Al would get a certain type of fucked up and start thinking about his future. He'd come up with some grand plan that just needed one little spark to set him ablaze with the inspiration he needed to launch his new life. He'd fly wild-eyed and vital to the computer and order up a brand new set of custom business cards, destined to arrive well after that burst of desperation had faded and made the little cardstock rectangles-- perfect talismans for the new life upon which he was about to embark-- emblazoned with things like "Albrecht Drue, Problem Solver." or "Albrecht Drue, Philosopher." or "Albrecht Drue, Hired Goon." obsolete. Inevitably, he'd tear open the boxes in a fury and they'd end up scattered on the floor, soaking up the grime, the sweat, and the filth of Al's shithole, tens of thousands of paper reminders of all the things he wasn't and would never be. When the booze was humming in his veins and the autumn breezes funneling through the hateful open window, they'd come together and swirl around him like a storm of tangible recriminations and Al would have himself a good old bout of poetic self-hate that would last him until he felt like doing it all over. This time changing the white to bone, and finally getting the type just right.

Because he had to do something with his life and his time, seeing how goddamned long it was taking for him to die.

Looking above him the ceiling fan was still. Must be cold out, he figured, or he would have turned it on last night. Al looked into the darkest corner of his shithole and saw that the computer was still intact. The TV was, too; in fact, it was still on, tuned to one of the Hitler channels because those stayed on 24/7, even if they did tend to show the same damn three-hour block of shows over and over. Today's block was about Bigfoot, and aliens, about whether Bigfoot was secretly an alien; Al had a hard time separating them anymore, but he was pretty sure that Giorgio Tsoukalos was on, and that guy wasn't saying the Bigfoot was an alien, but *it was aliens*. He fished around in the mess beside his bed and came up with a homewrecker of Aristocrat vodka, surprisingly unopened, unspilled, and undrunk.

"One thing about Aristocrat," Al said to no one, "if you're drinkin' it, you're not one." That made Al chuckle; Al had a way of making himself chuckle. Forcing himself to, really, because it made the day and the cheap booze go down easier. He uncapped the jug and took a swig, let it settle, then took another. Yep, that'd do him to get through his daily ablutions.

Suddenly, Al got the distinct feeling that he was being watched. Not just watched, but sized-up. Someone or something was taking his measure, and his buzzing head aside he was going to have to act.

It was that fucking cat at his window again. He looked over, and the thing stared him down. He was a big orange waste of breath that never missed an opportunity to shove his enormous cat balls in the face of anyone whose path he crossed. Maybe that's why Al liked him so much.

"Alright, Boyo," Al said, kicking a path through the crap on his floor to the window. He dug out a canister of dry cat food he kept on hand, dumped some in a bowl, and set it outside the sill for the little bastard.

Boyo complied, without even a thank-you. He just tore into the kibbles and scarfed them down, looked over his shoulder when he finished, lifted his tail erect, and sprayed the window with more urine than Al figured was necessary.

Well, that answered where the cat was; the only remaining question: where the fuck was the snake?

Al was the first to admit that his life was not only drunk and shitty but also kinda weird, even for Bitburg. Take, for instance, the snake in his mailbox. Ever since he was a kid, he'd been deathly afraid that, should someone choose to assassinate him, they would employ the time-honored method of hiding a deadly asp in his mailbox. If you thought about it, it was the perfect method for taking someone out: unsuspecting target casually-- probably in little more than gym shorts and a hoodie-- goes to check his mail, opens the box, and BOOM— a deadly asp bites him on the wrist, slithers away, and all you're left with is a dead Al. The fact that no one could pin on him anything warrant- ing assassination never played into Al's thought processes; it was just one of those fears that some people have. The perverse thing was that Al had indeed gone down to his mailbox, clad in only the finest of unwashed polyester-rayon shortpants and matching hoodie and found a venomous serpent in his mailbox not three weeks before Check Day. Stranger still, the thing had steadfastly refused to bite him, thereby ensuring that, should he ever again come across a snake in his mailbox, Al would ques- tion its heretofore obvious motives. The really weird part was that he'd allowed the thing to follow him upstairs to his shithole and generally have its run of the place. After all, if it hadn't killed him on sight, what were the odds it was laying the long con, waiting for him to drop his guard so that it could murder him in a way that had yet to be defined in terms of embarrassment?

Panicked, Al threw his gaze towards the computer: sure enough, it was open to a thumbnail porn site, his Deskbabes catalog, and the camchat site he went to when he wanted to watch drunk girls get naked. If he were going to die in a shame- ful fashion, this is exactly the scenario the snake would have had planned.

But his chair was empty, the space for his feet clear. The Aristocrat had obviously raised him above his station, so he figured, *fuck the snake*, and decided he better go ahead and get cleaned up so he could meet Ari at their prescribed time. After all, punctuality was the key to all social contracts, and Al was nothing if not punctual.

Punctual and generally mindful of fire hazards.

-2-

Charlene looked up from the sink and smiled her practiced smile at the buffoon flirting with her. The guy was pretty in a Guido sort of way, with a waxy faux-hawk and pecs like basketballs. He had a decent enough rack, she concluded, keeping up the smile as he prattled on about whatever the hell he was talking about. Charlene had learned over a long career behind the bar that it's usually better to not know exactly what a customer was saying unless the words "tonic" or "brewski" popped up. Faux-hawk definitely had the look of someone who would go up to a bartender and order a "brewski," or just as likely, "a round of brewskies for me and my bros." He didn't seem to be ordering anything though, so she kept washing out the glasses, dropping a "really?" or "wow" at seemingly appropriate moments, and thinking about more interesting matters. Matters like the acceptable parts-per-million of fecal matter allowable on glassware.

When the subject of ordering a drink at a bar comes up, most people don't think it likely that they'll end up getting a chunk of poop along with the onion dressing their martini. They also don't generally concern themselves with the notion that there are government agencies concerned with knowing and monitoring the allowable levels of scat on glassware, and when they find out about either, they're usually fairly horrified. That's a horror born of being oblivious and stupid, Charlene knew, because she bothered to think about things before reacting to them.

People touch glasses in bars. Jerks drop deuces in bar bathrooms, and horrible, feculence-flouting dickbags return to their glasses without thoroughly washing their hands. Said hands touch everything from toilet-flushers to doorknobs to handrails to tables to silverware on the way back to what is, more often than not, a "brewski" bought by one of the dickbag's bros. Other, more innocent hands also touch doorknobs and guardrails and tables and soon the whole place is awash in miniscule particles of human filth, and there's not a damn thing anyone can do about it. In a world of people, especially in a confined space where those people mingle, shit is inescapable.

So, Charlene did her best to make sure that every glass got washed in unsafely hot water, dried with a clean cloth, and placed as far from the shitty fingers of the customers as possible. She knew it didn't help much, but she firmly believed that her knowledge of the *Dookie Transference Principle* imparted on her a responsibility to minimize the chances that she would become part of the problem herself. That's why her hands were always too red for the rest of her gothly pale skin, and why her fingers could handle a steel-string acoustic for hours on end without even the slightest hint of wear.

"So, you in?" Faux-hawk said, plastering on a smile left over from the wardrobe room of every golden-era gameshow involving the words "newlywed," "dating," or any of their derivatives.

"In?" Charlene said, placing a rocks glass with utmost delicacy on the freshly-changed green plastic mesh that kept the rims from touching the surface of the shelf behind her. Like angels' feet on the base earth, no glass under her charge would ever touch anything even remotely unclean.

Faux-hawk did his best to look more hurt than he was; this wasn't the first time a hot chick had ignored him, and it wouldn't be the last. Hot chicks ignoring him had driven him to climb all the high peaks he'd ascended in life, and he'd learned just how to drive hot chicks in return... if you knew what he meant, bro.

"You haven't heard a single word I've said, have you?"

Shit. Charlene hated getting caught ignoring jerks. She glanced around the main room of the Cyclops and threw in a "dammit" for good measure when she saw that there weren't enough people around to successfully play-off her distraction; she couldn't even spot Lilith through all the bodies that weren't there at four-thirty on a Friday afternoon.

"I'm sorry," she said, blushing and sinking into her body in just as practiced and fake a show of contrition as Faux-hawk's wounded pout, but producing a much more disarming and attractive effect. "I was listening, really; I just, I don't know, saw something shiny and drifted away for a second. Something about ghosts, right?"

"Something about ghosts, right," Fauxhawk said, straightening up to his full height and ratcheting out his Chuck Woolery smile.

Charlene had to admit that he was a fairly impressive specimen; his chest strained to Partonian dimensions, and his biceps stretched his black t-shirt's sleeves to their limit. If it weren't for the all-over white barbed-wire design and Copperplate Gothic Bold lettering, which, while nearly illegible, always read "dickbag," he would have been a good-looking guy in a tight shirt. Most of the time, Charlene was fond of those. This was not most times.

"Allow me to re-introduce myself: Dax Vagance, lead investigator from *Ghostquest*."

Charlene drew back from the extended hand, offering upturned palms in reply. "Sorry, dish-hands."

Dax looked her up and down, not sure he wanted to keep going with this. Sure, she was a hot chick, but she was a hot chick with bright red dish-hands. Still, it never hurt to hone his cool on a substandard honey; he could always toss her to his bros if nothing better came along, and it kept his game sharp. He ran the hand through his faux-hawk and focused on her tits. They weren't nearly as big as his, but he bet they were pretty perky once they came out to play.

"You know, *Ghostquest*?" he said, making just enough eye-contact that Charlene couldn't help but notice every time his gaze flicked down to her chest. Still, he was a customer, and she was used to it. He was also an asshole, but assholes paid the bills. "We *are* the most popular ghost-hunting show in the US of A."

"Like, on TV?" Charlene said. She wondered what the acceptable parts-per-million of figurative fecal matter in a pumped-up dickbag was and began formulating a way to accurately measure it.

"On every TV you mean," Dax said, chuckling at his joke. "Actually, more people watch us than watch *Ghost Hunters*, *Ghost Adventures*, *Ghost Brothers*-- any of those guys. Along with my technical advisor Herman and JT, my fellow investigator--," Dax indicated a similarly-attired pair of bros in the corner farthest from the door-- "we go after the ghosts that send the other guys running."

Charlene pursed her lips, bobbed her head from side to side like she was separating an egg inside it. She figured that if she could measure the number of words spent saying asinine things versus things of any value, correlate it to the density and fragrance of hair product and Axe body spray, then find some way to control for whether or not the subject wore black jeans, she might be on to something.

"That's pretty neat," she said after getting the yolk and the albumen into their proper solitary half-shells. *Albumen was a fun word; a lot more fun than this conversation.* "So, you ever find any?"

What was up with this chick? If he didn't know any better, Dax would swear she had different-color eyes. Okay, she was almost definitely approaching the level of not-hot. Still, he was pretty sure that she was hiding amazing tits under that top.

"Find any what? You mean the dopest EVPs ever recorded? The hours of eerie noises we caught with our audio recorders? The literally tens of clips of unexplainable shadows we've caught on video?"

Inexplicable, you detestable guido. "Ghosts, I mean. Ever caught any ghosts?"

Dax found himself, once again, appalled at the ignorance of the public when it came to matters of the paranormal. Epic Tits or not, she was so becoming less hot. Who the hell even knew who Jethro Tull was, let alone wore one of his concert shirts to work in Twenty-Something? Still, the way she'd cut off the collar did a fine job of accenting what he was now positive were historically great tits. These weren't just hottish bartender chick tits, either: no, these were TV Tits.

"Our mission isn't to find ghosts or prove they exist, because we know they're there and we know they do.

"We have the best evidence of the paranormal ever discovered. But what we also bring to our viewers is a chance to get to know the people touched by the cases we investigate. For instance, we're actually interviewing Bitburgers who have actually been touched by the supernatural right now, and they might actually get to appear on our show. So, you ever been touched by the spirits of the departed, sweetheart? I say again: are you in?"

Actually, she couldn't have been less in, though if he tried to eye-rape her much longer or said "actually" one more time, his face was going to be *in* the damn blender. Charlene puzzled for a second, wondering if the blender still worked; it was mainly for show because Cyclops didn't play with frozen drinks. Flaming ones, maybe, if the one ordering them was worthy, but anyone who wanted a daiquiri could damn well go over to the Cheesecake Factory for that shit. Unless it was Christmastime, when they liquored up a hell of a lot of 7-11 Candy-Cane Slurpees, but that was a whole different story.

Crap, Dax Vagance was still here and waiting for a response. "Oh, in? Nope."

Then, brilliance: the perfect way to get this jackhole out of her face. Only one thing could scare off a douche-bro who so fancied the occult, and though she felt bad about invoking the almighty, it had to be done. "The only spirit that's ever touched me is the holy spirit of my personal Lord and Savior, Jesus Christ."

Dax lit up like he'd just won a lifetime supply of Drakkar Noir and hair gel.

Suddenly, TV-Tits McDish-hands shot right back up to the top of the hot-o-meter. "Really? That's actually wonderful to hear! *Ghostquest* is all about strong Christian values. Along with my Technical Advisor Herman and JT, my fellow investigator, we all consider ourselves Warriors for Christ-- we've actually had encounters with actual demons and never would have made it out alive if not for the blood shed by Jesus on the cross!"

Oh my stars and garters. It wasn't often that Charlene reflexively cribbed from the bashful, blue-furred Beast, but when she did, she knew she was in trouble. The look on Faux-hawk's face told her that he might have just fallen in love, and that was a hole she did not want to get dragged into. Her gaze darted desperately around the room, searching for any route of escape.

That's when he walked in, all six-feet-plus of wild-eyed Albrecht Drue, radiant in full-on happy-to-be-here mode. Charlene could never get over the modal disconnect between the Al that walked in with the sunset and the one who walked out with the too-bright lights of Last Call, but she also never got tired of seeing him like this.

He looked fantastic in his "mysterious barfly drag" as she called it: jeans that were "aired-out" but never washed, a black t-shirt with a simple, fist-sized logo (today it was an Imperial Snowflake) over his heart, the same hooded leather jacket he'd been wearing for the last twenty years, and a pair of scuffed boots. She loved that jacket more than she was willing to admit; it had, like, this monkish, grim-reaper thing going on, flat across the top, as wide as his shoulders at the bottom, then folding under itself to anchor at the collar. When he put up the hood, Charlene could almost believe the rumors about what Al did to supplement his income, especially when he slipped into the glare he wore when he'd been drinking for an hour or two.

But the hood was down tonight. He'd washed his hair, too, so that it bloomed and bounced to his shoulders like a bronze mop. If she looked closely, she could see where age and booze had made a droopy mess of his body, but there was no denying the mass of the muscle underneath all the flab. He still carried himself with an easy confidence that matched the welcome written on his face, like he wanted to make sure everyone knew that he wasn't there for anything but a good time, and no matter what your intentions were, he'd be happy to hear you out. He never showed his teeth when he smiled, and Charlene had been warned about people like that, but with Al, it didn't seem to matter. The guy just had a way of putting her, and almost anyone else, at ease. This version— almost five o'clock Al-- did, anyway. The only problem was that she'd seen enough of ten o'clock Al-- not so bad, just so much louder-- and midnight Al-- occasionally fucking terrifying-- to know not to get too drawn in.

The fact that Al stopped to hold the door for the people behind him added another layer to the rotten-cored onion of Charlene's feelings for him. He was a good guy; knowing what else he was, though, she couldn't help but feel a little sad every time she looked at him.

Charlene perked right up when she saw the group following Al inside: The Bitburg Supernatural Squad was the perfect escape clause for this horribly annoying dialog with Guido McFaux-hawk, Christ-Warrior.

"Ooh!" she said, popping up on her toes. It was just something she did; the top of her head was only about five and a half feet away from her heels, so, to emphasize things, she'd make herself taller. The surprise factor also made people standing too close get the hell out of her grill, so it had become part of her little coterie of body phrases; everyone has them, and the ones who use them without thinking are the ones you want to know. "I bet those guys would be perfect for your show."

Dax Vagance looked to the doorway, very consciously puffing out his chest and flexing his neck muscles as he did. Behind some pudgy, long-haired jerk, a bunch of ugly people streamed in like a melted ice-cream sundae onto freshly-pressed black jeans. Inside he groaned; outwardly, he just pumped up his Shit-Eating Grin.

It's like they were a super-hero team who, when joined together, had the powers of Social Awkwardness and Physical Repulsion, only with matching sweatshirts instead of tights: Hayseed Gargantua led the way, followed by Fat Girl Who Acts Like She Isn't Fat; Overly-Enthusiastic Little Black Guy with Glasses and Acne held the middle, yammering on in the ear of Almost Pretty Asian Girl Who'd Obviously had a Kid at Seventeen; Old Black Lady Who Probably Called Herself a Medium stopped to hug the long-hair; Shifty-Eyed Ginger Psycho in a Red Peacoat followed, making sure to cut eyes at everyone in the bar; Buzz-cut-san Japarean Jarhead and Regular White Guy brought up the rear. At least Regular White Guy looked regular and white enough that he might provide some useable footage for the show. The rest just screamed "set dressing," but the hand-drawn BSS sweatshirts guaranteed Dax had to interview them. According to the sweatshirts, they were the Bitburg Supernatural Squad, and the Producers loved it when he found some rinky-dink band of amateurs to make the Ghostquesters look good.

Taking care to pre-emptively placate his bosses would be particularly useful if the Producers found out about this unscheduled jaunt to Bitburg before Dax and his crew finished their investigation; better to ask forgiveness than permission, right? And 'I'm sorry' always sounds better when it's got a back-beat of 'look what I did, just for you!'

"I bet they would," Dax said, eyes following the BSS as they sat themselves around a table not far from his technical advisor Herman and JT, his fellow investigator. "Hey, why don't I go ahead and grab a round of brewskies for me and my bros and see what's up?"

-3-

Cyclops, Check Day

Al fucking loved the Cyclops. Time and booze had significantly diminished his capacity for loving anything, but if there was one thing that wasn't nachos that Al could say he loved with all his heart, it was the 'Clops.

Just around the corner from one of those for-profit art schools that occasionally churned out a graduate with marketable job skills, and adjacent to a high-rise that charged a couple grand a month for a studio apartment, the Cyclops drew a mixed crowd that reminded Al why he loved being alive. Art-school girls showed up after the daytime classes or before the nighttime ones, and the eclectic crew of Bitburgers who preferred to live and work in the city center commingled with them to create a nifty cocktail of lively conversation and potential face-punchings. Even the bar's sign--just the word "cyclops" spelled out in lower-cased courier-new text-- spoke to its understated, elevated vibe; no one would see the sign from the street and say "hmmm, that looks like a fun spot," but anyone who knew enough to look for it was probably cool enough to be there. Of course, "probably" is a fairly pointed word, but that's a story for a few paragraphs down.

The building itself was older than most in the city, dating back to when Bitburg hadn't quite existed yet, and the ancient stones held the resonating energy of all the generations that had passed while they just sat there being rocks. The basement was connected to the warren of shanghai- and transit tunnels that ran under Bitburg like a waffle fry buried in a mound of chili and cheese. The place had always been a bar, or a public house, or a speakeasy, and it had seen its share of atrocious and illuminating moments. All those things-- Al could feel them every time he walked through the front door or stumbled out the back. And every time he came in, one of his heroes was there to greet him: Malcolm X, smiling ear to ear, his mosaic portrait ten feet tall and made out of those little plastic things that hold bread bags closed, each one colored by hand by some long-dead heroin addict. Always there were familiar faces, and always new ones, and it filled Al with the kind of warmth usually invoked by whiskey or a good plate of *All the Nachos* when he first looked each new acquaintance in the eye.

He'd never admit it, solitary dignitary that he was, but the reason Al loved the Cyclops so much was that it felt more like a home than his shithole did. *What makes a home? The people in it.*

Even the regulars had grown on him after a while, whether or not they knew or liked it. Take, for instance, the Ghost Geeks, who had just now followed him through the door. Whatever they called themselves, they fit right in with the rest of the motleys whose butts warmed the stools. He wasn't so sure about the three bros huddled around their brewskies in the back corner, but Al even liked seeing them here; it never hurt to have someone around to punch.

Then there was Charlene.

What the hell could he do but be truly, madly, deeply, movie-title-quotingly in love with a girl who wore Jethro Tull t-shirts in Twenty-Something without even a touch of irony, and showed her dedication to his not drinking excrement with her pink-steamed hands?

She had these eyes, you know? One was green, the other blue, but you had to really look into them to notice it, and if you got that close, you knew that, in that moment, she knew you in ways you never could. That, and she had the most epic tits God ever saw fit to put on a human.

When she wore her hair back, one long blue lock would fall on the left side of her face and she'd spend half the night brushing it behind her ear, inevitably getting it tangled in one of the eight rings she wore from the lobe to the little stiff bit that covered the earhole. Then there was the way she could--

"Oh good, you're here," Ari said, bumping into Al as he stood there blocking the door and gawking at the object of his unrequited love. "Let's grab a seat, shall we?"

"Serious business, then?" Al said, forcing himself to stop his staring and follow Ari Jimenez to the closest table. Al hated sitting at tables in a bar; what the fuck was the bar for if not for sitting and meeting new people? Tables were too closed-off, too private, too lacking in opportunity for unplanned misadventure. Still, Ari had Al's check, and Check Day wouldn't be Check Day without the check.

"Serious business, indeed," Ari said, wiping crumbs and probably not too small an amount of unavoidable feces from his chair before seating himself.

Al swore Ari's back never flexed; his posture as rigid as a hard-on in a whorehouse. A Lucky Strike found its way to Al's lip somewhere between his standing and sitting, but he didn't light it, citing deference to his associate.

Ari Schlomo Jimenez wore a less-scrutable-than-his-normally-inscrutable accountant expression.

It's important to note here that Ari Jimenez was not a stereotypical Jewish accountant; in fact, he wasn't a stereotypical Jewish anything. He was just the son of Honduran immigrants who happened to be racist as fuck and decided upon the arrival of their firstborn that they wanted a son who could grow into a man with a good job who would make them money and proud, and what better way to make your parents proud and rich than to be a Jewish Doctor or Jewish Lawyer? So, being unintentionally and un-maliciously racist as they were, they'd named him Ari Schlomo Jimenez and sent him off into the world to make with the pride and the dollars. Ari had rebelled by refusing to become a doctor or lawyer, but could not escape his uncommon facility with numbers and their manipulation, and as such his racist parents had to settle for the fact that Ari Schlomo Jimenez, CPA was one of the most sought-after money guys in the city. Just who was seeking him remained mostly confidential, what with Ari's Achillean weakness for strippers, gambling, and most other vices, but such details didn't keep his parents from bragging about their "big-shot Jewish accountant" son. It was, in fact, Mr. and Mrs. Jimenez bragging about Ari that had brought Al to him in the first place, their less palatable common acquaintances not coming to light until much later.

"Ari, your expression does not say, 'here's your thousands, favorite client of mine,'" Al said. Usually, Ari looked like a slightly stuffy, impeccably tanned young professional, the kind of guy you have no problem entrusting with everything you own, and your sister if he liked her.

However, right now, Ari looked more like 'Ari Jimenez, Reluctant Bringer of News that Your Old Dog Just Ate Your New Puppy, then Choked on the Bones and Died Right After Shitting on Your Heirloom White Shag Rug' than 'Ari, Bringer of Checks.' The discrepancy wasn't lost on Al, who got that feeling he usually only got when he thought about what might be hiding in his mailbox. He looked over to Charlene for visual reassurance and to order booze, only to find his eyes staring straight into someone's crotch.

The crotch in question belonged to Lilith, wore its cranberry leather tights exquisitely, and gave off just a whiff of perfume from behind a low-slung half-apron.

"Heya, Recht," Lilith said, not through her crotch, but from the normal place words come out of a speaking person. Lilith said "Recht" like "wrecked," and was about the only person who could get away with calling Al that; Charlene could have, but wouldn't call him anything except 'Al' under most circumstances. Lilith had painted her lips thick and black tonight and had taken great pains to give herself the perfect red-ebony smoky-eye treatment. Her *Rainbow-in-the-Dark* hair would have made Ronnie James Dio proud, but what she'd spent on it that afternoon at *Peech Salon* could easily be made up on a Friday night. How she managed to make it through a shift without a single strand ever coming undone was something that defied both physics and Al's ability to comprehend the universe, but he had to admit, it looked damn good. Throw in the corset and fishnet sleeves, and she'd make the cover of any Vampire-fantasy cosplayer's hot rod calendar. She was fucking hot, for the vintage nineties anyway, and the way she brushed Dat Ass up against Al reiterated the standing invitation; thing is she just wasn't Charlene. She gave Al's companion a tip-increasing wink.

"Heya Ari."

Ari didn't give two square shits that Lilith wasn't Charlene. He'd already grown mildly uncomfortable with the tailoring of his slacks because of her and just hoped that he hadn't begun to sweat through them as well. "Hi, Lil," he said, making sure he kept his eyes on hers instead of the strategically exhibited parts he really wanted to see.

"Hmmm, now let me guess," Lilith said, scrunching her nose and nibbling on the veteran end of a red pen. Ari couldn't help but squirm and wish he'd been born a pen; Al just smiled up at the girl and wondered why he never said yes when she asked him upstairs after he walked her home. "For our regular, Double Fighting Cock, neat, and you, Ari, a Diet Coke with lemon?"

"Sounds just right to me, darlin'," Al said.

Lilith didn't know if he was cheesy or charming, but she liked it when Recht called her "darlin'." She slipped the pen into her apron and twirled, making sure everyone in the steadily crowding bar got a good look; after all, she'd spent hours getting ready for the shift, and Recht wasn't the only one she wanted to impress.

"Actually," Ari said, stopping Lilith in mid-twirl. "Scratch the Diet Coke and bring me a tequila, with a Guinness back."

Al didn't startle easy, but this caught him off-guard. Lilith just nodded and darted off, leaving both men a stunning view of her sweet, sweet leather-wrapped ass.

"Not your normal Check Day libation, Ari," Al said, sliding low in his chair and raising an eyebrow in what he hoped was a pointedly interrogative expression. He hadn't ever seen Ari drink anything boozified, and the last time he'd seen anyone drink tequila and Guinness? Well, such things are better left for prequels. "Something up?"

Acutely aware that Al had abandoned his sight-seeing earlier than necessary and turned his focus towards his own less-than scrutable visage, Ari slowly removed his Trotsky glasses and rubbed the lenses with a cloth he produced from his inside jacket pocket. Ari knew Al well enough that any real news, in order to be fully processed and retained by his client, would have to be couched with dramatic gestures and all requisite theatricality. So, while Al danced his mercifully unlit cigarette across his knotty knuckles, Ari made a show of cleaning his glasses before replacing them and boring a tunnel through Al's captive gaze.

"Up, indeed," Ari said. He must have achieved the appropriate saturation of gravitas because Lilith didn't even peep as she placed their drinks in front of them. *Hmm, maybe he'd over-gravitasified, but maybe that'd turn Lilith on; nothing else had worked so far.* He couldn't be certain if it was discomfort at the sudden tonal shift or just a drunk sweating for his next drink, but Al looked genuinely ill at ease. *Good. He'd love this next part.*

Ari drained his tequila in one quick go, turned the glass upside down on the table. "What's up is your annuity, in case you weren't keeping track. As in it's up, depleted, tapped the crap out."

Ari sipped at his Guinness, the low-alcohol bread-water instantly gelling with the Mexican napalm he'd just thrown down. It was true that Al had never seen Ari Drink, but that didn't mean he didn't know how; with his peculiar clientele, such displays of machismo were more frequently necessary than not. Guinness had served him well in many a vodka-soaked Russian warehouse, like milk chasing the heat from a batch of hot wings, but people assumed that "Porter Stout" meant "hardcore" instead of "keep the porters energized, hydrated, and sober in an era when water was toxic," and Ari had no problem using others' ignorance to his advantage.

Times like this, when Ari had to lie through his teeth, it helped to have some stage business. He didn't like having to put one over on one of the few people who considered him a friend, but Al had to buy into this whole-hog. If he didn't, it was Ari who'd be well and truly fucked, and Al's friend or not, Ari didn't want to be the one getting fucked.

Besides, to look at Al was to look at a guy who'd be dead in a week or a year, anyway. How he'd failed to succumb to booze or bullets by now was a goddamned miracle on its own.

"Ain't that a shot to the nuts," Al said, succeeding at looking far less terrified than he suddenly felt. Wasn't that annuity supposed to last, like, Al didn't know, forever? "So, no check?"

Ari tried to read the big drunk; he might as well have been reading his sister's kids' letters to Santa. Every year, he got one from each of them written in pictograms and chicken-scratch, and because his sister rarely had more than a bongload's worth of cash to her name, he answered as best he could, because it wasn't her fault their racist parents had completely ignored her. Finally, he closed the book of Al, reached into his jacket, and withdrew a small white envelope.

"This is the last one, Mr. Drue," Ari said. He laid the envelope in front of Al, then placed a fine-looking, engraved silver pen beside it. He sipped his Guinness.

Thank fucking Christmas.

As long as he wasn't flat broke, four-months-from-now-Al could deal with this happy horseshit; hell, if he was lucky, he'd be dead by then and not have to worry about it. Al snortled, eyeing the envelope, left hand absent-mindedly coiling around his drink.

"Well then, here's to not being completely and utterly fucked," Al said and threw four ounces of six-year-old Kentucky Straight Bourbon Whiskey down his throat. Fighting Cock was something like 103 proof, but smoother than Midnight Al thought he was. Still, there was a bit of a burn underneath, and that was enough to wrinkle his belly. Another few glasses, it'd wrinkle his mood. A few more, he'd wrinkle someone else's, and the whole place would end up an upturned laundry hamper that no amount of regret could ever iron out. Al could see that scenario laid out in front of him like a ten-dollar whore, and for an instant, his grin became a sneer.

Like The Man said: *Whiskey. It angries up the blood.*

Ari watched Al's face. He caught the sneer, even if no one else would have. As he understood it, that sneer was a rare but regular visitor to these parts, and never preceded good things. That's why Ari and Al were associates instead of friends. Yet Ari didn't have many friends or even many associates who weren't wanted by law or wanting to throw him through a window, so he couldn't help himself from letting out a sad little sigh.

This was the part of the plan that maybe made it okay for Ari to run a con on the guy who had, more than once, willingly bailed him out of the kind of shit he was unwillingly bailing Ari out of right now. The sigh was just a prelude, part of the sell.

Al saw Ari's posture droop just the littlest bit and tried to look perkier. For his part, Ari raised his glass, tilted it towards his client of the last eight years, said "To not being completely fucked," and mostly drained his beer.

"Neato," Al said, then turned his magic waitress-hailing eyes to the crowd in search of Lilith and more booze. He thought briefly about heading for the bar to flirt with Charlene, but his disappointment-to-alcohol ratio already leaned too far to the former. Lilith must have felt his eyes on him because she straightened up from the black-clad Bros' table where she'd been selling another round of brewskies with the spillage from her corset and winked at him.

Al didn't like the way the guy with the faux-hawk leered at Lilith's ass while her attention was diverted, and disliked how the three of them high-fived and hyena-laughed when she'd flitted away altogether. He kinda hoped they were gone by the time he'd finished a bottle of the Cock. Then again, he kinda didn't.

"Really, Al," Ari said, watching him watch them watch her. This was the part where, if he squinted real hard, Ari could look back and say the con had been just as much about getting Al out of his bullshit situation and making him do something with his life as as it had been about getting Konstantinov off his own back. "Have you given any thought to what you're going to do for money now?"

Truth be told, Al had pointedly and adeptly ignored that question since it became one. He knew he needed to figure out what to do with the rest of his life, but fuck all that. And fuck Ari for asking personal questions. *Whatever the fuck I do, at least I already got a card for it.*

"I's thinkin', I might become a gigolo," Al said. Ari rarely called him Al; more theatricality, he supposed. He always did this when he wanted Al to pay attention. "Maybe just a straight man-whore."

"Al," Ari said, emphasizing the familiarity even if it did make him professionally uncomfortable. After all, once Al signed the contract inside the envelope, there'd be no accountant/ client relationship, so he might as well get used to calling him by his first name. "This is pretty serious. I don't know how you've managed to live as long as you have on what you get, but that's gone now. How are you going to live?"

Al did his best Stallone, which was fairly weak, "Day by day."

Surprising everyone, himself included, Ari slammed an open palm against the table.

"Dammit, Al!

"Once you sign that contract, your income goes from pitiful to non-existent, and pitiful I could at least turn into livable. Non-existent stays at not-a-damn-cent, regardless of my supernatural talent for money-making. Legally, I won't even be able to accept a collect call from you, let alone handle literally every aspect of anything remotely resembling your business affairs. You understand that, right?"

Al decided that he didn't particularly like this version of Ari Schlomo Jimenez, Certified Pedantic Asshole. "Well, maybe if you'd handled them better— "

"Do not blame me for that," Ari said, regaining his composure and adopting a quiet, severe manner that reminded Al of the mailbox-snake that even now was probably slithering all over his unmentionables. "I'm not the one who got drunk and let your sole credit card loose on Kickstarter. For fuck's sake, Al, a fan-funded *Firefly* reunion series?"

He couldn't help himself; just the thought of such a miracle split Al's face from one dimple to the other. It wasn't enough to make his teeth show, but it was plenty to set Ari back to fuming. Luckily, Lilith's immaculate self showed up with another round, and she spared none of her cleavage on the table just because they were friends; she figured she only had a few years' worth of equity left in her girls, and she was going to get every dollar out of them while she still could.

Not quite used to booze and Lilith's boobs at the same time, Ari lost track of his thoughts for exactly as long as it took Al to remember that this was a friend, not some faux-hawk wearing *bro*. Ari hadn't quite earned a face-punching, at least not yet.

"Look, Ari," Al said, tucking his Lucky behind his ear. He sat up straight and leaned forward, wiping the bullshit off his face. He took a cue from his accountant, played up his own gravitas. "I know you don't understand me. But I do understand a few things. Things like the Universal Locomotive."

"Hun, waitasec," Lilith said, holding a finger in front of Al's face and thereby completely derailing his universal locomotive. Her hand spirited in and out of her apron, and before he could squee, started dabbing a clean napkin on Ari's chest; somewhere along the line, he'd managed to spill the dregs of his Guinness all over himself. She smiled right at him while she said, "No wonder you usually stick with diet Coke."

Lilith finished her dabbing and gathered up the empty glasses. When she left, the smile she dropped in Ari's lap was the kind that POWs think about to get them through their years of rat bites and bamboo splints under their fingernails.

Al waited for Ari's intoxication to almost wear off before he got back on his train. Ari was so blissfully unsettled that he just sat there listening and mentally doing the cost/benefit analysis of ruined shirts to being touched by Lilith.

"See, the Universe is a Locomotive. You get on, it takes you where it takes you, and when your ticket runs out you get the hell off."

"What?" Ari said, Al's being-Al-ness cutting through the lingering warmth of Lilith's touch.

Al was chugging on down the track now, pleased as punch and just about as full of alcohol. He leaned back to take a drink and make sure anyone within earshot could hear him. To his ultimate satisfaction, Charlene had moved down to his end of the bar now that the 'Clops was reaching capacity, and looked to be taking her own sweet time cleaning a glass with what he assumed was unsafely-hot water. As soon as they made eye contact, Charlene rolled hers and stuck her tongue out. Al wouldn't have expected any less.

"You only got one place to get on, and one place to get off, and as long as you stay on the train, you're always right where you're supposed to be."

"Again," Ari said. Lilith was leaning over someone else's table now, giggling. The warmth she'd left faded. "What?"

"Hey man, I'm on my train. If mine's the next stop, I'll get off. If not, I'll keep watchin' scenery, drinkin' my flask, and smokin' in the bathroom with the fan turned on."

Al sat back; arms crossed in triumph. Through the sudden-onset bourbon buzz and the successful employment of

metaphor in a social situation-- seven points in the Bullshit-
ter's Game Of Life, if you're keeping score-- the discontent
of Ari's fiscal revelation had all but erased itself from his
mind.

A few tables away, Lilith had her hand on some old guy's
shoulder. That's probably how she thought about Ari if she
thought about him at all. *Just some ... customer.* Ari gave his drinks
the once-over. He looked up at Al. It made him feel sick, and Al's
refusal to acknowledge the weight of what was happening made
the sickness even sharper.

"That is some seriously bone-headed bullshit," Ari said.
"Tell me this, Al: were you on the train when, after your first pro
fight-- a fight you lost, by the way-- you got drunk and walked in
front of a goddamned truck?"

That was a low blow, especially from Ari. "Well, it did happen to be a Coca-Cola truck, and the ensuing settlement has
supported me for the last eight years, as you kinda fuckin' well
know, so, yeah, I guess I was."

Al thought about that, chuckled, and scowled at the same
time. "And I didn't get drunk. I was already fucking shithoused
when I stepped into the ring."

Ari sighed, again, rubbing his temples with one hand so the
other was free to signal surrender. He knew Al well enough to
know that he was beyond reach, and likely would be until the
bender that started tonight worked its way through to its end
and left him curled up in a corner of the shithole apartment he
would soon be unable to afford.

Besides, he didn't know him well enough to admit that he
cared much. At least not enough to abort his mission to trick

him into signing over his only source of regular income to the guy he trusted to make sure the life he lived maintained a minimal level of comfort for the remainder of the long, slow suicide he'd stumbled himself into. Lilith was flirting with another table now, and he needed to go change his shirt before his meeting with Konstantinov. No sense in stretching this out any longer.

Ari pushed the envelope and the-- *dammit, where was the pen?*

Oblivious to Ari's sudden shift from exasperated grown-up to spastic first-grader, Al went through the envelope. His check was there, bigger than usual, along with a sheet for him to sign signifying the successful completion of his association with the accounting and law firm of Coleridge and Ditko. He assumed that's what it was, anyway; reading was for pussies and menus, dammit.

Al used his own pen-- way he saw it, a man's pen is like his penis, otherwise, they wouldn't be spelled that way-- to sign with a capital "A" and a lower-case Drue, then passed the papers back to his former accountant.

Ari looked truly shaken; he knew he'd put the damned pen his father had passed down to him on the table with the envelope, hadn't he? He'd had the thing for almost thirty years; it wasn't just an heirloom; it was his lucky pen. But he couldn't panic.

He breathed.

He breathed again.

If it wasn't on the table, that meant he hadn't brought it with him; if he hadn't brought it with him, he couldn't have lost it, right? Right. And Al was handing him the papers. Ari Schlomo

Jimenez, CPA, composed himself because that was the professional thing to do.

"You know," Al said, Ari giving him a tenth of his attention as he satisfied himself that everything was in order. "I'm thinkin' I might become a private eye. I mean, I drink hard, I quip; I could totally pull it off. All I need is a trench coat, a hip flask, and a shoulder-holster to carry my two best friends and I could be like, the scourge of the underworld. Or at least I could take pictures of guys cheating on their wives."

Ari folded the papers, shook his head, and looked Al straight in the eyes. It was kind of sad, the way the guy had no idea that he'd just signed away the rest of his shitty life. He didn't have a clue about the magnitude of what was going to happen to him as soon as this last check ran dry, and even with the fiduciary alchemy Ari had executed to squeeze as much as possible out of the last quarter's dividend, it wouldn't last more than a few months. Al didn't have anyone or anywhere in the world to go to when it dried up, and the worst part of it was that he didn't even seem to care.

"One," Ari said, standing and pushing his chair under the table. "You hate guns. Two, you don't own a camera. Three, you have the deductive skills of a slow-witted alpaca."

Al laughed, loud, hard, and real. "Tell me what you really think, dude."

Ari tucked the power-of-attorney transfer into his jacket, along with any regret he may have felt. Sure, Al might die when the money ran out, but Ari wouldn't live through the night if he didn't render unto Konstantinov what was Konstantinov's

"There's enough in that check to make it work for you. I don't know exactly what you're good at, but I'm sure there's a school for it or something. Use it, Al. Fuckin' monetize your aptitudes or something. Just because you can't make a living punching people doesn't mean you have to give up on life."

The accountant put forth a hand for his former client to shake, but Al was having none of it. Instead, he sprung out of his chair and gave Ari the biggest man-hug he'd ever gotten, and after a less-than-comfortable return, finally pulled back, holding him like his eyes were snapping a Polaroid.

"It's been good to know you, man," Al said, his smile so laden with honest affection that Ari couldn't help but let some of it overflow into his own. Hell, maybe Al would be okay; he'd made it this far through luck, charm, and beating the hell out of people, so maybe he'd just keep chugging along on that stupid-assed Universal Locomotive of his.

"Independently lower class, Ari," Al said, finally letting go. "That's all I need to be."

"Right, Al" Ari said and left the bar. He still had to get back to the office and change his shirt, and for that matter, retrieve his pen from where, if he hadn't brought it with him, it had to be safely locked in his desk.

Al watched him go. At long last, he lit the Lucky Strike he'd stashed behind his ear, opening, striking, and closing his Zippo in a flashy routine that, back in the day, had many times broken the ice between him and some eventually regretful young lady.

Ari probably had a point, somewhere in all his stern-faced nay-saying. Al could, he supposed, go home, dry out, and look at using this last bit of money he'd gotten in trade for his life and career to maybe try and start new ones. Yep, if Ari had a point, that would be it.

Fuck points; all the things that make you bleed have points, and Al had always preferred hammers. Or at least getting hammered. Fuck, they couldn't all be gold, but the internal wordplay was enough of an excuse for Al to keep smiling as he could have hoped for.

-4-

The Cyclops had filled up while Al talked with Ari. All the usual suspects and rejects were there, along with those three bros that Al had decided were definitely of the unsavory variety. The Ghost Geeks were locked in deep debate around the big eight-top, probably about something esoteric and pointlessly conjectural, but important enough to give them a reason for being together. Lilith moved like a vampire hummingbird between the little blossoms of humanity gathered around the tables, pollinating each one with her unique brand of unspoken promises no one expected her to keep. Charlene and the other bartender whose name and face seemed to change on a weekly basis danced a frenetic ballet behind the bar, surfing the tide breaking against the three-hundred-year-old oak shore before them. Someone had kicked the old-school juke to life and it belted out something appropriately forgettable but perfectly punctuated by the sound of pool balls clattering from the back room. Brother Malcolm looked out over his subjects, smiling.

Al took it all in, as he had almost every time he'd left his shithole these past eight years. He breathed in the life and the sustenance of the place with every drag on the Lucky, savoring it, knowing that this was as good as his life had ever been and that it was over now. Ari didn't have to say a word for Al to know exactly what he'd been thinking. Today was the last Check Day, and whatever else it had cost him, at least the accident that had ended his career as a fighter had given him almost a decade of this beautiful tableau of human communion in return. *Shit happened; shit ended.*

But it hadn't ended yet; it had also given him the previous Check Day, which meant that he still had a few hundred bucks to burn through if he didn't want to mix the new money with the old.

"Lilith!" he shouted, thereby ensuring every head in the place turned his way.

"Darling!" Lilith said, cooing and fluttering across the floor to fall into his arms. They posed like an unholy crossover between a *Twilight* movie still and a Harlequin Romance cover painting for just long enough to wrangle the crowd's attention, then Al spun Lilith to her feet.

"Whiskey!" Al said. "And for the room! It's my very last bloody Check Day!"

If such were the case, it had better damn well be one worth remembering, and Al damn well wanted to make sure it was worth remembering. Or at least entertaining when someone told him about it later, because if he remembered any of the rest of tonight, he'd know he'd screwed it right the hell up.

-5-

Charlene groaned and started laying out shot glasses, mustering up the best "woo-hoo!" she could and letting it join the chorus. Like The Man says, *"When all else fails, give people free booze and they're sure to love you."*

Sure enough, tonight's crowd embraced the notion and the gratis whiskey, and what already looked to be a Friday night spent knee-deep in the weeds bloomed into something even busier. Customers were already nut-to-butt with each other and more were coming in. The bartender looked over the ranks of heads at the antique clock on the far side of the room. She was unsurprised to see Al underneath, gesticulating wildly as he entertained some new friends with an animated recounting of one of his maybe true/maybe not exploits.

The clock told her it was 5:30 PM.

"Fuck," Charlene said. "Midnight Al is gonna be early tonight."

Interlude: A Pimp's Fate

Bitburg, Nineteen Seventy-Six. Because pacing

It was a dark and stormy time in the world, as *Star Wars* was not yet a thing and, as such, the world's economy was uncertain. There might have also been a thing about gasoline. Suckas and jive turkeys abounded, unrest lingered like the hookers on every corner, and rats died of dysentery from the garbage cooking in the streets. Summer in Bitburg was a grainy 8mm snuff-film of sweaty desperation and polyester psychedelia.

Yet a real pimp could still wear a fur coat with its matching hat and never drip a drop of Maxie's Relaxer on his fine-ass purple silk collar. If he was anything, Silky Cobra Watkins was a real pimp, the kind of OG P-I-M-P still inspiring poseurs and misogynists today, and he ruled Jennings Heights like some kind of funky Grand Poobah. From the penthouse of the Palace Majestic Hotel, he could look down on every motherfuckin' one of his subjects and know each and every deplorable nigger he saw owed their next breath to him and him alone.

Make no mistake: as a Black Entrepreneur and businessman of note, Silky Cobra Watkins knew the difference between a nigger and a negro and Black man, and the pusillanimous little shits who did their dailies in this magnificent aquarium were all niggers in his eyes, 'cause he'd gotten rid of everybody else.

Jennings Heights in the seventies was the kind of place Blaxploitation was invented to mythologize, an archetypal ghetto that curled around the base of the Fallfallow Hill like an unfed dog at the foot of the master's chair. Outsiders might have looked at the place and said it had seen better days, but the truth was, Jennings Heights had always been a fucked-up place. This wasn't Harlem; this was Watts on August 11th, 1965, three-sixty-five a year, if Watts had shared a cross-street with Hell. A few people associated its deadly reputation with its proximity to Cardinal's Crest, but really, everyone should have, because, after all, like everywhere else in the world, shit rolls downhill.

"Silky Cobra, my man," Willy Roderick said from his stoop. Willy was a skinny little dealer, shooting craps on the sidewalk with a bunch of other rats. Seeing the Smooth Snake himself out making his rounds was never a good thing, but the pile of lettuce between his knees said Willy had been lucky this afternoon, and that meant he could afford to be proactive. Hell, if Silky Cobra was in a good mood, he might even get to keep some of his winnings. He leapt up from his spot and held up his half of a high-five, "What it is?"

Silky Cobra stopped up short, a groovy locomotive pulled into its station by an expert engineer, his thick fur coat whooshing around his calf, silver-headed pimp cane resting easily against the concrete. His lips drew tight; his eyes followed suit. He did not back up Willy's proffer of greeting, but rested both hands on the silver ball atop his stick, cocking his head back as he did.

Willy did his best to withdraw his mitt without looking like a chump. The rest of his crew was watching now, the clatter of dice and smack-talk slinking off to some other gutter. The city's summer symphony filled in the empty space: distant traffic; kids playing; the secondhand stench of melting asphalt. Willy only just noticed, precisely ten paces behind the King of Jennings Heights and conspicuous in their attempts to look unobtrusive, the pair of funky flunkies serving as the pimp's escort. Suddenly, even with the heat, Willy felt cold. Then he remembered: he'd been lucky all morning, and Willy Roderick was never lucky. Silky Cobra showing up was just the part where his lucky day reminded him of that.

"What it is, Willy Roderick?" Silky Cobra said. His voice was maple syrup dripping off the end of a switchblade.

Willy smiled and motioned for Silky Cobra to wait, then scurried back to his spot in front of the game. Almost instantly, his palms were dampening a stack of worn bills, which he presented to Silky Cobra like a midwife would a newborn.

"Tribute, Silky," Willy said. He held out the money and kept smiling in anticipation of his boss's satisfaction.

"Today ain't Monday," Silky Cobra said. "Is it, Willy Roderick?"

Willy's skin seemed to be trying to escape Silky Cobra's glare by burrowing into his heart. The pimp's expression hadn't changed, nor his tone nor meter, but Willy knew that he might well have just fucked up. "No sir, Silky Cobra, no, today's Friday— "

Silky Cobra's cane flashed up, arcing from concrete to Willy's face in a glassy flash that left a crack on the air and Willy on his knees. Some of Willy's crew might have flinched, and some of the citizens on the street may have gasped, but anyone who did either tried their best to hide it. Languid as his name implied, Silky Cobra reached down a manicured hand and turned Willy's face to his. "Today's Friday, Willy Roderick. I don't do no collectin' on Fridays.

"Hey, Justin Thompson, what Silky Cobra do on Fridays?"

A chubby kid hiding behind the rest of the crapshooters stood up, careful to convey nothing but respect. "Everybody knows, on Fridays, Silky Cobra gonna see him the new talent."

Silky Cobra flourished his furs and shot the kid a smile. At his feet, Willy fought the nausea oozing into his guts. His face burned. Blood pulsed from his cheek, soaking into the cash in his hand. He could hear his heart beat right before the stinging in his face flared, but he couldn't hear anything else, and all he could see were the pimp's shiny snakeskin shoes.

"Look at you, chunky nigga," Silky Cobra said, all smiles and satisfaction. He waved his cane over the rest of the guys. "Y'all be watchin' out for this motherfucker; little half-smoke Justin Thompson knows what it is.

"On Friday, Silky Cobra gets his self ready for the weekend. That means seein' how my bitches is. It don't mean motherfuckers be given him shit he didn't ask for at inopportune moments."

Like a cane-reaper, Silky Cobra swept the silver end of his pimp-stick down, and the wet smack of metal against Willy's elbow echoed throughout the brick and concrete warren of The Jen. Willy collapsed, whimpering, cracking his jaw against the concrete. The pimp looked over the crew, gauging reactions and measuring loyalties.

Not a shirt or a pair of balls on any of them: just dirty wife-beaters and false bravado. Justin Thompson back there might have something, though. Seems he was keeping up in school, reading books, and shit like that. "Justin Thompson, you fall in line with Raj and Dumpsterdive, follow them around some."

Justin did as he was told, trotting off to join the funky flunkies ten steps back, making sure to bow a little and avert his gaze from Silky Cobra's gold-plated grin.

Willy managed to prop himself up on his good arm, using the sodden pile of cash for support. He'd been lucky all morning, dammit; *what the hell happened?*

"Now," Silky Cobra said. He slid the silver end of his stick under Willy's chin, ever so gently drawing the man to his feet. Willy could barely think, but he knew to stand, to stay quiet, to not puke blood all over the man in front of him. "Now, Willy Roderick, you understand what it is?"

"Yes," Willy said, bleeding and stammering. Quickly, he added, "I understand, Silky Cobra."

"Good man. Now you go get cleaned up, you look like something my dogs shit out."

Willy nodded, clutching at his sides, and sped off in whatever direction he'd been facing.

"And don't you be bringin' me no nasty-ass skungy bills come Monday," Silky Cobra said. Satisfied, he bent down and collected most of the money from the dice game, leaving just enough for the crew to fight over when he'd gone. None of them said a word.

"See y'all later, boys," Silky Cobra said, then sauntered on down the block. It was Friday, after all, and pleasant as this morning was proving, he still had talent to inspect.

Interlude Part Two: Bottom Bitch

Cherish Randall jabbed the little shiv at Junk-Mama's bare chest, growling. "And if you come near me one more time, you dyke bitch, I'm gonna cut your fucking heart out and feed it to that gaping old asshole of yours."

Even if she'd lost everything else, Cherish still had her gift for words.

The other girls watched with a mix of heroin-lidded disinterest and itchy dis-ease, scattered about the piss-elegantly palatial digs of the Cobra's Nest. Layers of silk and animal-printed velvet draped the penthouse of what had been the grandest hotel in Jennings Heights, a smattering of whores, in turn, draping the plush, garish sofas scattered around the room. The only piece of furniture that didn't look like it came from a New Jersey strip club garage sale was the gilded, seven-foot-tall steel safe that dominated the wall directly opposite the elevator; this was Silky Cobra's stash, set out where everybody could see it, where it could dare all the wretched little roaches to give the Psychedelic Serpent a reason to send them down to the basement.

Everyone back then knew about the Stash, and everyone knew about the Basement. Everyone knew that touching the one got you a trip to the other, and didn't nobody know what happened down there, except for what it sounded like when it did. Nobody who'd heard that sound ever thought about touching the Stash.

A film projector sprayed porn over a bare wall, a triple-chinned midget nearby keeping the reel fresh. The flickerstock lightshow danced with candleflames, the natural daylight conceding the place to less revelatory illumination. The girls weren't really whores so much as they were hos, and the Nest wasn't a brothel as much as it was a flop. Silky Cobra kept his penthouse rich, but the rest of the building leaked, stank, and seeped, much like most of the girls themselves. There were a few exceptions, the most notable and immediately relevant being Cherish Randall and Junk-Mama.

"Twenty bucks on Cheesy," one of the thugs guarding the door said to the other.

"Shit, man, bitch gonna get filleted," the other thug said, pronouncing every letter because he'd heard a Brit say it like that and he thought it made him sound sophisticated-like. "Junk-Mama gonna shove that shiv right up her cooch, you watch."

Junk-Mama strutted around Cherish like a cock in a pit, afro bobbing, hands on her hips, daring the little slut to make her move. Junk-Mama was the one Silky Cobra called his bottom bitch, not this skinny twat from the Hills, and she'd be damned if she was gonna take this kind of shit from a runaway honkee slut too good to spread her knees for Mama like everybody else.

"You wanna stay, little chicken, you gotta play," Junk-Mama said, words like frost skimming off her spear-pointed tongue. For having passed thirty, with most of those years qualifying as duly unpleasant, Junk-Mama still had all her parts in the right places, and she could intimidate as well as she could seduce. Cherish, though, she was maybe fifteen, her tight, mostly unspoiled body only hinting at what the bottom bitch had already begun to lose. And to crave. Junk-Mama opened her robe, letting a plump, heavy tit thunder out from behind the threadbare satin. "And you best be playing before the Silky Man show up, or he ain't gonna want to be playing with you at all."

Cherish might not have known how to spell revulsion, but she knew how to feel it. The last few weeks in Jennings Heights had taught her that, in addition to all sorts of other new feelings and skills. She'd learned how to give head, how to roll a drunk, and that drugs felt really good. She'd also learned that it's better to fuck for money than to be fucked by someone who didn't pay or even ask first. Still, the thing she clung to was the one thing that had made her come here in the first place. Cherish didn't like to be told what to do. Cherish stepped forward and plunged her shiv into that fat, weighty tit, then yanked it out.

Junk-Mama's eyes went wide; none of the other girls paid much attention. It took a second, but a single spurting scarlet ejaculation spouted from Junk-Mama's freshly-tapped tit, and Cherish up and lost her god-damned mind.

The projectionist midget cackled gleefully as the girl-- maybe ninety pounds of her, if you wrapped her in wool and dunked her in a pool-- sprang forward and started wailing on Junk-Mama. The ensuing caterwaul managed to wipe away some of the general haze in the room, and within moments the hos were joining in the savage symphony. Cherish wasn't nearly heavy enough to take Junk-Mama to the ground, but that didn't stop her from beating the older hooker's head and chest with her tiny, dirty fists, her shiv still in hand but mostly forgotten. Silky Cobra's bottom bitch stomped and shook and struggled, howling and yelping and spinning to get out from under the hellion.

"That's twenty bucks on you," the one guard said to the other.

"Fuck you, nigga," the other guard said.

The penthouse doors swung open, and the hooting from the bitches cut itself off. The wails of Cherish's ferocity fought with Junk-Mama's pained squeals for dominance until those, too, were silenced.

"What in the name of almighty Jesus do we have here?" Silky Cobra said as he glided through the doorway.

Close behind were the two funky flunkies, flanking pudgy Justin Thompson who couldn't help but quicken his pulse at the sight of so much naked female flesh. At first, he didn't even notice the two women intent on mutually-assured destruction; there were just too many boobies.

Cherish clambered off Junk-Mama and let her collapse as Silky Cobra passed, the pimp not yet deigning to acknowledge them. She momentarily locked eyes with the doughboy who trailed her pimp; he quickly turned red and his head, like he'd never seen a half-naked chick covered in blood straddling a mostly-naked whore bleeding from a pig-stuck tit.

"Half-stack, what we got this week?" Silky Cobra said, sidling up next to the midget.

"*Kylie Takes It In*, Silky Cobra," Half-Stack said, brimming with pride. If there is such a thing as a connoisseur of porn-- a pornosseur, if you would-- Half-Stack would be one. Silky Cobra watched Kylie fulfill the film's title for a minute, quietly nodding approval.

Cherish pulled herself off Junk-Mama. Junk-Mama just lay there on the floor, panting hard, each breath bringing a fresh spurt of thick red slow death from the hole in her tit.

"Did anyone tell yo bitch ass to move, Cherish?" Silky Cobra said, not looking away from Kylie.

Bitch could really take it in.

"No, daddy," Cherish said, trying to keep her voice steady. Between receding adrenaline and growing dread, she didn't know what else to say. The shiv in her hand was heavy and sticky and she couldn't remember why she had it in the first place.

Silky Cobra sighed, pulled himself away from the movie, crossed over to Cherish, and gave her the back of his hand hard enough to loosen more than a couple of teeth. The pimp regarded his bleeding bottom bitch with an appraising eye.

"Cherish," Silky Cobra said, crouching to run a hand through Junk-mama's hair. The whore saw real care in his expression; the pimp saw burgeoning bruises, scratches, and lumps all over the face of one of his top earners. "You know I hate that daddy shit. Creepy. Creepy as fuck. Anybody wants his bitches to call him daddy ain't nothing but a pederast, and an incestuous one at that.

"Damn, baby, bitch done fucked you up."

Cherish had managed to collect herself, the shock of Silky Cobra's pimp-hand jarring her back into the moment. She actually entertained the notion of sticking him with her shiv, but regardless of how things looked, she really didn't want to die at fifteen. "I'm sorry, Silky Cobra."

The pimp stood up, resting his hands on his hips. "Well, we gonna need a new bottom bitch. Raj, Dumpsterdive: throw this old ho in the street." Silky cobra waved, and his funky flunkies gathered Junk-Mama between them and headed for the doors. None of the other girls showed the slightest hint of surprise or emotion. Silky Cobra took stock of his merchandise.

He felt nothing but pride when he looked at his stable. He had black bitches, white bitches, Mexican bitches from Costa fuckin' Rica, a couple slices of genuine Egg-Foo-Yung pussy, even a pot-bellied sand-nigger. His Snatch Menagerie couldn't be beat by anyone in Bitburg, let alone Jennings Heights. The only thing he didn't have was an obvious choice for bottom bitch. He turned finally on Cherish, still clutching at her swollen jaw. There was blood on her clothes and on the floor. *Messy. Bitches always be messy.*

"I guess you thinkin' it should be you, Cherish?" Silky Cobra said. Cherish trembled under his gaze. "You beat the ever-loving fuck out my number one ho and now you gonna take her place?"

"No, Silky Cobra," Cherish said, stammering. "I just--"

Silky Cobra's backhand found its mark again, and Cherish crumpled hard into the floor. The sound of it was enough to make the guards at the door wince; even Half-Stack flinched, Kylie's acrobatics be damned.

"That ain't how it works, baby girl," the pimp said. "This ain't no hierarchy of hos. You didn't move yourself up; you cost your man some money is what you did."

Cherish tried to scramble away, but Silky Cobra moved too quick and too smooth. His snakeskin platform boot caught her in the stomach and she coughed up blood.

"Now," he said. "I was plannin' on savin' you for a while, you know, let you do some other kinda work 'til you was older. But, well, we gots to make up Junk-Mama's share."

Silky Cobra kicked Cherish once more before turning back to his bitches and his crew. He caught sight of Justin Thompson. The kid didn't look nearly as squeamish as he ought to, having just seen his new boss toss a dying bitch into the street and follow it up by kicking the hell out of a girl his own age.

"Justin Thompson," he called, and the fat little bastard snapped to attention. "You popped your cherry yet?"

Justin turned even redder than he'd been, which was in itself a bit of a feat. He swallowed and said, "No sir, Silky Cobra. I ain't. Not yet."

Silky Cobra looked the kid in the eye. "Well, just so happens somebody gotta break this bitch in before I turn her out. Get on that."

Cherish remembered her shiv, but couldn't for the life of her remember what it was for.

Well, Justin Thompson did as he was told, right there in front of everyone. If anyone felt any discomfort, they hid it well enough.

After a few seconds, Silky Cobra went about the normal Friday inspection. He lined his girls up, looking for sores and track marks; to anyone so branded, he just said "street," kissed her on the cheek, and sent her off to work. Those not afflicted were given room keys and reminded just how much Silky Cobra loved his girls.

He ordered the new bitches to his private suite for their baptism. By the time he'd finished, Justin Thompson was bathing

in a goofily-grinned afterglow and Cherish was a sodden, sob-
bing rag of flesh who couldn't even move from where she'd been
dumped.

"How was it, my chunky man? Cuz you a man now, that's
for damn sure." Silky Cobra said, taking in Cherish's shuddering silhouette.

"It was... really, really good, sir," Justin said. He figured he
ought to stand up and show some proper respect, but his legs
wouldn't cooperate.

Silky Cobra chuckled. The sound was gravel in a blender. "I
bet it was.

"Cherish, you understand now why we ain't allowed to beat
the fuck out the other bitches."

Cherish didn't understand much of anything right now.
The only thing she comprehended was pain and the unsettling
notion that Silky Cobra had never even asked what the fight was
about. So she nodded her head, every movement a punch in the
jaw and the cunt.

"Good girl. Now clean yourself up and get out there. You best
to come back with your share and Junk-Mama's, or I'm gonna let
Justin Thompson fuck you up the ass with that little sticker you
got in your hand," Silky Cobra said. He hauled Cherish to her
feet; she did not resist.

The pimp spat into a handkerchief, dabbed some of the
blood off the girl's face. "And if you don't come back, I'm gonna
send Raj and Dumpsterdive after you, and they're gonna bring
you back, and I'm gonna feed you to my dogs.

"Justin Thompson! Get ya'self a heater from the closet and
follow this bitch. You her bodyguard for the night."

Justin jumped to obey. Cherish stood shakily on her feet, blood running down her legs. Half-stack changed the reel. The pimp was satisfied.

"That's it, y'all; get out there and make Silky Cobra's money."

Interlude Part Three: Junk-Mama's Sweet Song of Vengeance

By ten that night, Cherish's wounds were just a dull memory compared to the indignities that had followed. It seemed Justin Thompson had been born for this kind of work: like an old-time carney barker or the Mister Popeil of illicit, abusive sex, he spotted his marks and one after another seduced them into dropping a few bucks for a ride. If they wanted to get rough, that cost a few bucks more. Every other trick, he took a turn on Cherish himself.

She didn't feel much, wasn't even really there. She was back in Poeper Hills, or she was at Disneyland, or maybe Paris. Paris would have been nice. By the time Justin decided to break for lunch, she'd worked up a whole scenario where she drifted like a wind-borne leaf through the streets of the City of Lights, weightless and fearless and beyond all hurting. When she squeezed her eyes hard enough, she could see the golden stars below reflect the silver ones above, and it was almost enough to make reality slip away.

Cherish was sitting in a vinyl booth at the Revolution Diner, where the night workers gathered. There's a certain type of person who works graveyard, and though it may be bad form to paint with such broad strokes, there is an undeniable commonality among them. They work in darkness because they don't want to see the things the light reveals. They learn to look away, or to look through, or just not to look at all. So the things that no one should have to see stay unseen. Nameless to man and god, they fester and grow strong in their anonymity.

Justin Thompson was cutting a steak and talking about some TV show when Junk-Mama walked in. He was in mid-sentence when she pulled a thirty-eight from her purse, held it to his temple, and splattered his brains across the big glass window and its view of the Cobra's Nest. Cherish gave a little "Humph" and a smile before her own skull exploded, drenching the man in the booth behind her. Before she left, Junk-Mama spotted another of Silky Cobra's whores and blew her away, too. No one had time to process what had just happened, let alone react before she was gone.

The hours between her then and her now were a patchwork of agony and rage, a tatterdemalion rag Junk-Mama bundled up around her. There'd been no choice but to stagger to the emergency room at Saint Eugenia's and let the doctors patch the wound in her chest. When they were done, there was a cop waiting for her, but Junk-Mama didn't have time for that shit, so she snuck out and headed for the apartment where she kept her kids. After ten years at Silky Cobra's side, performing whatever pernicious labors he set for her, she had time to do exactly one thing before the anger wore off and the blood she'd lost took its price.

"Just a couple hours, Lord," she'd said as she passed the chapel on her way out of the hospital. "Just a couple of hours and a handful of avenging wrath."

At home, she'd yelled at the kids for being half-dressed and unfed, then took five or six bumps of coke from the baggy in her nightstand. She grabbed the .38 and a couple of other things she'd need from her bedroom, then went across the hall to get some gas cans from Carlos. These she loaded into her blue '73 Caprice ragtop, filled up at the Texaco down the block, and drove back into the heart of Jennings heights. All the while, she kept dipping into the baggy, snorting away the pain in her chest. By the time she pulled her Chevy in front of the diner, her jaw was clenched so tight she broke her right front tooth. She caught a glimpse of that broken little whore Cherish through the diner window, went in, did her thing, and walked out.

Shots fired in The Jen on a Friday night didn't call too much attention, but Junk-Mama knew she only had a couple of minutes before the diner started going nuts over what she'd done. The two thugs standing guard outside the Nest were on their feet already, not quite sure what was going on but fairly certain something was.

Junk-Mama waved at the men; she'd known them for as long as they'd been in Silky Cobra's service, and even though they'd been there when he threw her away, they waved back without a thought. She lifted her hand-cannon and fired twice: the one's chest exploded; the other's knee disappeared and he dropped hard to the ground.

This round of gunplay did manage to draw some attention; someone started screaming, and soon johns and hookers and the few regular people who braved these parts joined in. Some of them even started running for their lives, not that they needed to bother.

Junk-Mama opened up the trunk of her blue Caprice, taking out a big cardboard box of bottles filled with gas and stuffed with rags. The two gas cans were next and took some finagling to fit into the box. Up the three steps to the nest, the other guard was writhing and hollering up a storm, so she set the box down, padded up the stairs, and put the last slug from the .38 into his left eye. She tossed the rod on her way back to the car, pulled the brand-new 1976 Remington 870 Wingmaster pump-action sawed-off out of the trunk, then tied the machete around her waist and grabbed the box of Molotov Cocktails. Hauling all this crap was a pain, but damn if she was going to make two trips.

By the time she stepped through the front doors into the Nest, Junk-Mama was effectively announced. Most of Silky Cobra's goons were out watching the girls on the street, but his Funky Flunkies were never far from his side. One of the idiots-- Raj-- came rushing at her right away; she caved in his skull with one of the Molotovs and he dropped. The less stupid of the two-- Dumpsterdive-- fumbled with a pistol at the top of the grand double staircase, but never managed to draw it; a load of birdshot from her twelve-gauge sent splinters and marble shrapnel flying all around him. The second load convinced him to stop resisting, while the third left him thinking, for as long as it took him to stop breathing, that he probably should have resisted a little longer.

Not quite finished, Junk-Mama faced the gas-soaked idiot just now getting to his feet in front of the door. She gave him a quick boot to the nuts, took a box of strike-anywhere matches out of her pocket, and lit the motherfucker on fire. His screams provided the perfect backdrop for the chorus of ground-floor doors opening up to let loose a disbelieving horde of hookers and tricks, but there was no way in hell they were getting past her.

Every one of these snatchrags had just watched Silky Cobra toss her in the garbage, and even if they could get past the wailing, flaming corpse in the doorway, she wasn't about to let them get that far. Two halls lead from the lobby to the trick-rooms, and it took about as many seconds for Junk-Mama to light another pair of Molotovs and lob one down each corridor.

She trotted up the stairway and hit the elevator button, leaving the flaming gaggle of hos to finish spreading the fire. It opened right up on a third funky flunky too slow to raise his gun before she let him have it with hers. She gave it to him in the belly, then dug her fingers into the lacey flesh that was left and yanked him out of the car. Junk-Mama toppled him onto the twitching remnants of the first guy she'd shot-gunned, then smashed one of the Molotovs on the floor, dropped another match, and sent them both to hell. The gun was empty, so she tossed it and hitched the box up on her hip.

The elevator didn't take forty seconds to reach the penthouse.

Half-Stack was there at his projector, getting head from a fat, one-legged Sri Lankan hermaphrodite who Silky Cobra kept on hand for when he was feeling bored. Still hefting the box under one arm, Junk-Mama drew her machete and had it buried in the Sri Lankan's skull before it dawned on either her or the pornosseur that someone else had entered the satin sanctuary. Because that's how bodies work, the dead whore's jaw muscles spasmed, and her last act as anything resembling a living person was to bite Halfstack's surprisingly formidable cock right off.

The midget howled, scrambling backward and knocking the projector from its stand. A quick jerk from Junk-Mama freed the machete, and a last tired swing freed the midget from the bonds of mortality.

Junk-Mama hadn't realized how much of an exertion revenge was going to be. It was damned tiring, in fact, and by now, her wounded tit was throbbing and most of the coke had worn off. She was surprised at how quiet it was up here in the penthouse; the sounds of the fiery panic six floors below didn't even register. Still, Half-stack had raised a hell of a ruckus, so she didn't have time to do any more than catch her breath.

The penultimate stage of Junk-Mama's spectacularly efficient revenge involved liberally dousing the sitting room with gasoline, which she did with particular abandon. She'd always hated this tawdry crap; if she'd had her way, the place would have been done up tasteful and understated, like one of those nice San Francisco brothels. Instead, Silky Cobra just buried them all in zebra stripes and leopard spots. Said it reminded him how he was a cobra, the perfect predator, and they were all his prey.

"Yeah, we're prey all right," she said, emptying the last of the gasoline. The box had gotten much lighter, down to one Molotov and a couple of the other things she'd picked up at home. "That's all I ever was to you, isn't it? Just a little animal to get eaten by the big, bad snake. Well, tonight I'm a mongoose, motherfucker."

Apparently, Junk-Mama had read a book somewhere along the way, but she really should have saved her one bad-ass line for the next room.

She tossed a match into the center of the sitting room, and the place went right the hell up. Something finally stirred in Silky Cobra's suite, so she pulled the last thing out of the box and waited for the door to burst open.

Burst it did, the groovy Poobah of Jennings Heights bursting right along with it. Bare-assed and dripping with sweat, a pair of pearl-handled forty-fives in his hands, he would have looked funny as hell if he'd been anyone else. But he wasn't anyone else, and the look on his face almost stopped Junk-Mama from finishing her tantrum.

"Bitch, what the hell do you think you're-" Silky Cobra said before the grenade Junk-Mama tossed to him cut off everything else. Reflexively, he dropped his guns to catch the thing, not quite recognizing what he'd caught.

"I'm not your bitch anymore, Silky," she said. "I'm not a dog. Dogs don't kill snakes. I been your bitch for ten years, but tonight I ain't that. Tonight, I'm a fucking mongoose."

Watching Silky Cobra's expression change from unbridled fury to dumb-founded consternation made the whole wretched day worth it.

The bomb exploded, blowing the pimp's arms clean off at the elbows and filling his chest, belly, legs, and face with shrapnel. He tried to stand up, blind and deaf from the flash and the bang, but Junk-Mama, again, didn't have time for that shit.

She grabbed him by the hair and drug him into his suite, where one of the new girls-- a skinny, luded Filipina-- howled bloody murder from her hiding spot behind the bed.

Junk-Mama hadn't counted on the grenade being so loud, or on the whore-décor being so flammable; she couldn't hear anything over the ringing in her ears, and rich black smoke brought darkness thicker than the night's to the penthouse. Her stitches had popped, and she couldn't breathe. But she still had one more thing to check off her list.

Junk-Mama chucked what was left of Silky Cobra onto the bed, and the Filipina went wild, leaping around like a cornered rat. Whatever Silky Cobra screamed was lost to the yowl of the blaze. Junk-Mama caught the whore by the ankles and threw her out the window, the fresh air breathing new life into the fire.

In an instant, the conflagration engulfed Junk-Mama. Her hair caught first, crowning her in a halo of flame. In his terror, before his eyes melted, Silky Cobra watched her smile as she anointed them both with the last Molotov.

Interlude: Epilogue

That was pretty much the end of that. Jennings Heights' heyday ended a few years later. Much like the charred carcass of Cardinal's Crest, the Cobra's Nest is still there. It's still surrounded by the ghetto, resisting all attempts by the cancer of gentrification to remove it from the sight of the world.

There are plenty who remember the night Junk-Mama went shithouse on her pimp, but it's not a subject anyone likes to talk about. The Nest isn't a place anyone ever goes into, either, even with the rumors of Silky Cobra's stash still hidden somewhere inside. It's not so much that they're afraid the place will fall down around their ears; it's more the fact that everybody knows the place is haunted, and the only thing scarier than a living, evil motherfuckin' pimp is an evil motherfucking pimp-ghost.

And just like they do with Cardinal's Crest, the people of Bitburg keep the Nest on the down-low, keep their eyes looking the other way, keep their home living up to its nickname: *Bitburg, the Quiet City*.

Chapter Two: ghostpuncher begins

-Verse 1-

Cyclops, Twenty-Something, a Couple of Hours After Chapter One

"For the last time, they are not zombies, dammit," Jeremy said, smacking the table for emphasis.

"Of course they're zombies," Sarissa said, rolling her eyes in dismissal. She had a way about her that could drive anyone nuts, the smug, self-enamored certainty that came from honestly believing that everything she said or did was right. "They're dead. They eat people. Hence, they're zombies."

"Zombies don't eat people!" Jeremy's exasperation knew no bounds at this point, thanks to yet another round of free whiskey. For some reason, he found himself, though otherwise at the end of his rope, quite fond of Albrecht Drue. Sarissa squeezed her eyes closed and smiled a tight, wide, patronizing smile that she hoped would let Jeremy know what an ignoramus he was.

"He's got a point," Eldon said. "Zombies don't eat people; ghouls eat people."

Grigsby, Eleanor, Lyric, Cletus, and Dave all groaned over their beers. Well, Lyric didn't; she groaned into her tea. They knew what was coming next. Only Jeremy showed a positive reaction because while he had picked up the smack in this particular discussion, Eldon was about to lay it down; Sarissa might believe she knew everything, but as far as anyone could tell, Eldon did.

Sarissa balked. "What are you on about, Ellie? Romero invented the modern zombie, and all his zombies did was eat people."

"They did lurch a lot, too," Lyric said, peeking over her tea. The fatter Ghost Geek glared at her, so Lyric dove back into the cup.

"Yes, but Romero had the good sense not to call his monsters 'zombies,'" Eldon said, sitting up straight. As he elucidated, his speech became rapid-fire and excited. "See, *Night of the Living Dead* was originally called *Night of the Flesh-Eaters*. And he never wrote the title or copyright on any of the script pages, so all anyone had to do to show it was change the name. Which is why it went into the public domain and it took like thirty years for Romero to see dime one from it.

"And he never, ever called them zombies. The closest he ever came was 'ghouls,' which actually fits the mythology. See, whereas ghouls are mindless, animate corpses possessed of only an insatiable hunger for flesh, zombies are totally different."

Dave leaned forward, much against his better judgment. "So why are they so hungry for brains in particular?"

Eldon beamed, tail fully wagging. For such a runty little guy, he managed to take up a lot of space when he got rolling on something like this. Most of the time, he just disappeared into the group, content enough to see what everyone else did. "They don't! That came about with *Return of the Living Dead*, Romero's cash-in he made to make up for all the money he didn't get from *N-O-T-L-D*."

Grigsby drained another beer, snapped his fingers for the waitress. *Fuck how crowded it was, and fuck how hot she was; if a barmaid couldn't keep his pint full, then she damn well better find another job.* "Then what's a fuckin' zombie, oi?"

"You wanna take this one, Eleanor?" Eldon said, tipping his pint towards her with a conspiratorial wink.

"What, just because I'm an old black woman I'm supposed to know about zombies?" Eleanor said, affecting all the indignation she could muster. "I'm from Indiana, not Port-au-Prince, dammit. Racist little nigga."

Eldon's eyes went wide, and he panicked on the inside. He hadn't meant anything by it, and he tried to make his mouth convey as much, but nothing would come out. The table went silent.

Eleanor couldn't hold it in any longer; she burst out with a loud, long, guffaw that cut through the Cyclops's din like a plus sign on a pregnancy test through a teenager's post-coital euphoria. A number of the other patrons looked over at her, not least among them a table full of bros and a rather ebullient ten o'clock Al, who had managed to insert himself into a group of barely-out-of-high-school art students.

"Of course I know about zombies," she said. "I am an old black woman, after all. And my mama *was* from Port-au-Prince.

"Zombies are the bound souls of the newly dead, raised by a gris-gris man to do his nefarious bidding."

Eldon felt much better. "And what do zombies eat?"

Eleanor rolled her eyes. "Not people, that's for sure. Gotta be feedin' 'em the blandest foods you can find, or the physical sensations will remind 'em they dead and poof! They just march back to their graves and shuffle off to the other world."

"So no brains then?" Grigsby said. He was positive that the waitress was ignoring him, and he was about to get pissed.

"Nope," Eleanor said. "Maybe some of Lyric's hippy tofu bullshit, but that's about it."

Dave said, "They drink?"

"Fresh water," Eleanor said. "Or maybe a Bud Light."

"Enough!" Sarissa said, annoyed that the conversation and the attention had drifted away from her. "It doesn't matter what the technical definition is: when people hear 'zombie' they think 'brain-eating walking corpse,' so that's what a zombie is."

Eldon was about to say something against the erosion of meaning by the effluence of common perception, but Dave caught sight of that intent and sidestepped it with a deft shift of parlay.

"Hey, y'all have all heard the new EVPs, right?" he said, parrying Eldon's intended lesson with the skill of a master swordsman. "I think we really got something this time."

"I ain't heard shit," Grigsby said. He finally locked eyes with Lilith; the smile she shot him went straight through the heart of his irritation, and he suddenly wondered how he could ever feel anything but the purest of lusts for such a remarkable girl.

Dave threw on his "check this shit out" face. "Now, I got this after asking, 'Is there someone here who wants to communicate?' It's faint, but you can hear it pretty clear."

The Bitburg Supernatural Squad leaned together as one, Dave setting a digital recorder in the middle of the circle. From the corner where the least extricable chair sat in almost complete darkness, Cletus bent his six-and-a-half feet of silent, unintentional menace to join the huddle. Even Sarissa betrayed a touch of excitement, though she made certain not to show too much; it simply wouldn't do to get all worked up in front of the others.

"This one is so cool," Dave said, a dreamy veil laying itself over his face. He turned the volume up all the way, held out a hand for silence. Static, broken by an unintelligible gurgle, flowed from the recorder. Dave couldn't believe he'd caught something so clear and clarion, but there it was. He looked from one face to another, watching their reactions. Just for good measure, he played the EVP again.

Sarissa couldn't quite make it out, but if Dave said there was something there, there was something there. She adopted a contemplative air and looked to Eldon.

"Get out of my house? Maybe," Eldon said, not sure at all.

Eleanor shrugged. Grigsby snorted. Cletus nodded. Lyric barely looked up from her tea. Jeremy, having served his purpose in this narrative, ceased to exist. He was not missed.

Dave's crest fell, leaving him crestfallen. Made sense. Still, his enthusiasm would not be dampened. "I can't believe you don't hear that. It's plain as day it's a male voice saying, 'Don't turn around.' Listen again."

Dave played the recording, and this time the rest of his crew did hear something, very clearly. Another play and they heard a man say, "Don't turn around."

"Where'd you get that?" Lyric said. She'd set her tea down and lit up a clove cigarette; Sarissa made a show of coughing, so Lyric sank into herself and stubbed it out. How could she be so dumb as to forget Sarissa was allergic to smoke? She coughed every time she saw someone smoking, even if they were on opposite sides of the street in a windstorm. Sometimes, Sarissa coughed when somebody smoked in a movie, so she had to be really allergic, right?

Cletus leaned back into the shadows. The darkness around him rumbled, "At Barringer Manor."

Eldon's hurt was palpable; he was the one who'd done the legwork to get Mrs. Barringer to call them in the first place. He had plans for that place, and Dave hadn't even asked him before he went and dove headfirst into what-- if all his research into the supernatural and the arcane proved correct-- promised something way beyond the scope of anything they'd seen so far. "You went without us?"

"We just did some preliminary scouting. I'm telling y'all, that place is packed with paranormal," Dave said. "I think this is gonna be the one that really puts us on the map. Take a look at this." Dave produced his smartphone, swiped a few times, and held it out for the rest of the group to see. Sarissa choked a little on her Chablis.

A pulse of giddy exhilaration beat through the Bitburg Supernatural Squad. Sure enough, right there on Dave's phone was an image of a white mist in a vaguely humanoid shape, with no fewer than five multi-colored orbs clearly visible in the frame. "How fucking cool is that?"

Eldon's eyes glazed over with a salty, wet, lachrymal discharge. They'd been at the ghosthunting game for years, and while they had a few good EVPs and a couple of photos that had made the rounds on the internet, not to mention a metric shit-ton of anecdotal evidence, this was far and away the most compelling proof he'd seen yet. Just the thought of finally coming face-to-face with the unknown and thereby knowing it turned him into the wide-eyed kid he'd been way back before he'd known the difference between a zombie and a ghoul, let alone a ghost and a residual haunting.

"Have you ever thought about what you'd do?" he said, looking up past the ceiling, the roof, all the way past the stars into the endless infinity of the universe. He got like this sometimes, lost in imagining, talking to everyone and no one all at once. He snapped back to the then and there, locking eyes with Lyric. "Really, what are you going to do when we finally come face-to-face with an honest-to-God ghost?"

Shoved into the spotlight, Lyric fumbled with her teabag, eyes big and darting in their sockets for an escape route. Everyone was looking at her, so she figured she had to say something. "I don't really, well, I'm not... I guess I'd try to just watch it, you know? See what it did. I don't know."

"I'd take a picture, of course," Eleanor said. She made a habit of saving the poor hippy from uncomfortable social situations, which, for Lyric, meant nearly all of them. "Take a picture and sell that son of a bitch for millions."

Grigsby, desperately in need of a beer, said "Shit meself, then go get a drink. Speaking of which..." before leaving the table for the bar. Lilith may have been gorgeous, but she was a terrible fucking waitress.

"Seen a ghost once," Cletus said, his words a part of the shadowy blanket his corner afforded. It wasn't his fault he came off so spooky; the light hurt his eyes, and the noise confused him some, but as long as he kept his back to a wall and his front mostly in the darkness, he could manage. That's why he liked ghost-hunting: plenty of dark, no extraneous sounds. "Didn't do anything. Shoulda said hello, I guess."

Sarissa decided Cletus had finished talking. "I know what I'd do. I would know, once and for all, that there is an after-life, and I'd live the rest of my life not having to worry about anything."

Sometimes, Sarissa said some stupid shit. Dave usually let it slide, but not always. "Not having to worry about anything? I'd be worried even more, mainly because if there's ghosts, there's prob'ly also some God, and I'm pretty sure that if there's a God, there's a whole bunch of crap I'd have to make up for doing."

Sarissa didn't know how to respond; she should have waited to hear what Dave said before she spoke. She thought up a way to make their answers mesh and was just about to repair her gaff, but never got the chance.

"Whattup, the Ghost Geeks?" Albrecht Drue said, dropping himself into Grigsby's empty chair like Little Boy hitting Hiro-shima. "What's good?"

Sarissa turned her nose up at Al because he was a low-life and Dave was watching; Eldon brightened, all but visibly glow-ing; Eleanor, thanking fateful proximity once again, wrapped an arm around Al and gave him a good long squeeze. Lyric man-aged a quivering grin. Dave darkened.

"Hey, Al," Cletus said, tipping his glass in Al's direction. Because he was Al, Al clinked it with a half-drained bottle of Fighting Cock, waited just long enough for a "no" that never showed, then sloshed some potable napalm into the two remaining fingers of beer. "Thanks."

"So, what are we talking about?" Al said, adding whiskey to glasses until he got to Lyric's teacup. He gave her a conspiratorial look, which transformed into jubilation when the little mouse sat up and said "Okay, but just one."

Al filled her cup, and by the way she slugged it down, you'd have thought he'd filled it with water. Al giggled.

"We were just trying to imagine what it would be like to actually meet a ghost in the flesh. Or ectoplasm," Lyric said, warming to her drink.

"Yeah, wouldn't it have to be more of a zombie if it had flesh?" Al said, taking a draught from the bottle. His free hand, in less time than it takes to tell, produced, lit, and perched upon his lip a Lucky Strike. When he exhaled, Sarissa didn't complain a bit.

"Not this shite again," Grigsby said. He had a sixer of Budweiser longnecks arrayed expertly against the webbing between his fingers, and very little intention of sharing. "And get yer bloody ass outta my chair, ye wank."

Al popped himself up, but before he could take a step away, Eleanor reeled him into her lap.

"Baby, I'm all the seat you ever gonna need," she said, biting her lip in a playful way.

"Baby, you keep talkin' like that, ain't neither one of us gonna be doin' any sittin'," Al said, returning the ogle. He wasn't exactly sure what he'd do if the old lady ever took things any further, but he was pretty sure they'd both regret it. Still, even if you're not going to the party, it's nice to be invited.

"So, what would you do, Al?" Eldon said, genuinely interested. He looked at Al the way a pee-wee hockey player would look at Wayne Gretzky, for reasons no one who'd known their own father or ever had a brother could possibly understand.

"What would I what?" Al said, acutely aware that Eleanor's hands were overtly kneading his thigh. He had to admit, for an old bird, she still had nimble hands... and he was pretty drunk...

"Yeah, I'm interested, too," Dave said. He gave Al the same look he gave every tough-guy civilian who never had the sack to enlist. "Just what would you do if you saw a real-live, honest-to-god ghost?"

Al met Dave's glare gamely; it wasn't a secret that Dave thought Al was an obnoxious drunk, or that Al couldn't have cared less if caring less came with a free toaster. He didn't mind Dave at all, mainly because the rest of the Ghost Geeks were chill kids and he'd been deflecting Dave's shade for years.

"Lemme ponder on that a sec," Al said, adopting a pondering posture. He swirled the notion around in his head like vintage wine in a dirty glass, examined its legs, then came to a decision.

"I reckon," he said, "I came across a ghost, I'd punch it right in its goddamned ghost face."

Grigsby cracked up, choppy British chortles that rang throughout the bar. Eleanor squeezed both of Al's hips, which he took as an opportunity to bail the hell out of her lap, which, truth be told, had gotten a little too warm for propriety.

"I bet you would at that," Dave said, holding up his glass and nodding to Al's bottle. He didn't know why he disliked the guy so much; Dave got along with everyone, even Sarissa. There was just something thoughtless about him that reminded him of every loudmouth bully he'd had to deal with growing up, coupled with a situational unawareness that would have gotten him and anyone around him killed in Afghanistan. The United States Marine Corps had taught Dave to see the world a certain way, and everything from how Al just barreled his way into the conversation to the way he encouraged Lyric to take a drink even though he knew she was only twenty was absolute anathema to his way of thinking. Al might have been a fighter, but he wasn't a soldier, and as far as Dave was concerned, that made him less than a man.

"Cheers, dude," Grigsby said, holding out his own pint. "You do the ghost-punchin', I'll do the pants-shittin'. And the bottle-draining."

Al poured for the guys, then emptied the rest into himself. He probably shouldn't have, but he wasn't going to feel it for another couple of hours anyway, and, like he said, he had an image to maintain. "Speaking of which, some fucker's done gone and emptied this one. Guess I'll have to remedy that."

With a bow and a flourish, Al left the Ghost Geeks to themselves. The flourish may have been one touch too many because his brain didn't quite stop spinning when the rest of him did and he ended up knocking full-force into a wall of meaty Ed-Hardy-ensconced Bro-hood.

"Sorry, mate," Al said, rocking back on his heels. Faux-hawk, he realized with equal parts satisfaction and resignation, comprised the meat in question.

"Hey, don't worry about it, bro," Dax Vagance said, SEG in full effect. He had a pair of pitchers in his hands; somehow, not a drop had spilled. "You look a little shaky there; you doin' alright?"

A plastic mannequin smile under plastic mannequin hair, Faux-hawk could have been a display at Hot Topic. Even through all the beer and cigarette smoke, the guy reeked of Axe body spray. Even worse, when Lilith spun up to where the two were faced off, she hugged up against him like she'd known him for years. What was it Al had been thinking about party invitations? Al's fist was cold and white, squeezing the neck of his bottle just shy of hard enough to break it; Dax's eyes were making an invitation to the kind of party where no one danced, no one got laid, and the music always sucked, but where Al found himself showing up over and over anyway.

"Oh, baby," Lilith said to either or both of them depending on which one you asked, slinking in between the pair. She may have been a shitty waitress but did have a talent for putting out fires with a soft word and a pair of soft but remarkably firm boobies. "Al's always doin' alright. Hey, how could he not be; it's Check Day!"

It was Check Day! Al got all warm on the inside and forgot that Faux-hawk existed. "I do believe that calls for a celebration."

"Ooh, almost forgot," Lilith said, aiming Dax at his table and talking over her shoulder. "Charlene said something about a smoky-treat. Maybe you should see what she's talking about?"

Lilith hated giving Al even more of a reason to go fawn over Miss Dish-hands, but she hated the idea of him bashing Dax's skull in even more; the guy was cute, and he had a huge tab open. As many things as she was, she wasn't a meteorologist but didn't need to be to see the cloud forming over Al's head to know what was coming their way.

"Many thanks, Lilly Love-Goddess," Al said, bending over to plant a kiss on Lilith's hand before ambling up to the bar. Though the place was as packed as it ever got, a momentary lull had stolen over the actual bar, of which Charlene took advantage by furiously scrubbing out glasses in a sink overflowing with unsafely hot water. Al watched her work, single-minded and unwavering, and lost himself in the rhythmic movements of her back and arms. After a moment, she looked up, caught his eyes, and turned him into balmy pudding with a smile.

"I figured it out, darlin'," Al said.

"What's that?" Charlene straightened up, satisfied that her wrathful labors had cowed any errant feces from her glassware. Then she put her hot, moist hands over Al's, leaning close so they wouldn't have to shout.

"You make me feel like a big cold scoop of vanilla ice cream melting over a warm brownie," Al said. He meant it, too.

Charlene rolled her eyes. "That's either the worst pick-up line anyone has ever used in the history of ever or the sweetest thing you've ever had come out of your mouth."

Al smirked, blushing, "Made you smile, either way."

"Yeah, but maybe I was smiling to keep myself from laughing at you," Charlene said. She tossed a glance at her partner for this week, a chubby guy with a goatee and sleeve tattoos who made a hell of a mojito, assured herself that he could handle things for a few minutes. She did her best sexy face. "Smoke me, baby."

Al sniffled, jutted out his bottom lip. "I don't know if I can if you're just gonna laugh at me."

Charlene just grabbed him by the wrist and led him down the length of the bar, arms stretched above the heads of the folks lined up in front of it. The irregulars might have complained, but everyone who'd hit the 'Clops more than twice knew Al and Charlene's halftime ritual. They passed through the kitchen, down the stairs into the basement, then up through the storm doors into the alley out back. There among the vermin and garbage, Al passed Charlene the one cigarette she allowed herself each day, lit it, and waited silently for the first drag to have its way with her.

-2-

Eight years ago, Charlene had been a smoker. She'd been a lot of things back then but one thing she never was was without a cigarette. But because the universe works the way it does-- or maybe just because her besty liked to meddle in the lives of others as a way of avoiding her own issues-- she'd stopped being a lot of the things she'd been before that night back in Twenty-oh-Something.

Deep in the throes of the most heinous nic-fit she'd experienced since she'd stopped being pregnant, she'd met Al right on this very spot. She'd popped out of the hatch and there he was, perched like a gargoyle on top of the dumpster, a smoke on his lip and a bottle at his hip.

"Hello, darlin'," he'd said, without a trace of the predation normally associated with large, drunk men in dark alleys. Regardless, she didn't feel particularly social; her mind was on the pack of Kools in her jacket pocket. She reached for her smokes, determined that she didn't give two square shits about whether or not she could ever carry a fetus to term if it meant she had to deal with the tribulation of having to give up the one thing that had kept her sane since she was twelve.

"Mother of whores!" she said, rather invectively. The fresh, unopened box of minty, delicious cancer sticks had been replaced by a pack of gum and a note that read *You'll thank me later--Lil.* She might say something nice at her funeral, but she sure as fuck wasn't going to thank her ass.

"No," Al had said. "Son of Texans.

"Problem, darlin'?"

Even all twisted up in rage, Charlene had the prettiest face Al had ever seen. It cut through whatever malingering alcohol vapors clung to his brain the way headlights cut through the life expectancy of a deer on a two-lane Pennsylvania backroad. She wasn't, by any stretch, the prettiest girl in the world; her nose was a little lop-sided, and her mismatched eyes had a disconcerting effect on the viewer. She carried a few more pounds than current fashion would approve of. Charlene wasn't, by any standard, perfect.

But she was perfect for Al.

He hopped off the dumpster and strode towards her, leather hood bobbing with the dismount. Charlene had already taken hold of the pepper spray attached to her keychain and knocked a particularly barbed arrow to the bow of her tongue, but a random turn of the clouds above the alley shone a spotlight on her inadvertent companion and she stopped short. He was huge, almost menacing, but the way he moved, the utter lack of ill intent, told her not to be afraid. She unclenched her hand and let out a short, exasperated sigh.

"Yeah," she said. "People who think they know my business better than me."

"Those people suck," Al had said. From somewhere inside the slick skin of his jacket, he birthed a pack of Luckies and put one to his lip. "Lucky for you, ain't none of them about."

Charlene's green eye lingered on the tantalizing roll of tobacco and sundry other poisons just long enough for Al to notice, so he produced a second and held it out for her. "Smokin'?"

The release she'd felt when Al had lit her cigarette rivaled any orgasm Charlene could imagine, let alone any she'd actually experienced. She wasn't proud to be such a minion of her addiction, but sometimes, nothing feels better than just giving in to your body, and the consequences can all go lick their own assholes for all they matter at that moment of pure, indomitable bliss.

They didn't talk while they smoked; Charlene's mind was on the smokin', and Al's was on Charlene. Her puffs were graceful sips that savored the vespers once on the inhale and once on the ex; every time Al drew, the cherry flared red and the sound of paper burning crackled in the quiet dark. Finally, Al steadied himself against the wall, lifted his foot in a figure-four position, and stubbed the butt against the sole of his boot. Charlene remembered clearly how tickled she'd gotten when he went over to the dumpster and, after making sure the last ember had been extinguished, properly disposed of the litter; fire safety was kinda one of her things.

He smiled at her, lips together but not pressed, and she couldn't help but smile back. "Thanks," Charlene said. She immediately ended her smoke, cutting it off with a dramatic inhalation. She would have normally flicked the butt away but found herself instead rubbing it out against the wall and tossing the remains in the dumpster.

"Albrecht Drue," Al had said, quite unprovoked, and held out a hand for Charlene to shake.

Well, at least that answered who this weirdo was, if not why he was hanging out in the dark behind her bar. She didn't know what else to do or want to be rude, so she shook the proffered hand. She couldn't help but smile a defenseless smile when his lips parted to reveal a chipped right front tooth. The goofiness of that grin squashed any lingering doubts she had about the guy; she liked him; creepiness be damned.

"Charlene Godwin," she said. "Hey, why don't you come in and have a drink? I think I owe you one. For the smoke."

Al drew back, tossed his hair with a dismissive shrug. He had noticed her Led Zeppelin "Icarus" t-shirt that hinted at a shared appreciation for the finest music ever written. "Sorry, darlin', but I've healthy drunk a thousand times, and it's time to ramble on."

Charlene shook her head, rolled her eyes, stuck out her tongue. Albrecht Drue blew her mind a little when he half bowed before skipping off down the alley, singing Zep's *Ramble On* with great gusto and absolutely no regard for key, pitch, or proper lyrics. For the rest of her shift, her nicotine craving remained abated; when it flared, she just thought about Al and it died again.

The next night, the craving was back. She'd made sure to bring an actual pack of smokes this time, but when she popped out of the hatch halfway through the night, Al was right back where he'd been. She didn't have time to even open her Kools before Al had a Lucky for her; she accepted it gratefully and stashed the box behind some crates. They shared a smoke and some chitchat, and this time Al accepted her invitation for a drink. Inside the Cyclops, Charlene mostly ignored everyone else to listen to Al's too-impossible-to-be-true stories, but never hinted at her disbelief.

That's pretty much how it went for the next eight years. Charlene never officially quit smoking, but she figured the one a day she shared with Al didn't count. As time wormed its way into their lives, Al became a fixture at her bar, and Charlene became a pillar in his life. Things changed, because age and inclination destroy everything, but almost every night, they went back to that alley and sucked down a Lucky Strike.

Now, that was going to end, and Charlene didn't have any illusions on how her friend would take it.

He looked almost exactly the same as he had eight years ago, but something was missing from those bright brown eyes of his. Sure, he'd added a few pounds, lost a little hair, maybe, and the bags under his eyes were newish, too. But for all the things age had put on him, it had taken something as well.

"Lookin' luminous as ever, darlin'," Al said, managing to keep most of the slur out of his voice. He'd been knocking it back pretty competitively for about five hours by now, but as long as he kept moving and talking, Charlene knew he'd be alright; it wasn't the drinking that was Al's problem, it was the stopping.

"Thanks babe," Charlene said, just to melt Al's heart a touch. When she smoked, she held her business elbow in her support hand, keeping it tight to her belly. "You look like you're having a good time. How is the freshman crop, by the way?"

Al blushed, thinking back to the art school girls he'd been hanging out with. "Young. Seems like every year, they look a little more like kids and a little less like targets."

"That's because you're getting old, Al," Charlene said.

"Better than the alternative," Al said, mostly meaning it. He felt the weight of his final settlement check inside his jacket and wondered if that was true after all. "But I been old for a while now, so it's up for debate."

He grinned at her, but she saw through it. Four or five years ago, she would have pressed him, would have wanted to know more. But that ship had sunk a long time ago, and Charlene didn't have it in her to dive in after it any more.

There wasn't any need to wait any longer, or anything she could think of to get out of saying what she had to say.

"So, I'm getting back together with Jake," Charlene said all at once, slapping the grin right off Al's face. "We're moving to Atlanta in a couple of weeks."

He recovered quickly enough; Al had an uncanny ability to take a punch. He hid his color-drain behind a brutal drag on his Lucky, lit another on its tip. He flicked the burning butt towards the open end of the alley, because fuck fire-safety.

"The DJ?" Al said. *Of course it was the goddamned DJ; who else would it be?* He must not have been as good at hiding his emotions as he thought, because Charlene read every word he didn't say in that flick of the cigarette and the way he stiffened his back.

"Come on, Al," she said. "You know who Jake is; it's not like he hasn't been a huge part of my life the entire time you've known me."

That was true; at least once a quarter, Jake the DJ showed up to screw with Charlene's life. He'd hit it big-- at least as big as a DJ can hit it, anyway-- about the same time Charlene had lost her unborn kid, then sacked off for the touring life as quick as he could. That didn't stop him from calling her up whenever he was wasted in Phuket or Ibiza or Detroit, and sure as hell didn't keep him from dropping by whenever he landed in Bitburg. The fucked-up thing was two-fold: Charlene didn't hold a single grain of ill-will toward him; and even Al liked him well enough, in small doses, when he was drunk enough to forget just how crappy he treated Charlene.

"You really think that's a good idea?" Al said a little sharper than he meant to. "I mean, isn't he just gonna be in and out like he always is?"

Charlene gave Al a rare look of disapproval. "No, that's not how he's gonna be. He's done touring. In fact, he's got a studio set up down there and he's been doing some producing, and it looks like we're gonna be able to settle in one spot and, you know, be grown-ups."

"Unlike what you are now?" Al said. "You're the most grown-up person I know; for Christ's sake, everyone in the bar thinks you're their frikkin' mom as it is."

"But I'm not, Al," Charlene said. Her eyes bulged with an indeterminate pressure; the back of her throat got hot and tight. "I want to be someone's actual mother, you know? And Jake promised me we could start a family now that he's not going to be on the road."

"He promised that huh?" Al said, having given up on trying to fight his sudden-onset emotions. He wanted to grab her and shake her, yell at her, remind her that this was the same guy who'd promised to never leave her, only to conveniently take his furlough when she miscarried his child. This was the same guy who'd left her to fend for herself while he was out living it up with his dick in every hole from here to Nepal. As long as Al had known her, Charlene had never been with anyone, not even Al, regardless of how hard he tried or how much she wanted to. But reminding her of that would be kind of a dick move. Still, he was drunker than he should have been to hear this, and he couldn't filter out all the anger. "I guess if Jake the DJ promised that, it's got to be true."

So many feels. He didn't have to throw any more garbage at her to see that, even censored for her benefit, he'd already heaped enough of the same things on her that she'd been burying herself in since she started making this decision. As out of the blue as it was for him, the Jake thing had been with her for some time. Maybe she looked a little less fresh than she used to; maybe she was a little more exhausted every time she closed the bar. Maybe Charlene had outgrown the job she'd taken as a kid fresh out of that same art school around the corner, and maybe she wanted something more out of life than serving drinks to washed-up never-wases like Al. She certainly deserved it.

But dammit, Al wanted more, too. He wanted her, because when she breathed the same air he did, getting old really was better than the alternative.

Charlene was still looking at him, her expression somewhere between hurt and desperate. He wasn't going to say anything to change her mind, and even if he did, what then? He had his entire future in his jacket pocket, and it sure as hell wasn't going to last long enough to give her the things she deserved. Besides, what the hell did he care, anyway? Charlene was his friend, that's all she'd ever been, and there just wasn't any damn reason to make her feel bad for sharing what, at least to her, was happy news.

"No, really," Al said at last, stubbing his barely-smoked Lucky against the bottom of his boot. "Jake's a good guy; I'm sure he's got his wanderlust out of him. Y'all are gonna be happy, I know it."

Charlene finished her smoke, the weight in her eyes and the strangling discomfort in her throat abated. She nodded, shivering against the chill that came as much from her friend as the night itself. Not cold enough for snow this late in the spring, but cold enough that the rain waiting up above would make for a miserable walk home. She should have felt relief at Al's tacit approval of her plan, but a big part of her had hoped he'd make more of a fuss. She'd known all along how he felt about her; it's not like he'd ever tried to keep it a secret. There had even been times when she'd come close to admitting she had the same feelings for him. It's just that Al was... well, he was Al, and Al wasn't the kind of guy who could give her the future she wanted.

She'd gone to school. She'd worked hard every day of her life. She wanted to be with someone who had done the same things she had, not some man-child who'd literally been hit by a truck full of money and not lifted a finger ever since. She wanted to be a mother to her own children, not to her lover. And if Al wasn't even going to try to talk her out of it, all his acquiescence did was tell her she had made the right choice.

"Thanks, Al," she said because that's all she could think of.

Some vagrant spirit must have possessed him at that moment, because suddenly Al had his arms wrapped around Charlene in an embrace so strong and pure that, for a moment, all the girl could do was tense her body and try to shrink back into herself. Instead, she found herself melting into him. He was fresh November coffee, siphoning the chill away, filling her with the liquid warmth of hot melting butter over straight-from-the-griddle pancakes. The physical contact was more than she'd ever seen Al show anyone, and way more than she ever thought would pass between them. She unclenched her body and let it flow into his, all the affection they'd shared these last eight years spilling out like the deathbed confession of a lifelong sinner.

In that moment, she almost forgot the name of her DJ, but then Al pulled away, and the moment was over.

"No problem, kiddo," Al said. Charlene wondered if he'd ever call her 'darlin' again, then figured it didn't much matter. "I'm happy for you, you know? Like, it sucks that you're not gonna be my sweet angel of booze any more, but that was kinda getting old anyway. Jake the DJ's gonna make you way happier than this place and this bunch of drunks ever could."

Charlene, separated from Al by three feet and the end of their embrace and the respective regret shared by two people who never did what everyone they knew assumed they had, felt the cold again. She shrugged, doing that little shimmy people do when they want to move things along. "You're really happy about it then? Because I want you to be. You know, Al, you're important to me, right?"

Yep. Important enough to just leave-bomb me without so much as a howyadoin'.

Instead of saying that, Al just mustered up his biggest closed-mouth smile and waved her towards the basement hatch. "Yup, I'm a regular load-bearing post in the wall of your existence. Now let's us go get drunker, woman; it's Check Day and last I looked we're still celebrating, after all."

"Oh right!" Charlene said. "I almost forgot today was Check Day; just don't get skimpy when it comes time to settle up tonight-- I've got a down-payment to put down on a house, you know."

Wrong thing to say, she realized, but Al let it slide.

He'd stopped giving a shit three paragraphs ago, and all he cared about now was making this last Check Day count.

-3-

It was the peanuts that did it.

In the time-honored tradition all bars share, the Cyclops had its way of making sure people kept buying drinks long after they'd reached peak thirst-quenchedness. Some places put out pretzels, banking on the fact that dry, salty twists of flavorless crunch that turned to glue in the mouth would convince an otherwise sated drinker to order up another pint. There were some states in the union that went a step farther, legislating that bars had to make a certain percentage of their sales through food and that usually meant cheap, fried garbage that tasted fantastic with another beer. The Cyclops's owner, however, was neither bound by law nor given over to tricking his customers into staying longer than they wanted. Long ago, he'd embraced the notion that if he made it so they wanted to stay at his bar, they were likely to order drinks for as long as they did.

So, he gave them peanuts. Those hundred-pound burlap sacks leaning against every post and hunkering in every corner weren't just for decoration but had in fact become a beloved aspect of Cyclops lore. Right about eleven o'clock every Friday and Saturday night, the music would stop, the lights would go up, and Lilith would blow an elephant-sounding trumpet to call everyone's attention.

"Alright all you demonic little bastards," she would say, brandishing a wicked little dagger over her head, "it's time to grab your nuts!"

Then she'd gut one of the sacks, and a hundred pounds of unshelled peanuts straight from Jimmy Carter's wettest dream would spill across the floor. Veterans of such ghastly sacrifices would move with great haste to gather into handy tin buckets the legumes Lilith spilled, and soon enough, even the neophytes would be tearing into the sacks and filling their shiny buckets of togetherness. What ensued was a festival of shelling, eating, and ordering more drinks, followed by the inevitable melee of whipping peanuts at everyone in range. It was a good time, and just about everybody who wasn't an asshole loved it.

It was this scene that saw Charlene return to her station at the bar, slightly annoyed that her partner had let her dishwater grow cold. Al came right behind, looking moderately sober.

This was something Grigsby could not abide. Al never looked that sober this late, and he couldn't recall a time he'd ever looked less than stupidly happy after sharing a smoke with Charlene. He got up, intent on finding out what was up, when Eldon caught him by the elbow.

"The fuck you want, kid?" he said, giving Eldon an eyeful of Scots hooligan.

Eldon was undeterred. "Check it out, Grigs," he said, cocking his eye at the bros at the back table. "Is that who I think it is?"

Grigsby had no idea who Eldon thought it was, but they looked vaguely familiar.

"Isn't that Herman the sound tech and fellow investigator JT from *Ghost Quest*?" Eldon said, brimming with excitement.

Grigsby squinted and decided the kid was right. "Oi, so it is. Guys look even cuntier in person."

Eleanor was next to catch sight of the Ghostquesters, following Grigsby's eye-line as a means of extricating herself from whatever Sarissa had been talking about; probably something to do with how she had a story that better illustrated the point Dave was trying to make than he did. Soon enough though, all of the Ghost Geeks had spotted their televisual heroes. Even Cletus gave an impressed nod in their direction.

"But where's the cute one? I swear, that boy has got a set of titties that'd make a girl question her orientation," Eleanor said. Lyric giggled profusely at that, snorting a little bit of whiskey out of her nose, which, in turn, brought on another fit of giggling.

"I'm gonna go talk to them," Eldon said, scrambling to his feet.

"Hold on a second there, Eldon," Dave said, staying him with a hand around his wrist. "Show a little professional courtesy here; those guys are just relaxing out in the civilian world. Leave 'em alone."

Eldon's heart sank, but he wasn't going to argue with Dave. Besides, it's not like the real star of the show was there, anyway.

"Nonsense, man," said a voice from behind and above the table. Eldon could barely contain himself when he turned around to see and say

"Dax. Fucking. Vagance."

Dax laughed at that. "Actually, my middle name is Chet, but I get that a lot. I take it you guys are fans of the show." His vocal punctuation was, in fact, a period, because Dax Vagance was the kind of guy who never asked questions whose answer he didn't already know.

"I'm a fan of whoever it is paints those shirts on you, baby," Eleanor said, drifting close.

Dave stood up, reached out to shake Dax's hand; he didn't miss a beat when Dax ignored the gesture, masking his rudeness by taking a broad gander at Sarissa, whose baity eyes were turned up to eleven. For a chubby chick, she was kinda hot, but he'd leave her for JT; the poor bastard hadn't gotten laid since he got married. "We're all huge fans of the show, Mr. Vagance; in fact, your Ghost Quest inspired me to take up the mantle as well."

"Is that a fact?" Dax said, winking at Sarissa in a way that made her lady-bits tingle. He turned back to Dave, who had reclaimed his seat not even slightly put-off. This was *the* Dax Vagance after all; *so what if he didn't see you offer your hand?* "Well, I'm a fan of yours, too. Those EVPs you posted on our website were frikkin' amazing."

That's all it was going to take to get these guys riding his dick, and Dax knew it. He sure as hell had never heard any of these amateurs' EVPs, but it was a safe bet they'd posted something on the show's site. These guys were perfect for the role of small-time wannabes, the archetypal identification vessel for all the losers who tuned in week after week, and he wanted to make sure he worked them into the show; Gargantua Hayseed alone could sell a promo, and the old black lady would open up a whole new demographic.

The collective high felt by the Bitburg Supernatural Squad could've made Timmy Leary blush, all except for Grigsby, who just drained his last beer and got up to grab another. He slapped Dax on the back as he walked by, just hard enough that it might have been just a friendly tap but probably wasn't. "Nice meetin' ya, mate."

Dax turned back to the BSS, making a mental note to cut that guy from the show. Before he could come up with another way to wrap these yokels tighter around his finger, Eldon broke the glee-boner for him.

"Holy crap, Mr. Vagance;" he said, still awash in the adulation of his idol. "What are you doing in Bitburg?"

"Glad you asked, little man," Dax said. "*Ghost Quest* is going after one of the least known, most haunted places in America, and it's right here in your fair city."

Cold rain fell from a sudden cloudburst, snuffing the mood of the adoration club like a lantern in a hurricane. Dave and Eldon shared an uneasy glance, but it was Lyric who chimed in before either of them could find the right words.

"You don't mean Cardinal's Crest, do you?" she said, then emptied the last of her unholy tea/ whiskey amalgam into her mouth and proceeded to freak everyone at the table right the hell out. "You'd have to be seriously fucking deranged to go up there. What? I can cunting swear all the fucking fuck I want to. Poop."

"What she means," Dave said, nearly knocking over the table as he lunged forward to block Lyric's further attempts at speech; he knew it was a bad idea to let her drink, and if he could, he'd punch that bastard Al right in the mouth. "Is that no one goes up there. I mean, it's haunted."

"Really haunted," Eldon said. "It's not like normal places where people hear weird noises or see shadow people or any of that. It's cursed, you know? It's... evil."

Dax chuckled. These guys were pure gold; he wished Herman had brought their gear because this was too good not to air. "Like we always say, *Ghost Quest* takes us into the heart of the unknown, where the other seekers of truth fear to tread."

Eldon shook his head emphatically. "Do you know why it's one of America's least-known haunted houses? It's because no one who goes there to investigate it ever comes back. At least, not capable of talking about it, anyway."

"What about you, mama?" Dax said to Eleanor, mainly to distract her from rubbing his thigh. "You think the Crest is really all that terrifying?"

A rigid calm cascaded over Eleanor, tightening her features and effectively killing her desire to touch the pretty man. "I don't know about all that, but I do know I wouldn't set foot on those grounds on a bet."

Something in the old lady's mien crept through Dax's façade, threatening to upset his shit-eating grin. He needed to get these guys on camera.

"Wow," he said. "Really, wow! Do you guys think you could say all that again? We're not on the clock until tomorrow, so we didn't bring any of our gear, but you would make for an awesome Pre-Quest segment."

Another wave of giddy disbelief washed over the BSS, all except Eldon, who continued to look at Dax with a mix of fear and incredulity... and Lyric, who was licking the rim of her teacup in the hopes that it had absorbed some of the delicious.

Dave beamed. "Sure we could, Mr. Vagance; we could even help with--"

"Awesome," Dax said. Benny from the Network would love this, and if Cardinal's Crest was anything like the BSS thought, *Ghost Quest* might beat out the big boys on *Syfy* for once. He'd talked a big game to Charlene, but the truth was that his show was never more than a bad episode from cancellation, and the Producers made sure he was aware of that. It was for that very reason that he'd made the executive decision to divert to Bitburg instead of heading off for another New Orleans investigation.

Sometimes, it was like the Producers sent them to the same places-- places where they never found anything, but which the Producers swore up and down that the viewers wanted to see-- over and over again on purpose. It's like they cared more about their ratings than his reason for seeking out the supernatural. Bitburg, though, was going to be different; the BSS made him sure of it.

"Then it's settled; why don't we meet up here again tomorrow afternoon?"

"Dax," Eldon said, forgetting all about his idol-worship. "I don't think you understand what Cardinal's Crest is."

There was always one of them, like the creepy old guy in an eighties horror flick, screaming about curses and evil and oh the unholy terrors that awaited them in Castle Whatever-the-fuck. This kid was making it hard for Dax to keep up his SEG.

"Save it for the cameras, kid, and don't worry: I've faced down demons before, and come out stronger for it."

Eldon wanted to say more, to convince Dax that Cardinal's Crest was just not a place to screw around with for a TV show, but the first shot in tonight's peanut fusillade had found its way into his half-empty beer, effectively ending the conversation.

-4-

A couple of minutes earlier, Grigsby had gotten up to grab a beer and evade that ponce, Dax Vagance. He couldn't stand him or that bullshit circus of a TV show. With a constancy usually shown only by the sun's refusal to not rise a few hours after it set, *Ghost Quest* delivered absolutely fuck-all in terms of evidence of the paranormal. Worse, it regularly shone a spotlight on the kind of freaks and weirdos that made his chosen vocation look so pathetic.

Speaking of pathetic, what the hell was up with Al? The guy looked like someone had just kicked his football into the sewer. Grigsby hadn't seen Al sitting alone at a table in ages, and the last time he had, things had gotten downright entertaining.

The ginger Scot elbowed his way to the bar, propping himself in front of Charlene, who looked almost as unlike herself as Al did. He put the pieces together quickly enough that he could've avoided saying something inappropriate, but that had never stopped him before, so why start now?

"Heya luv," Grigsby said, flashing Charlene a hungry grin. "You're lookin' a bit south o' happy tonight; Al still keepin' his balls in the freezer?"

Charlene didn't expect much from Grigsby, so she wasn't surprised by what he said. Annoyed, repulsed, even a little offended, but not surprised in the slightest. "What are you drinking, Grigsby? And for the record, I'm the last person who cares what Al does with his balls."

"Alcohol," he said, perfectly content to have gotten under her skin. As far as he cared, Charlene was a cunt of a tease who'd been leading his mate on for years; not that he cared very far, but everyone else made way for Queen Charlene and he just couldn't abide that kind of deferential fakery. "Made from wheat, barley, and hops, served warm in a pint glass, preferably from a tap that says Newcastle on it. And for the record, you might want to make sure Al knows that, cuz he looks fuckin' bothered over there."

Grigsby jerked a thumb at Al, and Charlene looked out of reflex.

It wasn't her fault, and it wasn't her problem, no matter what Grigsby said. Still, she got a little lump in her chest at seeing him look so abjectly dejected. Because occasionally God freelances as a cinematographer, a void had formed around Al, the drinkers and dancers kept at bay by the unseen force of his dolor, because that's what happens when a guy leaks out so much of what can only be appropriately described with a word like 'dolor.' Al slumped in a worn chair, left arm dangling at his side, a crown of grey smoke constricting his head beneath a low-hanging lamp. An empty bottle of Fighting Cock stood at mute attention on the table before him, its shadow shrouding an ashtray overrun with crumpled cigarette butts. Al's right hand unconsciously flicked his Zippo open and shut, open and shut, in a clinking litany of aimlessness. His head hung down, long copper hair hiding his face from the light above.

'Bothered' didn't quite cover it.

Charlene shrugged, pulled Grigsby's beer from the tap; she decided to forego her customary glassware inspection this time. "You know Al; he gets moody when he's been drinking this long."

Grigsby dropped a five on the bar, took his Newcastle. "Yer right, luv, I do know Al, and that ain't drink weighing on him;

drink looks different. Lots more fun. Throw's a bottle o' that Cock shite, too; Al's tab, o' course."

Charlene complied, setting the bottle down in front of Grigsby. He left the bar, drinks in hand, ambled over Al's way. The bartender watched him go, sickly mud filling up her guts. If there was any justice in the universe, Grigsby's glass had all the dysentery in it, and he'd spend the rest of his miserable life with his bony ass glued to the filthiest toilet in the city. Who the hell was he to go sticking his nose into her business? Even her friends kept clear of the subject of Al, and Duncan Grigsby was the last person she knew that she would call a friend. He wasn't even Al's friend. Seriously, what the hell right did he have to talk to her like what he said mattered? She took a little bit of solace in the peanut that caught Grigsby square in the forehead, but it did little to thin the muck in her belly.

"Fucking moppet!" Grigsby said, rather loudly. He reached into a hundred-pound sack of peanuts and chucked a handful in the general direction the shot had come from, and after that, the melee was officially on.

-5-

A wet red ire poured over Al as he settled into a chair at a lonely table off to one side of Brother Malcolm's giddy portrait. His empty bottle croaked a listless thud on the tabletop, so he looked around for Lilith and another, but gave up far more quickly than he would have expected. He didn't feel like another drink right now. What he felt like was stomping over to the bar, grabbing Charlene, and telling her what he really felt about her running off with Jake the DJ. More immediately, he felt like picking up the table, walking over to the yahoos in the corner, and pounding the ever-loving shit out of them with it.

Bros are bad enough, but they usually confine their douchebaggery to ultimately innocuous activities like cheering for whatever NBA team is currently popular or wearing shorts in public. They're mostly showing off to and for each other, because, well, that's how they roll. Yahoos, on the other hand, are never content to keep it in the family. They get loud, they get vulgar, they like to cat-call women and "accidentally" spill drinks on guys smaller them. They grind girls on the dancefloor and yearn to be the guy who gets picked to serve as a prop in a *Girls Gone Wild* video. They're pack-traveling assholes looking to take down the weakest prey they can find, and Al knew them the instant he saw them. This particular lot was new to the Cyclops, yet they strutted and swaggered like they'd built the place.

A pack of yahoos like this was enough to make him forget all about Dax Vagance and his bros.

The yahoos hadn't been here when he'd gone outside with Charlene but were already laying the yahs down thick. The art school kids Al had been sitting with earlier remained blissfully oblivious to their presence. The kids were having a fine old time, laughing and winging peanuts at one another, mostly hitting their friends. It was the few errant shells that were going to cause a ruckus soon enough, Al could tell because if there was one thing a mob of yahoos couldn't resist, it was an excuse to pick on somebody. And Al couldn't resist an excuse to play the hero, especially if it meant beating Hell out of someone he'd never met and already didn't like.

"Fucking moppet!"

Grigsby's voice could cut a hole through glass, or occasionally one-hit a bad mood into submission. Things were lining up perfectly, as the yahoos had begun to point and sneer at the kids. Peanuts were flying from and to every corner of the room, with most of the folks joining in or just trying to stay out of the line of fire. This shit happened twice a week, and no one ever complained. *Who the hell were these guys to come in and start talking shit?*

"You still hung up on Miss Heterochromia Iridis USA?" Grigsby said, snatching a chair from a nearby table and plopping himself down next to Al. He drank a quarter of his beer, topped it off with a liberal dose of whiskey, then passed the rest over to his *mate from Texas.*

Al reconsidered his desire for another drink and took a long swig from the bottle. On some level, he knew it was likely not a good thing that he didn't feel the burn in either throat or belly, but his mind wasn't on whatever level of inebriation that might have indicated. It was on how one of the yahoos had moved to the perimeter of his pack to get a better eye on the art students.

"You still got the rest of the Ghost Geeks convinced you're bloody Scottish?" Al said, wiping his mouth with the back of his hand.

Grigsby laughed, loud and short, dropped his accent. "Yeah, I'm kinda stuck with it now. Serious though, what's up, man? You look like my asshole feels after a binge at Taco Bell."

Al didn't answer right away. A second yahoo had strayed from the pack, joining up with the first. The two glowered amongst themselves, gesturing at the kids. Al stood up, casually, took the empty bottle in hand. "Not a damn thing that ain't always been up, man."

Grigsby followed Al, the two of them, he noticed, drifting towards a knot of assholes in the corner. "So, yer dick then?"

Al snorted; they were close enough now that he could make out the conversation between the two free-range yahoos. Surrounded by her friends, one of the girls-- a pretty blonde Al half-remembered as being named Sheila-- wound up for a vicious shot to a buddy's head but missed convincingly. Her spent ammunition found its way to one of the chittering yahoo's chest, and Al got himself ready. Maybe-Sheila didn't even notice, and just went back to her fun night out.

"Left," Al said to Grigsby.

Grigsby smirked. "Howcum I always get the big one?"

"Because I'll be done with the other one before he gets a chance to hit you. Wait for it, now..."

The yahoo on the left flexed his massive arms inside his long-sleeved Tapout T-shirt, cracked his neck from side to side. The yahoo on the right, complete with a backwards white Yankees cap and a popped white collar, spoke loud enough that anyone nearby could hear.

"I swear, another one o' those bitches hits me with another motherfuckin' peanut, I swear to god I'mma choke a bitch."

Tapout agreed. "Truth man, bitches be ridin' my last nerve."

Al staggered up to Tapout and Whitehat, his usually pleasant grin subbed out for something a little more threatening. "Now that's a hell of a thing to say about a little girl, chuckles. You really gonna choke a bitch over some peanuts?"

Whitehat tilted his head and pursed his lips. It was meant to look intimidating. It did not. "Lucky I don't slap you, faggot, now walk your long-hair-havin' ass back to your seat and mind ya bees, bitch."

"Mind my bees?" Al said. "The fuck's that even mean?"

Tapout cocked his arms and shrugged his shoulders forward, the quick, jerky battle-cry of the yahoo. "He said step off, motherfucker. And take ya boyfriend with you."

Grigsby was playing his part and playing it cool. By now, the rest of the pack could sense that something was up, and began turning their attention to the nascent ruckus. Grigsby tipped his glass to the biggest of the lot, winked.

"So, this is the nineties then?" Al said. "You want me to step off, and take my boyfriend with me?"

"That's right, fool," Whitehat said.

"I'm afraid that ain't gonna happen, my homophobic atavist friends. But I'll let you and all your buddies walk out of here if you do it now, and do it quiet."

Steps one and two--namely the callout and the rebuttal--were complete. All that remained was for Whitehat to initiate fisticuffs, or walk away. For a fearful second, Al thought

Whitehat might actually do the latter, and he sure as hell couldn't have that, now could he?

"And suck my dick before you go."

Whitehat shoved Al but didn't even unbalance him. Al smashed the empty whiskey bottle over the yahoo's face, cracking his skull loudly enough to shock just about everybody in the bar. He made sure to bring a knee up and catch Whitehat as he plummeted to the floor; he hadn't intended the bastard to bite through his tongue, but at least he couldn't use it to go around threatening teenagers anymore. He held up the bottle for all to see: it hadn't even cracked.

"See?" Al said to an understandably stunned Tapout. "That's how you know this bottle was made in America."

"Cry Havoc and all that shite!" Grigsby said, howling as he launched himself into Tapout. Grigs wasn't a big guy, but he was vicious, and if he'd had a shit to give about what happened to him, he'd have traded it in on something more entertaining. Momentum carried him and his target flailing into the ranks of yahoos, who caught their boy and sent Grigsby reeling back. Grigs grinned and ducked.

Al lobbed his bottle full-force at Tapout's face. It shattered this time, and anyone in the place who had yet to tune in to the brawl now found themselves a part of it.

Some girl-- Sheila, Al imagined-- screamed, and anyone not yet alerted to the fracas took up the call. Al sprang at the closest yahoo, throwing short, snake-strike jabs to his face and throat. The poor bastard never even put up his hands to defend himself, just started swinging wild haymakers that might have hurt if they ever hit anything but air. He went down faster than an Italian wedding dress. That left just three targets from the original pack.

Grigsby decided that he didn't quite want this to end so fast, so he grabbed Herman the equipment tech by the shoulder, spun him around, and popped him a good one in the mouth.

The Cyclops erupted: random punters punching people who'd pissed them off tonight or sometime in the past; potential escapees clambering over one another to flee the flying fists; those too stoned or drunk to react just getting in the way of or providing cover for those doing the actual fighting. Because someone at least had a sense of humor about the mess, they slid a quarter into the juke and queued up War's *Why can't we be friends*. It was probably Grigsby, who still had his beer in hand.

One of the yahoos planted a ham, or maybe just his fist, on Al's nose, splattering it in a pimple-popped flare of blood and twisted cartilage; Al smiled, grabbed him by the back of the head, and forced it with all necessary haste into the wall, ticking another off the list. He didn't have time to lock on to another candidate before someone wrapped him up in a full nelson from behind and spun him to face the crowd.

Momentarily immobile, all Al could do was stare down the penultimate yahoo and the six inches of straight sharp steel in his hand. Another instance where there was always one jerk who had to ruin it for everyone else. *When did humanity decide that it was okay to bring knives to a good-old-fashioned barroom brawl?* Al figured it was probably right about the time the first guy in a brawl realized he was getting his ass kicked.

A hand the size of most people's heads seized the yahoo by the wrist. A quick twist, the sound of bones cracking, the clatter of the knife on the floor, and a painful yelp preceded the yahoo's collapse. Cletus stood tall in the spot he'd come to occupy, his weathered-asphalt face showing not the slightest emotion.

"You should probably get out of here, Al," Cletus said.

"One sec," Al said. "Kinda busy."

Blinking away the fireworks behind his eyes brought on by the tightening hold wrapped around his shoulders and neck, Al slid his left leg back between his captor's feet, clenched his stomach muscles as tight as he could, and yanked his head towards the floor. The yahoo tumbled over him, sprawled on the ground. A rabbit-punch to the throat took him out of the fight.

Al got to his feet, took in the carnage: most everyone had fled, and all five or six of the yahoos were down or gone. Blood and wreckage painted the Cyclops in vibrant hues and textures. Grigsby had already retaken his chair, refilling his pint with Al's whiskey. Al wasn't even thinking about Charlene any more, just enjoying the thrill of battle and the liquid electricity pumping through his veins. He looked around for Faux-hawk, banking on a little extra credit. He spotted Dax hiding under a table and set his sights.

"Neato," he said, a devil's mask on his face.

That's when Charlene stepped in front of him, her face a warped wreck of revulsion.

"Go, Al," she said. "Somebody's called the cops, so go! Just get the hell out of here!"

Just like that, all the battle-joy dissipated, leaving Al with only a sour twist in his stomach. So, he did as he was told, but not before swiping the rest of his bottle out of Grigsby's hands. The last thing he saw before the cold air of the vernal night slapped him awake was the bubbly visage of Brother Malcolm smiling at him above the wake of ruin he left behind.

Al stumbled onto the street; someone popped him in the eye, but he didn't see who it was. He just staggered onwards into the night, sidestepping a taxi, bouncing off obstacles real and imagined. The rapid cut-off of adrenaline had brought every extra shot of booze right to the front of his metabolism, and he felt it all, all at once.

Sirens wailed from downtown, the Finest of the Fifth Precinct confirming that some jerk had felt the need to get the law involved. That meant Al couldn't head right, seeing as how he didn't particularly feel like spending the night puking in a cell; his shithole was only a block away, and on the left, but the thought of lying at home with the room spinning didn't offer much comfort, either. Besides, the night was still young, and the boundless possibilities of the city's copulation with the darkness promised distraction enough, at least until he could pull himself together. Al caught sight of the moon, framing Bitburg's silent sentinel atop Fallfallow hill, and lurched away, more or less in the direction of Cardinal's Crest, because that was as good a direction as any.

A couple of blocks down the street, Al passed a tattered wino huddled under the eaves of a ramshackle bodega. Ageless and filthy, he looked Al over with eyes that had once seen everything but saw nothing now. The sight of the man-- bearded, gaunt, devoid of everything but the stubbornness of a heart that wouldn't stop beating and lungs that refused to give up on drawing breath-- struck Al hard enough to almost sober him up.

"You look like warmed-over dogshit," the wino said with a voice made of broken glass and duct tape.

Al pondered that, wiped blood and snot from the rubble of his nose on his sleeve. "More than likely," he said after a minute.

"I'm cold," the wino said. "Gimme that bottle so I don't freeze to death."

"You didn't freeze to death last night," Al said. The wino, underneath a cardigan of indeterminate color and a mud-caked wool overcoat, wore a *Bitburg Batwings* hockey sweater. That seemed out of place, like maybe a long time ago he'd been a real person who went to hockey games and had a girlfriend he cheated on and maybe parents he never talked to.

"Wasn't raining last night," the wino said. "I'll trade you for it."

Al hadn't noticed the rain, but true enough, it had begun to mist, and the sky promised to open up sometime soon. "What you got to trade?"

"Wisdom, kid, wisdom," the wino said, coughing up a little bloody phlegm.

"Keep it," Al said. "Doesn't look like it's done you no good." He dropped the bottle into the wino's lap, ignored the words that spilled out of his wino mouth, and trundled on back the way he'd been headed.

It struck him, then, that maybe the old wino's wisdom had served him well enough, after all. Remember now, Al was pretty fucking drunk, a bit hung up on the facts that Charlene had basically told him to fuck off for a fucking DJ, and that after he'd burned through the check in his pocket, he'd have pretty much lost every damn thing he had in this world. He didn't even know that he'd just been conned to death by a good friend, but the other two facts were shitty enough to play with his head on their own.

So, he did the kind of shit he always did. Al took the Last Check from his jacket, endorsed it with the pen he kept next to the flask of emergency Fighting Cock, and handed it over to the wino. If he was going to end up broke and alone anyway, why put it off?

The old bum took a look at the check, sniffed his derision.

"I look like a fuckin' bank to you?" the wino said. "What I'm gonna do with this?"

"You look like a pile of human shit, you ungrateful cock-rash," Al said. "It's made out to cash, so fuckin' wipe your ass with it for all I care."

The wino shrugged, folded the check, ink running in the rain, and stuffed it into his sodden parka. "Fine, but you gotta take something from me for it."

"I don't need no goddamned hepatitis," Al said.

"Yeah, but you gonna take this," the wino said.

Without so much as a Diddle-Eye Joe, the old bum hacked up a mouthful of lung-butter, spat it in Al's face, and started cackling like a complete asshole. Before Al could react, and with surprising agility for someone of his smell and condition, the wino sprang off into the rain-mottled nightscape of the city, giggling and waving the check like a flag.

Al-- all reasonable emotions sublimated by the wino's fuckwittery, and as such no longer gripped by his usual self-destructive impulses or this peculiar feeling of disquiet-- chased after him.

-6-

By the time the cops fought their way through the crowd gathered outside the Cyclops, there wasn't much for them to do. The bar was a bit of a mess, but pretty much everyone involved with the actual fighting had already disappeared. They took a few statements, but not even the yahoos would identify just who it was that started the fight. Grigsby saw to that, making sure they all saw that he had the knife their boy had pulled on Al and leaving no doubt that he'd rat them out if they said word one to implicate him or his friend. It might have helped that he didn't hide the Beretta nine-millimeter pistol silhouetted in his inside pocket, but either one likely would have sufficed.

To his credit, Dax worked the cops like a champ, finding a fan among them and talking up *Ghost Quest*. A few promises to put them on the show, a couple of autographs, and a wink in the direction of a homely lady cop sealed the deal, and the Finest of the Fifth didn't even write the incident up, just told the crew running the joint to shut the doors for the rest of the night. Dax promised to meet them at another bar after their shift, and that was that.

That left Charlene and the rest of the staff to clean up the mess, the same way she always had to clean up Al's messes. Cletus offered to help, along with the rest of the Ghost Geeks, but Charlene shooed them away. She'd have to call the owner, and it just wouldn't do to have customers hanging around after she closed the place. It also wouldn't do for her to break down in tears in front of them, especially not in front of that asshole Grigsby.

What he didn't understand, what none of them did, was that she hadn't been leading Al on. She'd never hidden anything from him, and he'd never really tried to make a move on her. She knew how they gossiped and how much the ones who only knew him in passing liked Al and saw her as some kind of witch just playing with his emotions. Most of them had never seen Al the way he'd been tonight, but she had, a dozen times; maybe now they'd understand a little better how, no matter how much she cared about him, she could never be with a guy whose method for dealing with his emotions was to start punching things.

On her way out, Lilith broke character and gave Charlene a little hug and a squeeze. Neither of them could come up with anything to say, so Lilith waved good-bye and headed home, the rest of the Cyclops crew not far behind.

Alone with the empty, not much worse for wear Cyclops, Charlene mixed herself a vodka tonic and waited to see if Jake the DJ would remember to pick her up.

He didn't. Charlene called a cab and headed home around three, leaving the last of the scattered peanuts for the morning crew to sweep up.

-7-

He walked, cloaked in a blue razor vortex of invectives and incoherence, aimless and looking to incite. What he wanted to incite, he didn't know and didn't care. All he knew was that he was tired and the fun part of his booze had worn off, and all he cared about was not going home. He walked through streets devoid of light, unpopulated, vacant but for the rats and the dogs and the forgotten men who had no shelter from the rain that came down like pine needles in a wildfire. The sodden cold dug into him, clattered his jaws, stung his broken nose, clung to him like unfinished sex.

It had been hours since Al lost track of the wino or even recognized the streets through which he stumbled, almost as long since he'd had to shove past another body or had some sleep-interrupted citizen shout at him from a slammed-open window. The farther away from the Cyclops he got, the darker the night grew, the harder the rain and recrimination fell. Townhouses and boutique storefronts gave way to tenements and boarded windows. Cramped, overgrown lots teemed with coyotes and carrion feeders, and shadows found deeper places to hide from whatever moonlight dared venture earthward. Dimly, distracted by the fact that he'd been kicking the crap out of a stray garbage can for the last few minutes, Al realized he'd just crossed Marin Luther King Boulevard. Just to be sure, he checked himself: he hadn't been shot yet.

Jennings Heights crowded all around him; one condemned building holding up the next, all of them waiting for the rogue gust of wind that would bring the whole ghetto down. Cars hunkered in the downpour, rusting and abandoned where they'd been stripped years or minutes before. Some of them had people inside, others maybe corpses. Al didn't look too closely.

A skinny, destitute hooker spied him from a doorway, offering her wretched wares with a series of gestures more ridiculous than seductive. Al didn't acknowledge her but saw her give him the finger as he trudged past. She disappeared an instant later, and Al knew she'd gone off to tell someone what she'd seen wandering around the hood. He didn't belong here, and the locals would have no qualms about reminding him of that.

He had to get out of here, but the storm had grown into a deluge, getting stronger every second. He'd meant to lose himself tonight, and he had; hours of turning down random alleys and blindly loping off after anything that caught his eye had stolen all sense of space and direction from him. There was no way he could find his way back home in the dark; he'd be lucky if he could get out of Jennings Heights without getting rolled. If it weren't for the rain, whoever the hooker had run off to tell about him likely would have already done the honors.

But a little rain never dissuaded a pimp for long. The thought did a fine job of sobering Al up, and he began to move a little faster. He needed to get off the street, out of sight, find a place to hide.

Al ducked down an alley, desperate to elude whoever was or wasn't chasing him. The general slanting dilapidation of the buildings offered a little cover from the rain, and Al found he wasn't the only one taking advantage.

"Hello, children," Al said like Chef from *South Park*, waving to the three kids huddled beside an overflowing dumpster. He couldn't tell if they were boys or girls thanks to the deplorable state of their clothes and hygiene, but they were short, and probably not yet teenagers, which was a good thing because the only people worse than teenagers were adults and preschoolers. They might have been midgets. "Don't mind me, just trying to get away from an army of killer pimps."

One of the kids, gaunt and overburdened by a green parka five sizes too big, shrugged. Based on the voice, Al guessed it a boy, and probably not a midget. "Ain't no pimps 'round here."

The other two, smaller still, and dressed in rags that envied being a coat five sizes too big, had their hoods drawn low. They chittered among themselves, keeping to the relatively big one's shadow.

"Then who protects the hookers?" Al said. He found a dryish spot and sat down, bringing him to just below the speaker's eye-level.

The kid laughed a grimy, gutty, choking noise. "Ain't you know Heights girls don't need no protection? S'like *Sin City* up in this bitch since the seventies, man."

Whatever shelter from the wet the alley coughed up did nothing to stem the chill. Sitting had been a bad idea; the physical exertion that had kept his blood circulating had also served to more or less keep the alcohol in check, and now that he'd stopped, the world began to spin and lose cohesion around the edges. Blood-thirsty pimps or not, he needed to get somewhere he could crash. The other end of the alley opened onto a wide thoroughfare, across which stood the burned-out remains of what Al assumed had been a fine hotel at one point. It'd do, at least until the rain stopped; *any goddamn port, right?*

"Shit, man," the bigger kid said. His companions had fanned out from behind him, scuttling on all fours, effectively blocking either end of the alley. If Al hadn't known better, he'd have thought the little bastards were purposely flanking him. "Been all sorts of crazy in the heights since the seventies."

"Blame it on disco," Al said.

He hauled himself up the wall behind him, or at least tried to, but discovered rather abruptly that his legs weren't working right. The kids were drawing closer, something like ragged hisses fogging the air in front of their faces.

"What happened to your face, man?" the big one said. He hadn't moved since he'd stood up. In fact, he seemed to have planted himself directly in front of his new friend, his stance solid and not at all in line with the casual manner he affected. "Looks like somebody got his ass kicked."

Al felt dizzy, and not just from the liquor. There was something wrong with this kid and the way he just stood there with his minions slithering around him.

That's when Al finally got a good look at them; they'd gotten within arm's reach, grown silent. Underneath the hoods, their eyes-- cave-black marbles set in shadow-- seemed to cast a faint darkness. Their mouths were lipless slits, their noses sharp, bony, without nostrils.

"What the hell kinda crack you little bastards been smoking?" Al said, struggling again to find his feet. Too late, he managed to drag himself halfway up the wall.

The kids were on him like dogs on a bleeding puppy, ripping with fingernails like talons; snarling, snapping, biting.

"You don't belong here, man," the big one said. He still didn't move, but a slow smile stretched across his ashen face.

"I'm guessing you don't either," Al said, "you demonic little cunt."

Al kicked at the kids, sending one flying against the far side of the alley. It hit hard, then slammed into the concrete, but was on its feet and charging as soon as it did.

"Alright, enough o' this happy horseshit," Al said, "I'm cold, and I'm drunk, and I ain't in the mood to get murdered by a bunch of prepubescent thralls of Satan!"

If there was one thing Al could do even when he was drunk, tired, and not in the mood, it was screw. If there was another thing he could do, it was fight. He grabbed the second kid by the neck with his left hand, brought its head up to slam the first one under the jaw. His right fist wrapped itself around the kid's ankles, and he swung the little bastard's body like a bat, smashing the first kid back into the wall. This time, it didn't get up.

Taking one ankle in each hand, Al bashed his impromptu hammer against the ground until it stopped squirming. He hoped to god this was a dream and not just a hallucination, because there was no damn way it could be real, and he didn't want to sober up to the bodies of two dead non-possessed kids.

"You're an asshole, man," the big one said. His smile had faded away. It almost looked like he was going to cry. "My sisters were hungry is all, and you go an' smash 'em up like that? Fuck you, jerk."

"Well, I'm a lot o' things, but I ain't dinner," Al said. "Shit, I ain't even Fourthmeal."

Al stepped forward, hefting the gory, pulpy meatsack by its legs and bringing it down as hard as he could onto the big one's skull. What he got for his efforts was a shower of milky grey-green goo as the body exploded.

The big one didn't budge. Al's fingers went numb, dropped what was left of the kid-thing. He should have run, but he found himself rooted in place. The big kid shook off his too-big coat, revealing two more miniature black-eyed delinquents, standing on each other's shoulders like they were trying to sneak into an R-rated movie. The talker tore off his fake nose.

"Demons," Al said. "I'm about to get eaten by demon midgets. "You have absolutely got to be shitting me."

With a spastic shriek, the three of them bolted at Al, who did the only thing he could think to do just then: he pissed himself and ran the fuck away.

Newfound energy surged through him, and Al sprinted towards the far end of the alley, kicking trashcans over, vaulting debris, doing anything he could to slow his pursuers. Nothing helped; they were on him like pasties on nipples at a Virginia strip club. He burst onto the deserted street, instantly slipping on wet asphalt and crashing to his knees.

One of the things nipped at his ass, and Al kicked back hard. On hands and knees, he pulled himself across the tarmac, waiting to be overtaken and devoured, but not quite ready to give up.

Thank god for the Universal Fellowship of the Drunk. Whether they knew it or not, every alcoholic, binge-drinker, and wino was a member, and half the shit they did when they were wasted was subliminal groundwork laid down for a Fellow's future use. So, if you see some waffle-faced pisher carelessly toss a bottle out of his bindle or car window, just leave it alone; odds are, like everything else, he's dumping it for a very specific reason.

Al's hand closed over a discarded MD 20/20 bottle, then smashed it into a functional enough shank. He rolled over onto his back, raising his blade.

"Great fucking Christmas," Al said, his words redolent with breathy disbelief. "I'm going to be eaten by a Demonic Midget Voltron."

The three demons had been joined by the two Al had done his best to fuck up beyond repair, and they were indeed pulling a Voltron on him. Flesh separated from bones that cracked and splintered, twisting into hideous caricatures of limbs. The scraps of skin and muscle wriggled like worms in a light socket, braided themselves together with a sickening sucking slosh. Al sat there watching like a dumbass as the thing became not five vicious diminutive demon boofuters, but a single titanic monster with gaping, dagger-fanged mouths for hands and feet and a leering, featureless maw where its head should have been. It would have been pretty bad-ass, if Al hadn't known he was most likely going to end up inside it in the next few seconds, and not in the way he'd always imagined himself inside Voltron, either.

Running hadn't quite worked out so far, but Al compared his broken bottle to the thousands of snapping teeth pointed his way and decided to give it another go. Body screaming, he shot away from the monster, aiming himself at the hotel he'd seen from the alley. He'd never really cared much how long he was going to live, but at that particular instant, he wanted as many more seconds as he could get.

A tall, wrought-iron fence separated the derelict hotel from the sidewalk, but Al parkoured right the hell over it, not bothering to remind himself that he didn't know how to spell parkour, let alone demonstrate it. He hit the ground hard, and his knee gave out.

"Well," Al said, panting and dazed. "That's me done."

"Kinda wish I'd smoked more."

Al laid back on the concrete, rain washing over him. He dug a Lucky out of his jacket, careful to keep it from getting wet, and managed to find his lighter. He lit up, drew in, and let out a long plume of cottony grey smoke. He wondered if, when he'd boarded the Universal Locomotive, his ticket had read 'Last stop: eaten by Demonic Midget Voltron after pissing himself in an alley in Jennings Heights.' He closed his eyes and gave in to what was coming next.

That turned out to be not a damn thing.

Half a minute of lying in the rain having not seen him taking the long dirt nap, he sat up. The demon was gone, vanished. He sat alone in front of the hotel, soaked and in a rather exorbitant amount of pain, but so far uneaten and thoroughly un-murdered.

Actually, he wasn't quite alone. Squatting in the once opulent doorway of the gutted hotel, an old Filipina lady ate cat food straight from the can. She watched Al with calm eyes, absently scooping her meal into cracked, chap-latticed lips. Apparently discomfited by his staring, she held the can out in a hospitable gesture and motioned him over.

Al declined the snack but accepted the invitation, limped out of the rain to share her shelter. The doors, their glass long ago shattered, were bronze portals looking into an inky void. It was weird that nobody had bothered to even hang up plywood to keep the animals and bums out; it was also weird just how tidy things were, without a speck of graffiti or even a chunk of wind-blown rubbish. The old lady shrugged, kept on eating. As Al started inside, body and mind just about at their limit, she grabbed him by the wrist with more strength than her apparent frailty would have suggested.

"That's a bad place, kid," the old lady said. She was calm, free of the normal tics and visible madness he expected. Her only affectation seemed to be punctuating her sentences with bites of Fancy Feast. "Stay out here. Warm enough out here; and food tonight. Rain's bad, but not that bad. Better here."

"Did you see what just happened?" Al said.

"Saw you jump the fence," she said. "Saw you smoke a cigarette. You got another cigarette? I'd like one of your cigarettes."

Al gave her one.

He flicked open his Zippo, but the old lady shied away from the flame. She tucked the Lucky into the tangled mass of thick black hair and swept her fingers along the inside of the empty can, sopping up every last drop of juice.

"I give the cigarette later to the man. The man gives me food. Sometimes cat food, sometimes leftovers. His wife won't let him buy his own, so when I get one, I give it to the man and he gives me food and I keep his secret smoking secret from his wife. It's bad to lie because we are both daughters of someone, but she's a bitch for not letting the man smoke so it's okay."

The storm wasn't lessening. Al didn't even know if it could be called a storm. There was no lightning, no thunder, no wind, just a constant, ceaseless downpour, like someone left the shower on and the hot water had long ago run out. He wobbled on his feet, very much aware that if he didn't crash soon, he was going to topple over where he stood. There was warmth inside, he knew, and regardless of the old lady, he was going to find it.

"Don't go in the nest, I said," the old lady said. "The snake is in the nest."

"Sweetheart," Al said, "after what I just been through, I'll eat a fuckin' snake if it means I can get a little sleep."

"Bad language," the old lady said. She let go of Al's wrist, wiped her hand on her clothes. "Eat the snake then. You eat the snake; I'll move into his nest. Maybe find the stash I left in there. Probably broken now. Everything is broken in the nest, but not the snake."

For the first time, Al noticed that the old lady wasn't sitting there at all. Her legs had been removed at mid-thigh. Al wondered how she managed to get around, but the pile of empty cans and his burgeoning awareness of a vengefully foul odor told him that she probably didn't. He tossed the remainder of his pack of Luckies into her lap and left her for the warmth he could feel emanating from inside the hulk that once been a place where people found shelter when they were far from home.

That's the thing about hotels, or inns, or hostels: whatever else they might be, from the shittiest roach-coach to the grandest Budapest, they offered haven to the homesick and weary. People didn't live in them, but they let their guard down almost as if they did. They fucked and killed and slept beside each other with a communal anonymity that lingered long after they left, never giving much thought to who'd been there before or who would be there next. They were the ports in the storm where anyone with a few bits could find shelter, but where only the saddest among them stay longer than they had to. Check in, check out, onto the next.

"Sure thing, darlin'," Al said as he went inside.

The old lady watched him disappear into the inner darkness, counted five long smokes in a white box. "Shoulda told him about the ghosts," she said.

-8-

The Cobra's Nest still reeked of the carnage Junk-Mama had wrought, the stench of death and fire heavy on air staled by time and neglect. In the dark, the only sound a muted whisper of wind through heat-cracked walls, the smell was all-consuming, a rotting dust that cloyed at the back of the throat. You could taste the brutal memories of the place, the only reasonable response to them being to flee someplace where the living still had business.

Unless, of course, you were well past drunkenness, exhausted to the point of utter systems shut-down, and had just been attacked by a Demonic Midget Voltron.

Al found a dry spot near the door, mainly because the rest of the lobby had opened into a vast pit when the upper floors collapsed in on themselves some forty years ago. The wrecked elevator shaft stabbed down from the thorny rafters. A dim, incongruous light shone from the roofless heights, illuminating just the rim of the sinkhole and sharpening the black beneath. None of the winged things -- not the owls or bats or any of midnight's hunters – roosted up there, nor did any of the belly-crawling vermin of the earth scuttle across the splintered floor. The Nest was a mausoleum without mourners, a silent witness to the eternal scars of rage. To Al, it kinda looked like the gaping anus of a corpse whose cause of death was better left a mystery.

"I've literally found the asshole of Jennings Heights," Al said as he stretched himself out to sleep. Sleep came quickly, with a vivid vengeance and as lucid a dream as he could have in his current state.

They came to him almost instantly, and at first, Al thought it was going to be the kind of dream where he woke up sticky and pleased. Floating, he saw the rich decrepitude of the hotel's glory years layer itself over what remained, like transparent slides lain down one over another to make a time-lapse picture. The girls materialized like pale bodies floating to the surface above a new-sunk ship, one at a time at first, then in twos and threes, until he lay at the center of a white-limbed carpet of moonlit flesh. Fingers stroked him, lips brushed his, cooing voices whispered promises of delight into his ears. All in all, Al rather enjoyed it, right up until the Pimp showed up.

The celestial flesh-peddler descended the staircase that no longer existed, resplendent in the finery of madness. As one, the phantom whores drew back from Al, gossamer tendrils of smoke drawn into the lungs of some ancient, wrathful god. All at once, the force of Silky Cobra's presence overwhelmed the dreamer, and all he could do was lie there in his paralysis and watch as the ghost or memory or fever-dream of the monster descended upon him.

"Been awhile since Silky Cobra's seen any kind of flesh, boy," the pimp said, his words oozing like embalming fluid into Al's frozen soul. "Now that I seen some, reckon I got me a hungerin' for it."

Al struggled in the place between waking and slumber, forced the words from his mouth. "I got a Snickers bar in my pocket, man; have at it."

All semblance of humanity exploded from the image of Silky Cobra, a scream like steel pressed on dry ice shattering the still. The Snake hissed, drawing back. Suddenly, Al was aware of a new presence in his dream, one that bore the faintest light, a light that drove the monster back. He tried to see what had come, but it was no use; with a choking gurgle, the dream dissolved, leaving Al sweaty and breathless, awake and hanging precariously over the edge of the pit.

He scrambled back, scattering bits of ash and refuse into the void. He could have been asleep for minutes or days; the darkness remained impenetrable, but his weariness had been salved, the throbbing in his knee rendered dull and forgotten. Rain dripped from above, tentative, like it didn't want to disturb whatever rested below.

A light, feeble and unsteady, hovered not far from him, a crystalline orb of silver that pulsed with the weakness of a dying heartbeat.

"Hello, light," Al said because that seemed perfectly reasonable given the situation. "You one o' them ghost-whores from my dream?"

The radiant ball didn't speak; it was, after all, a ball of light. But it pulsed a little brighter, began to drift away from Al into the depths of the building. Al followed, because hey, he was already awake, and it wasn't every day a will-o'-the-wisp showed up to lead him into the abyss beneath a burnt-out seventies whorehouse. He figured he was probably still dreaming, anyway, and had never believed in the whole "if you die in your dreams, you die in real life" thing.

Gradually, Al became more aware of his surroundings, the illumination cast by his glowy new friend weaving shadows into shapes. His heart caught in his chest as he realized what it was that crunched under his feet and scratched at his jeans. Bodies lay where they had fallen decades earlier, sculpted forever in the throes of their agony, blackened statues that, at the slightest stirring, disintegrated into piles of ash. This was a bad place, and the wisp was leading him ever deeper into it. They circled counterclockwise around old wooden floors warped into a wall-hugging spiral, the light and its follower walking widder-shins around the grave-pit, delving ever deeper below the street outside.

Finally, Al splashed into calf-deep water, the glow of the orb leaving an oily trail on the black velvet rippling out from where he stepped. He kicked something, tripped, ended up on hands and knees in the sludge and runoff. He could feel bones scrape against his hands, hear them clattering against the walls, stirred by his thrashings. Then the light vanished, leaving him shivering and alone.

"Dick move, firefly," he said, struggling to his feet. Most people would be terrified, abandoned in a basement sepulcher, surrounded by the dead. Yet Al wasn't most people, and he wasn't afraid.

"I've spent the last eight years in darkness," he said, stretching his arms out to find a wall. If he could find a wall, all he had to do was follow it and he'd be out of this place. Then again, he didn't feel any particular rush to leave. His hand closed around something thin and cold and rough, gritty, decayed; he drew back, still feeling the residue on his skin. "I mean, metaphorically, but there was a couple months where I kept forgetting to buy lightbulbs, so not just metaphorically."

The orb reappeared in a slow rush, forming itself at first into its familiar shape, then expanding slowly like a balloon filling up. As it grew, it lost its edges, color fading, and began to take on a new symmetry of contour. Al watched it coalesce into the dizzying, TV-static image of a girl no older than fifteen. She was pretty, but for the hole in the side of her head. Pretty and naked and sad; Al turned away, embarrassed at seeing her in such a state.

Her light's intensity flared and leveled out. For the first time, Al got a good look at where the ghost-girl had brought him. Though crushed under tons of rubble, this place couldn't hide its secrets any more: it wasn't a basement: it was a dungeon, and not the fun kind. The ruins of torture devices antique and new-fangled jutted like gravestones from the still grey waters. Cages lined the walls, their bars like broken teeth stained with rust and blood. With his horror rising for the first time, Al looked at his hands, covered in the same rust, then at the cage, not a foot away from where he stood. In it hung a body, bones held together by twists of desiccated sinew that should have rotted away decades ago. He stumbled backward, bounced off something, felt a body slide off the rack where it had lain to splash beside him.

"That shit ain't right," Al said.

Rising like a headstone from the sewage, a filth-caked monolith of steel and hubris loomed over the center of the pit. The undead glow of his personal Beatrice pooled on the metal hulk of the mammoth safe, fingering the massive wheel that had long ago given up its job of locking up whatever remained of Silky Cobra's Stash. Inside the breached door, that pale luminosity tickled the outlines of shiny things. Al wasn't a Bitburg native and didn't know shit from Shinola when it came to its legendary treasures, but a goddamned Martian would have recognized the rich stuff ready to spill out of that box.

Instinctively, Al took a step towards the Stash, only to find himself stayed by the presence of the lingering spirit who led him down here.

"Sure thing, darlin'," Al said. "Ain't gonna be no looting before I do what ya brung me here for."

The ghost-girl lingered before him, expressionless. He felt her, the flickering revenant of her soul, in his own. There was no longing, no desire, nothing at all in her. She simply existed in this place, and somehow Al knew that it wasn't a pleasant existence.

A red and rending force bubbled up inside him, his belly a cauldron of boiling oil spiced with nitroglycerin. Something shifted in the darkness. The ghost-girl's ethereal features erupted into a mask of distilled terror so primal that it almost cut through the fury building in Al's heart. Then she was gone again, the faintest shard of her luminosity persistent on the stagnant air.

"You -- You don't belong here!" the voice, a steel-scraping sizzle on the stillness, barked from nowhere and everywhere all at once. A cold blast of wind slashed across Al's face, tracing a crimson streak along the left side of his jaw. The force was like a prize-fighter's jab, flinging him off his feet. He hit the water with a splash, crashed against the concrete below. Bones shattered with the impact; not his, but it still hurt like a mother.

Choking on the rancid flood, Al fought to find purchase, only for another hoary blade of wind to stab him through the chest. He couldn't breathe, couldn't see, couldn't hear anything but the rasping hiss of his attacker.

"This ain't your place, honkee-nigger," the voice said.

"Fuck, man," Al said, hacking up fluid that somehow tasted worse than Zima as he pulled himself up to his feet. "You just won the racist Olympics with that quip."

Al heard a rumbling across the cellar, and half-blinded by pain, saw a chair, its seat and arms limned in rusty spikes, hurl itself at him. He dove for the floor, but the heavy block of wood and metal caught him square across the back, stealing his breath along with any chance to fight back. He tried to fight the kaleidoscopic spiderweb dancing a merry jig in front of his eyes, tried to fight the encroaching blackness at the edges of his vision, but it was no use. Face down in the murderous contamination of a pimp's dungeon, Al had only once considered this might be the way he finally went out. At least it hadn't been from a snake in his goddamned mailbox.

Cold, ethereal fingers pried around his neck, lifted Al into the air. He gazed into the eyes of his killer, unbowed by the sight that awaited him. The face was almost human, shreds of burnt skin and hair clinging to its black skull like melted wax on a candlestick. Its body, insubstantial as the air, billowed and ruffled in the stillness, a living cloak of shapeless black. The leering skull snapped its teeth at Al's face, a resonant, scraping sniggering welling up from the depths of its chest. Al's limbs had gone numb; his heart was a spastic, broken-winged bird in his chest.

"Now," it said, "You gonna die real nice, white-boy."

"Looks like, you dead pimp cock-smoker," Al said.

The ghost reared, drawing Al higher off the floor. All around them, tiny, crystalline orbs like the one he had followed to his death, floated up from the water. The light they shone brought the room and all its horrors into crisp relief. One by one, like the first, they grew and took on the glimmering shape of women and girls. Every face looked wan and bereft of anything resembling joy. Every eye turned to Al, every stare full of pity and abject disappointment. The ghost held him a moment longer, flexing its grip on Al's throat.

It shouldn't have.

Hanging on the lip of mortality, a gaggle of dead whores gawking at him, their dead pimp laughing... well, it all kinda pissed Al off. So, he did what he said he'd do: he reached back, balled his fist, and punched that ghost right in its goddamned ghost face.

Al hit the ghost of Silky Cobra so hard that he literally knocked the black right off him. Al dropped to the floor, and the pimp-ghost flew out of its own body. What remained wasn't some ghoulish monster, just the unsteady image of the man as he'd been in life, a gaudy spectral poon-trafficker with a stupid, mean look on his face. That expression changed immediately to one of stark, dumbfounded astonishment, which mirrored Al's perfectly.

"What the fuck, motherfucker?" Silky Cobra said, his shock radiating off of him.

Al popped him a good one to the mouth, just to make sure the first shot hadn't been a fluke. Judging by the way Silky Cobra swayed under the blow, it hadn't.

Al looked at his hands: they thrummed with a strident glow, pulsing, waves of tangible sunlight swirling about them.

"Neato," he said.

He threw a left to distract his opponent, then pushed forward off the balls of his feet and drove his right straight through the pimp-ghost's head.

Silky Cobra reeled, howling in pained, impotent rage. The incorporeal whores' light grew stronger, their eyes wider.

"Enough with this shit!" Silky Cobra said, bellowing. He lashed out with every bit of his unholy strength, smashing Al with a wall of rancid wind that hit like a bulldozer. His body heaved, stretched, knotted itself into a new shape more fitting his namesake.

A monstrous, glimmering cobra, as wide as a man was tall and as long as ten, coiled where the ghost-pimp had stood. Its hood flared, forked tongue danced around fangs as long as Al's arm.

"I mean it this time, you funky freak," Silky Cobra said. "Now, you die, then all these bitches gonna get it worse than they ever got."

Al shrugged, licked his thumb, took aim. "No, now I punch, and these ladies gonna watch you take it like the bitch you are."

Silky Cobra snapped himself in attack, and Al met him with a straight right. Gold light exploded with the impact as Al's blazing, fiery fist blossomed with supernatural defiance. He followed up with a flurry of overwhelming punches, some dim part of him suddenly lit up with muscle memory sloughing off the years of disuse.

The snake vaporized, leaving only a stunned, pitiable remnant of a pimp-ghost behind.

The shade of Silky Cobra reeled. Behind him, the outline of a doorframe traced itself on the air, a matte red rectangle humming with electric malice. Misty clouds of crimson roiled inside the frame, backlit by an unwholesome light. Al's hands flared, bright as any wished-upon star.

Al could feel strength flowing through his veins, pumping from his heart into his fists, a power greater than anything he'd ever known; it was like he held in his palms a pair of '69 Shelbies, straining against the slips to be let loose. The door hemmed and whined in hungry anticipation.

Al stretched backward, energy thrumming, solar flares arcing from his fist. He lunged at Silky Cobra, the pimp-ghost's staticky face a mask of terror, threw his fist forward, and screamed:

"GHHHHooooooOOOOOOoooooooooooooSTT PUNCH!"

because he'd seen enough anime to know that when you really, really need to end the kicking of the bad guy's ass in one fell strike, you damn well better shout a bitchin' battlecry to name your finishing move.

The blow struck Silky Cobra with the force of a thousand Japanese cartoon anti-heroes, thunder echoing about the chamber. Silky Cobra exploded backward, flew through the air, and disappeared inside the red-rimmed doorway. With a cosmic belch, the door shuddered once, then both it and the pimp-ghost were gone.

Al heaved, fell to his knees, the orgasm of ghost-punching anointing him in an afterglow of untethered release.

"Too much sturm," Al said, panting, as he eyed the door, making sure the ghost was truly gone. "Not enough drang."

All around the room, the glimmering spirits of two dozen dead hookers began to waver and steam. A second red doorway appeared, exactly as the first had, then another not so red one. The third door drew itself in blue, the clouds inside it calm and languid in their movements. Each spirit, in turn, passed Al in silence, drawing closer to either of the portals. The last to pass through was the little girl who had brought him here. He couldn't read what she wrote upon her face, but he figured it might have been something like thanks. *It damn well fucking better have been thanks.*

His hands hurt, but in the way your muscles hurt after a particularly spirited fuck. Otherwise, he felt pretty good; in fact, he hadn't felt as good as he did now since back before he'd turned pro when he fought just for the fun of it. Even his squashed beak had stopped hurting. Still, as he regarded his hands with a mix of awe for what they'd just done and nostalgia for what they used to, he couldn't help but wonder what the hell had just happened.

"Well," he said, shaking away the urge to try and explain the inexplicable to himself. "That's new."

Al grimaced, chuckling as the doors faded away, leaving him in the dark place, the only light streaming from his hands and getting fainter as he watched. He stumbled towards the collapsed floor that led back upstairs, ready to be anywhere but here.

"That just fits, don't it?" Al said, clambering towards the exit. "I unbind an entire bordello's worth of undead hookers from the thrall of their ghost-pimp, and not even a handy to say thank you."

Because sometimes the universe is listening, a ribbon of moonlight fluttered down into that dark place no longer given over to the evil it once housed. Al followed the light as it skimmed the liquid filth to shine on the open door of Silky Cobra's Stash.

Al smiled like he meant it, looked back up through the gaping asshole to which he'd just applied a fist-sized ghostly enema of Texan exorcism, and tipped an imaginary hat.

"But I guess the loot'll buy me at least a handy, at that."

-9-

The man who walked out of the Cobra's Nest that morning wore the same skin as the one who'd walked in yesterday, but there was something different about him. The rain still fell, Jennings Heights still reeked of desolation and fear, but the man was different. It might have been the pockets and bags full of plastic-wrapped blocks of seventies-era hundred-dollar-bills and the trail of gold coins and uncut gems trickling behind him, or it might have been the goofy sense of self-satisfaction that dripped along beside.

The old Filipina lady looked him up and down.

"You found him," she said. "You found the snake, huh? You kill the snake? Shoulda killed the snake."

"No," Al said. He cocked an eye at the box of Luckies still propped on the cripple's lap. She passed him one, after great deliberation with whatever voices kept her company. She'd changed, too, looked just one shade closer to alive than she had the night before. He lit the cigarette with a Bic and inhaled as he tried to conjure up a proper response.

Al was hungry, thirsty, and not quite sure what the fuck had just happened, but damned if he didn't enjoy the first puff of that smoke. "But I'm pretty sure I punched his ass straight to hell."

Chapter Three: Dax Vagance, Douchebro at Large

Cyclops, Saturday Afternoon

"You sure it's okay for us to be in here?" Eldon said, in a tone that made Charlene crinkle up her face the way you would if your foreign exchange student asked if it was okay that he took a dump in your bathtub without invoking the house divinities beforehand. "I mean, with all the stuff that went down last night, I didn't know if we're allowed back."

Charlene shook her head and pushed the Bud Light tap as far back as it would go, hoping the bros wouldn't notice all the foam, suddenly struck by the fact that she might have to change the keg since Al wasn't around to do it for her. That had to be the worst part of his benders; he'd disappear for a week after a brawl, then come creeping in like some recalcitrant dog that just shat the living room carpet, and because Lilith and the Cyclops's owner couldn't resist a stray and she didn't know how to stay mad at him, she'd just sulk until he turned on the charm. He'd earn his way back into her good graces by doing things like changing kegs and eighty-sixing rowdy drunks that weren't him, and everything would go back to normal. There was some kind of connection to be made between changing the Bud Light keg and Al not being around to do the heavy lifting, and it probably had to with the proclivity of yahoos and Bros toward drinking shitty beer.

She set the pitcher on the tray and thanked Eldon with her eyes when he picked it up, even if the *vox populi* told her she shouldn't have been so eager to let a man do all the work for a *poor widdle girl* like her. But fuck that noise; she'd been up 'til six waiting for Jake the DJ, and if it eased Eldon's weighty conscience to make the trip back to his table for her, then who was she to deny him a little well-earned sense of chivalry?

"If we banned everybody who got caught up in a ruckus started by Albrecht Drue, there wouldn't be anyone left to drain our Bud Light kegs.

"Besides, I don't remember you being part of the problem, well, ever," Charlene said.

It was true: if you had to pick the one guy out of any given line-up who absolutely, positively, had fuck-all to do with starting the shit in question, you'd pick Eldon.

Unless you were a racist.

Down at the far end of the bar, Lilith knocked over an entire flight of beers with a wild swing of her girls, soaking her linen puffy-shirt to the delight of the Ren Faire troupe who'd been occupying the back booths for the last hour and a half. Great merriment was expressed by all, with many a 'Huzzah!' ringing from the peasant masses; Lilith even added a deft curtsey to punctuate the show.

Charlene couldn't help but smile, showing her teeth as she rolled her eyes over the rest of her customers; it was a pretty good crowd for a Saturday, the regulars having just stumbled in, and before they closed for the night, she and her trusty sidekick would serve them all through whatever madness or mundanity they'd conjure up. Almost ten years she'd worked with Lilith-- ever since they'd wandered over after class at the art school around the corner-- and she still couldn't get over how easily and shamelessly Lilith made her money. A wink here, a batted eye there, and Lil would go home after four hours of waitressing with more cash and solicitations of high-quality casual sex than Charlene got in a whole weekend tending bar. Every lady-leaning eye in the place followed every move she made, except for maybe the ones firmly ensconced in the front of Eldon Garvey's skull. Those were still locked on Charlene, calmly prompting her to some end Charlene didn't quite fathom.

"Check, ma'am?" Eldon said all twelfth-grader nervous like he hadn't been coming here and ordering drinks for years.

"Alton, you're on Dax Vagance's tab," Charlene said, putting her fists on her hips and pursing her lips before she waved a falsely admonishing finger in the kid's face. "And what have I told you about calling me ma'am around here?"

Eldon blushed, declined to correct Charlene's misappellation, and pushed his round-rimmed Harry Potter glasses up on his nose before he made off with the tray. He handled the beers and shots with a surprising amount of dexterity, navigated the clutches and smatterings of packed tables and drifting bodies like Frogger on a mission across the interstate. For a gawky kid who looked like he'd never put a basketball through a hoop or a biscuit in a basket for the entirety of his life thus far, he avoided every bump and jostle and collision with the fluidity of a punt-returner on speed, and as far as he was concerned, he owed it all to the stiff lump of fur and bone sewn into the pocket of his *Naruto* hoodie.

It hadn't been lucky for the bunny, but after a few words cribbed from a book almost no one but the Old Ones could read, a bath in cuttlefish oil, and a ritual performed with the utmost faith in the subjective nature of reality, the rabbit's foot made Eldon as nimble and fleet as its totemic nature implied. That tickled him to no end, whether he believed it or not because it meant he hadn't tripped over his damn shoelaces once in the whole damn time since he started carrying it around.

Back at the big eight-top, he dealt out drinks to Faux-hawk McDouchebro, fellow investigator JT, Herman the equipment tech, and Sergeant Dave like a champ. Then he stepped back to take in the visual expression of the realization of the second biggest dream he'd ever had: the camera was rolling, and he was actually going to be on a big-time paranormal investigation TV show!

Sure, the discovery of life-after-death would be momentous beyond all imagining, but Eldon Garvey had already discovered so much of the world's hidden mystery that he knew ghosts would have to show up sooner or later. *But this was freakin' Ghost Quest, man! THE Dax Fucking Vagance was right here, interviewing him and Dave!*

Mostly just Dave, but still.

Herman had his monster JVC HD mobile camera on his shoulder, working his angle to make sure he framed up his shot exactly how he wanted it. Meaning, he had Dax in just the right spot for the forward spotlight to limn him in a subtle halo, while the dizzy motion of the bar blurred into a miasmic backdrop that just slightly bled into the fuzzed edges of Dave's outline. It was an ever-so-gentle reminder to the viewers' subconscious perceptions that a yokel like Dave could only fumble around in the darkness of ignorance until the hero of *Ghost Quest* shined his light on the scene.

Or some shit like that; Herman gave up on anything remotely resembling artistic cinematography the moment he signed up for this crap show, and the only thing not running on autopilot right now was his hangover. That had developed a mind of its own and seemed to be running on an all-encompassing hatred for the universe.

"Ready to go in three, two," Herman mouthed the 'one' and Eldon had to restrain himself from geeksploding all over the room.

"Along with my fellow investigator, JT--" Dax indicated the skinniest of the three Bros, who froze halfway through his Jägermeister like a bookend on the other side of their subject-- "I'm here with Sergeant Dave Paek," Dax said, eye-fucking the camera like he wanted it to cum first. "Formerly of the United States Marine Corps, now the commanding officer of the *Bitburg Supernatural Squad*."

"Ooh-Rah," Dave said. He mugged and puffed out his chest like he was *born for this shit*. "But hold on there, chief. I enlisted; I work for a living. And there's no 'formerly' when it comes to Marines."

Dax ate some more shit with his smile, flexing his gym-tastic pecs to remind everyone watching who had the biggest pair at the table.

"Point taken, Sergeant Dave," Dax said. "But tell me again what you said about the most haunted site in America that no one's ever heard of. Tell me again why even the bravest paranormal investigators in the city refuse to set foot inside Cardinal's Crest."

Dave couldn't tell if Dax was fucking with him or not, but only because he wanted for Dax to not be fucking with him. If Eldon hadn't been so caught up in the giddy squee of potentially being on TV, he might have taken offense for his friend. As it was, he stood behind Herman and tried to keep mum while Dave held up a shield of spread fingers to deflect any aspersions.

"It's pretty simple, really," Dave said, splitting his focus between Dax, JT, and the camera in quick succession. "Cardinal's Crest isn't just haunted; it's possessed. There's a demon who lives up there, and some things just aren't worth it."

Good job, Dave.

Dax shot him a look, and fellow investigator JT went all boggle-eyed and consciously half-choked on his beer. He leaned into the shot, somehow managing to make eye contact with both Dave and the camera. "You mean to tell us that people have experienced a demonic force in the castle?"

Dax bumped his chest, a look of pure gallantry lighting on his brow.

Dave looked at the both of them like they'd just asked what flavor of syrup he wanted on his diarrhea sundae.

"No," he said. "I mean there's a bat-winged Fiend of Hell that roosts up there, and it kills everyone who ventures near. I know it. Eldon knows it. Everyone in Bitburg knows it. That's why no one goes up there and why Cardinal's Crest is the hauntedest house in America no one's ever heard about."

Dax rolled his eyes and dismissed his interviewee with a wave. "Well, it's like we say: when no one else has the guts to, *Ghost Quest* strides boldly where even the bravest fear to tread."

Dave started to object but really wanted to be on TV with Dax Vagance and his crew. A crack appeared in the glowing crystalline shell of hero-worship Eldon had erected around himself, and it got wider with every word out of Dax's mouth.

Herman took a silent cue, scuttled around the table, made sure to tighten his focus according to the meter and cadence of his boss's voice. Whatever else you said about Dax, he did have a flair for drama, and Herman knew how to capture it in digital.

"Ghosts, evil spirits, demonic entities-- whatever paranormal dangers may stalk the night, we don't back down. The *Ghost Quest* crew has the gear, the experience, and the faith to stand up to the forces terrorizing this city.

"Now, don't feel bad about--"

Dave turned white and made a taint-check for errant poop-juice as Eldon barreled his way into frame; Dax and JT reared back, Eldon's tiny shoulders and massive sweatshirt filling the image like tear gas in a crowd of urban youths with *#blacklivesmatter* signs.

"We don't feel bad about anything," Eldon said. He could barely hold himself together, to the point that, for once, even Dave kept his mouth shut. "And we certainly don't lack the gear or the experience to investigate anything. What you don't understand is that we know what's up there, and we are telling you not to go."

Eldon suddenly realized what he was doing, who he was doing it to. Dave gaped at him like he'd just whipped his dick out at the dinner table; Herman the equipment tech and fellow investigator JT sat so still and pregnant with expectation that even Eldon wanted to know what he was going to do next.

Dax Vagance, though? He had this smile on his face like a kid who was this close to convincing his parents to let him stay home alone while they went away for the weekend, like he could already taste his first underage drink, dry-hump, and On-Demand adult movie binge. It wasn't the shit-eating grin that usually squatted under his nose; this smile was one of utter satisfaction.

Eldon knew there wasn't a thing he could do to dissuade Dax and his crew now. Not anything he could explain, anyway. He also knew that if the stories were true-- the urban legends, the first-hand accounts he'd stumbled on during his all-night perusals of the city's secret archives, the things he'd glimpsed from afar during his more esoteric investigations of the Quiet City-- he was about to watch the stars of his third favorite ghost-hunting show march off to their doom. And it would have been way out of character for Eldon Garvey to allow that to happen.

He didn't know if what he was going to do would work but didn't have any reason to think it wouldn't. So he balled up his fist, reached it into the pouch on his hoodie, and wrapped his pianist fingers around the fetish sewn inside. He could feel the energy that had once been part of the living animal, began to channel his own roiling energy into it. The technique wasn't one that he'd tried before and he'd never attempted anything like it in such uncontrolled conditions, but the principle was the same as what he did back at home, and he had to try to stop Dax Vagance from getting himself killed. Besides, he really, really wanted to know if he could do magic, or if it was all just because of the weed.

Dax started to speak. Eldon began to mouth the words to a spell he'd read in one of his old tomes. If he really believed he could, he reasoned, he would imbue the words with the mystical energy inherent to all things and stored inside his lucky rabbit's foot, channel that energy into a tangible form, and use it to make the *Ghost Quest* crew forget all about Cardinal's Crest. That is assuming he was some kind of wizard, and not just a skinny nutjob with a degree in metaphysics and way too much faith in the underlying magic of the universe.

"Dax Fuckin' Vagance!" someone yelled.

Eldon's heart leaped, and whether he was a whack-job or some kinda sorcerer became a question for another time and not right now. He also let out a ripping fart, because all that tension had to go somewhere.

A cyclone blur of cocaine and sleaze coalesced into the shape of a man who slapped both bejeweled hands down on Eldon's shoulders and spun him around before wrapping him up in a big-ol' hug, planting a chapped-lip kiss on each of his cheeks, then do-si-doed his black ass out of the way. "Dax Fuckin' Vagance, you slippery shit! You have any idea how long it took me to find your chiseled ass?"

"Benny?" Dax said. That was all he could get out before the grey-suited invader hauled him out of his chair in as expansive and affectionate an embrace as was allowable by public decency. To that end, Benny repeated his greeting with Dax, then dropped him back down in his seat. He turned a greasy smile to each of the men gathered around the table, then whipped out a wad of Benjamins wrapped around a *Ghost Quest* logo-emblazoned money clip, and started feeding them onto the table like an automatic card-shuffler.

"Fellow investigator JT, you old sycophant!" Benny said, his Armani shades disguising the actual object of his gaze. "How's Dax's cock taste today?

"Herman! You eat any small children today? Who'm I kidding? Of course you did!"

The coke-nado stopped moving, but even as he planted his hands on his hips and sized up the pair of strangers dappled among his colleagues, you could almost see the individual molecules comprising his physical presence swirling in place.

"Daxy-Dax, who's your friends here?" Benny said, staring back and forth between Eldon and Dave like he couldn't decide if they were turds or fresh scoops of chocolate ice cream.

Dax gulped. If Benny were here, that meant the Producers knew where he was. If the Producers knew where he was, he was in trouble, and all the effort he'd put in to getting a chance to investigate Cardinal's Crest would be for nothing. He went cold all over, his brain kicking itself into overdrive as he ran through every possible excuse and explanation for being in Bitburg when he was supposed to be thousands of miles to the south. Finally, he scolded himself and reapplied the mask of his shit-eating grin.

"This is Benny, Benny from the network," he said to everyone assembled. Dax stood, bulled his shoulders wide, and half-flexed as he bent over and slapped a hand each on Eldon's and Dave's shoulder. "This here is Sergeant Dave and Eldon from the Bitburg Supernatural Squad, just a couple of intrepid paranormal investigators who happen also to be *Ghost Quest* superfans."

"No shit?" Benny said. Behind all the sweat, razor stubble, and ignored bodily exhaustion, he might have looked impressed. "You guys are fuckin' legendary!"

Benny made a show of double-clasping the pair of Ghost Geeks' hands as he shook them, muttering with a happy incoherence about how much he was impressed by the work they'd done and the EVPs they'd gathered and how awesome it was and how he hoped they'd stick by their phones because he was totally gonna call them about a show idea he had in mind. All this he did as he funneled them out of their chairs, through the early-evening/late-afternoon barflies, out the door, and into the cab he'd left waiting at the curb.

He stood there on the sidewalk outside the Cyclops for just long enough to blow a couple of kisses in quick succession at the bewildered Dave and Eldon.

Inside the cab, the pair shared a confused, dumbstruck silence for as long as it took Eldon to realize that Dave was waiting for him to explain what the fuck had just happened.

Since Eldon had no clue on that score, he could only shrug and inwardly thank his lucky stars that Benny from the Network had shown up before he had to find out the hard way that he didn't really know a magic spell that would have wiped the thought of Cardinal's Crest from one of his heroes' mind, regardless of what he wanted to believe.

Benny let them get out of sight before he twisted the ruby top off the ring on his left pinkie, dipped in an extra-long right pinkie nail, took a bump of coke, popped a toothpick in his mouth, and stormed back into the Cyclops.

"Nice cans, baby-doll!" he said as he whooshed past an appreciative Lilith, who still hadn't done anything about the newborn transparency of her top. He snatched Dax out of his chair by the crook of his arm and led him off to a relatively quiet corner of the joint with JT and Herman left gobsmacked where they sat.

"Bubbeleh, babycakes, boychick," Benny said, all intense and Jewy-- his words-- like he sometimes got. Dax didn't know how to respond, react, or retreat; he just kinda stood there and let the perpetual energy machine that was Benny from the Network drive on to whatever end it was driving to because, after years of bussing off from one ghostless ghost quest to another, he'd learned not to get in Benny's way, especially when he was this goddamned high. "Daxy-Dax-- what the fuck are we doin' here in fucking Bitburg, baby?"

Benny had him pressed into a corner, in every sense of the words. He rummaged a glance at his crew, who were sitting around the table like the couple of innocent bystanders they were.

"Whatever you do, boyo," Dad had said so many times. Usually, he said it when he was drunk and going through photos of his Phantom wing back in 'Viet goddamned Nam.' Why he was saying it in Dax's head now, when he was long dead and Dax assumed unwillingly sober, he didn't know. But he could guess. "Don't you be a blue falcon. Don't you fuck your buddies just so you can get ahead."

His fellow investigator JT and equipment tech Herman didn't have a goddamned clue they were off the reservation on this.

"Questing for ghosts," Dax said, his face awash in a concretion of honesty. Dax knew he wasn't the brightest bulb on the tree, and that he didn't have the guile to keep up anything resembling a charade. "It's what we do, right?"

Benny's neck twizzlered and his head went all askew.

"But this isn't no New Orleans," he said, guiding the pair of them into a handy booth just outside the splash zone of the Renaissance smack-talk bubbling over from the cosplayers. "I mean, you got a buncha weirdos in costumes and a buncha booze and a buncha fine boobies, but there's something about this joint that that does not scream of *bontempses roullezing*. And I'm pretty sure the Producers wanted you in New Orleans, correct me if I'm wrong, and since the Producers pay for *my* booze and drugs and boobies, I kinda have a responsibility to make sure that you are in the place the Producers expect you to be."

Benny leaned back in his chair, took off his shades, tried not to fidget too much or crack open his ring right there in front of King Butter-nuts the Fifth and the Court of Nerdonia or whatever the fuck those guys were. Dax knew he'd done wrong, knew that he'd been caught, and didn't have an excuse for what he'd done. *So why the fuck couldn't he just come out and say it?*

When Dax couldn't do anything but squirm and make shapes with his lips that looked like they wanted to be words but couldn't decide which ones to be, Benny from the Network squeezed the bridge of his nose between his thumb and forefinger and rolled his red-rimmed eyes. They landed on JT and Herman, a couple o' dumb hangers-on who would have followed Dax into Hell itself if it meant not having to think for themselves. They were perfect Network employees.

"From the looks of it, I'm guessing Merry and Pippin over here have no idea you've gone rogue and taken them right along with you?

"Cuz you know that's what you done, right? Zimmern and the rest aren't gonna excuse them any more than they're gonna let your sorry ass off the hook."

Finally, Dax couldn't take it anymore; he might not have known what to say, but he had to say something. "Off the hook for what? For using a couple of personal days to go sight-seeing?"

"No, for diverting Network assets, Network money, and Network employees for your own personal bullshit. You think I wanna be here in Bitburg? Fuck no, nobody wants to be in Bitburg! Ain't shit in Bitburg worth seeing, hearing, or talking about-- Ain't nobody want to see this shit."

"And how is that any different from every other goddamned place we've ever gone?" Dax said, nearly knocking over the table with the force of his reaction. "Do you really think we're going to find anything down in New Orleans but a bunch of zydeco tourists and fat emo chicks in leather corsets?"

"I enjoy a curvy woman in a leather corset, and so do you, Daxy-Dax," Benny said. "And the people out there in TV-Land like to watch their big dumb beefcake Ghost Quester make eyes at fatties while talking about spooky bullshit. That's what you do, Dax; it's all fake, and everyone but you seems to get that. So you tell me why I don't just call up Mister Zimmern and the Board and let them know I've found their little golden boy?"

Dax froze from faux-hawk to toes when he heard what Benny had said. "You haven't told them yet?"

Benny leaned back in his chair, watching the cosplayers, checking out the hottie black goth waitress, soaking up the smile on Brother Malcolm's face. He decided that, aside from having some of the best coke on the East Coast, Bitburg had a few things going for it that maybe New Orleans didn't. "Fuck you think I am, some kinda narc?"

"You're a producer," Dax said, not particularly accustomed to the strange feeling of hope suddenly spilling into his doom.

"Exactly, with a little-p," Benny said, looking around for that waitress with the big soggy tits. "But like I said, the big-P Producers sign my checks, so I have a certain obligation to ensure their interests are protected.

"But I'm also a titty-honkin' drug-fiend who likes to get up to some shady shit now and again, and in all the time I been baby-sittin' Dax Vagance, douchebro, I ain't never seen you step off the straight and narrow to go lookin' in the shade. So, I ask again, what the fuck are *we* doin' in Bitburg?"

Belief in what he was hearing had a slap-fight with his fear of punishment, so Dax hung there just outside the ring and waited to see which one would win out. He'd never expected an ally in a guy like Benny, but then again, he'd never expected himself to con his friends and steadfast companions into running off on an unsanctioned adventure that could nullify their contracts, destroy their reputation, and end whatever hope they had of finding the one thing they'd been searching for since his dad died.

The only way he'd convinced himself to stray from the Producers' leash was to quite literally look himself in the mirror and ask himself the question out loud.

"What if I actually knew, like, really, completely, unquestionably knew that there was a place where we could do a Gravewalk and actually find a real ghost?" Dax said, pretending Benny was his mirror.

"I'd ask you to share what you were smokin', that's what. There ain't no ghosts, Dax. It's all just TV, and you know that." And just like his reflection had done, Benny showed the tiniest hint of doubt.

"Don't you ever get sick of it, Benny? That feeling like we're just going through the motions out there? Lying to everyone the whole time.

"Sometimes, it's like nobody wants us to find anything, and it just kills me dead. But I keep doing what they tell me to anyway because I gotta believe that what we're doing is important."

Dax paused for effect, trying to give that spore of doubt time to grow into something more substantial. He could tell it would take a little fertilizer, but as a veteran TV host, if there's one thing Dax Vagance knew, it was grade A bullshitting.

"As soon as I heard about Cardinal's Crest, I knew I had to come here. I've been asking since season one for the Producers to send us to check it out, but every time I ask, there's an excuse for us not to. But now, they're sending us back to places we've already been, for fucksake, and do you know why?"

"Because your ratings are shit," Benny said, which was true. The one bad episode between Ghost Quest and cancellation got closer with every week. Even if Benny didn't give a half a square shit about whether or not *The Truth (Was) Out There*, he did care about having money for booze and titties and Cartagena Stardust.

"Exactly," Dax said. "People are tired of the same old shit. Even if the Crest turns out to be a bust, at least it's something new. Now, if it's not a bust, just imagine what the Big Man will do when we bring him real proof of the paranormal!"

Benny's buzz had died down enough so that he was able to see the real expression on Dax's face. To his surprise, it wasn't desperation he saw. It was resolve. Dax Vagance looked like a man who believed everything that he was saying, and through all the drugs and years and the general malaise of being a grown-up in a world full of 'em, Benny caught himself feeling just a little bit of that belief. And a whole shitload of desire to become ridiculously more inebriated because of it.

"Look, Daxy," Benny said. He twisted the ruby off his pinkie ring and candied up his nose with the rest of his supply. "The Producers know where we are. Well, me and Marianna anyway. And I ain't gonna stick my neck out just because you're having some sort of quarter-life crisis and have decided to go out running around looking for 'The Truth'."

Dax felt that strange hope slip away, felt a more familiar stultification ooze in to cover up the space where it had been. He should have known better than to think he could get away with doing anything but what the Producers ordered him to do.

But Benny continued, "Thing is they don't know I've found you yet, and as long as I check in with 'em every twelve or so hours and tell 'em you're still somewhere out here on the lam, I figure it'll be at least a day or two before they expect me to move on and probably forget about *this* here all."

"What does that mean?" Dax said, holding his breath, not wanting to let that hope rise up again just for Benny to stomp on it.

"It means, who gives a fuck where we are?" the producer with the little 'p' said, finally wrangling Lilith away from the King and his court with a wave of a hundy and numb-toothed grin of lurid intent. "Look, I'll give you twenty-four fucking hours to go hunt your sure-thing ghost. Fuck-- if I can score some more of this amazing Bitburg Battle-Flour, I'll even go with you. Shit, if you're as right as you think you are, I'll want to be right there with you as we'll be fuckin' television heroes. Just like you was sayin'.

"And if you're wrong, you get to be the one to explain to Mister Zimmern exactly how I found you on the very precipice of misappropriation and talked you back before you flung their whole franchise into the abyss."

"Either way, you toddle off and I spend the rest of the night doing coke off a black girl's tits and knockin' on her back door so loud she don't have a choice but to open up and let ol' Benny in."

Dax wanted to say something big and deep and meaningful that would express the overwhelming joy he felt at Benny's unexpected collusion, but all he could think of was "Fuckin' A, bro!" so he said that instead.

Benny refused the high-five that followed and shooed Dax away with a flick of his empty ring. "Now scoot; Daddy's gotta go find his Aunt Bernice, and I'm pretty sure I know just the right ebony Vampiress to show me the way."

The sudden arrival of the busty beauty in question derailed any further discussion, so Dax just accepted that, for once, the Universe had nodded in his direction. All that remained between him and the fulfillment of his quest was one more night. And maybe a bat-winged Fiend of Hell.

"Mister Vagance," Lilith said, all smiles and technicolor sexuality. "Who is your adorable friend?"

Benny stuffed the hundo in between The Girls and pulled an enthusiastic Lilith down into his lap.

"That all depends, baby-- what do you call a guy with a corporate expense account, a yen for yayo, and a hard-on that could pound a two-inch nail through ten feet of drywall?"

After that, Dax toddled off to get his shit in order pronto, his fellow investigator JT and Herman went off to do whatever the hell they do when Dax isn't around, and Benny spent the night doing coke off Lilith's tits and ass, with the record of whether or not she opened up the back door remaining sealed until such time as propriety dictated its revelation.

Chapter Four: Monetizing One's Aptitudes

A Shithole

Somewhere outside the thrumming darkness of his universe, a dead man sang a dirge for everything. The Lizard King decried the end of all that was and all that would be, and flame devoured nature at man's behest.

Saigon.

Shit.

Wait, that was someone else's thing. And while Al found himself drifting up out of a soul-searing haze of ambiguity where dream and memory lost their borders in a blurry miasma of doubt and recrimination, the ceiling fan that served as his anchor to the waking universe was the one that hung from the roof of his Bitburg shithole, not some South Vietnamese flophouse.

Something tiny and dry and smooth flicked at Al's earlobe, subtly reminding him that he was alive and that his body resented its condition. Straining with the effort, he rolled his head to the side and stared straight into a pair of vertically slit glowing yellow-green eyes. A comparatively long, forked purple tongue flicked in and out of the narrow mouth underneath, slip-slapping at his brow.

"Good morning, mailbox snake," Al said. "I don't suppose you're here to kill me unless you've an uncommon flair for snake theatrics."

The snake, being a snake, didn't answer. It just coiled in on itself, burrowing into the caseless pillow, apparently satisfied that Al had indeed woken up.

Sitting up was decidedly more of a struggle, and swinging his legs over the edge of his bed proved almost more than he could handle. For some reason, Al wasn't even slightly hungover, but his entire body hurt and the room swam around his head anyway. It occurred to him as he groped his way to the bathroom that he didn't usually sleep bare-assed, but his dick was swinging free and he couldn't quite remember how he'd gotten home, either. About halfway through a truly epic piss, it hit him that the last thing he could recall was the old Filipina outside the wrecked hotel and that thing with the pimp-ghost.

The rest of that thing with the pimp-ghost came back all at once, bringing a whole shit-ton of minor aches and pains along for the ride. Al rarely remembered his dreams, but it was even less common for him to remember what he'd done the night before. Moving way faster than he should have, he drunk-skidded to the spot by the door where he usually found his jacket.

"Well fuck me sideways and call me fancy," Al said because Al had a fondness for vaguely redneck-sounding exclamations of disbelief.

His jacket was there, wrapped around three bricks of seventies-era hundred-dollar bills wrapped in waterproof plastic. He turned out the pockets, and a goddamned hoard of rings, brooches, watches, and loose gemstones scattered itself amongst the garbage inexorably becoming one with the carpet as mold, lichen, and whatever else could grow in the conditions afforded by Al's shithole continued to build its nascent ecosystem.

The loot was real. If the loot was real, that meant all the other shit had to be, too.

In the same instant, he came to grips with this universe-rewriting epiphany, Al thought he saw someone sitting in his chair, and wondered briefly who it might be.

But rubbing his eyes revealed that, like every other time he felt unseen eyes on his bare balls, it was just Boyo. The cat gave him the scantest of acknowledgments. The TV was on, turned down low, still tuned to one of the Hitler channels. This time, it was a bunch of hillbillies on the trail of ghosts. Or maybe the ghost of Bigfoot, who they claimed was really an alien Templar Knight working for the G8 and the Illuminati to stop the next Reptoid Ascension.

"Well cat," Al said, scratching the fat bastard behind his ears. "Turns out ghosts are real. And I can punch them.

"Brekkies?"

Cats may act like they don't, but they understand every damn word that's said to them. As soon as Al invoked food, Boyo transformed himself into an orange blur and might as well have teleported to the fridge. Al dug through about a hundred beers and assorted diet sodas, found some sniff-approved raw chicken strips, tossed these into a pan with a stick of butter, and turned the heat on underneath.

"You know, one of these days, I'm just gonna eat you, you hobo," Al said. Boyo did not approve, throwing up his tail and spraying a spiteful amount of urine on Al's bare legs.

Right. Pants. Maybe a quick shower first though, what with the cat pee.

The snake, a black ribbon of indifference, glided past man and cat and fixed on a crack underneath one of the kitchen cabinets. It disappeared inside, and in less time than it takes to relate, ended the life of some unlucky spot of vermin with a whipcrack and a squeak.

"Brekkies for everybody," Al said.

He reached back into the fridge, cracked himself an Olde English tallboy; *if you were gonna live ghetto, be ghetto.* He leaned back against the crook between the stove and the fridge, pondering. Well, more blanking out and vaguely ruminating about all the dead hookers he'd seen. Al had seen enough horror flicks and read enough comics to get that he'd probably freed them from some kind of post-mortal hell-on-earth the ghost of Silky Cobra had trapped them in, and he guessed that was probably a good thing. Even if some of them had marched straight through the same door the pimp had, a few had gone through the other one. It dawned on him that he may well have just seen proof of Heaven and Hell, which was kind of a heady revelation. It even made up for the loss of his final settlement check, which pretty much would have condemned him to a life not dissimilar to the one lived by the bum who ran off with it, if not for all the loot.

That could have been a problem, but fuck it now-- loot was loot.

He sprinkled a little pepper and some garlic salt over his chicken, flipped the pieces.

"Better keep that shit to yourself," Al said, ostensibly to Boyo, who sat sentry before the stove, not giving a single fuck what Al did with his new knowledge of the afterlife. All Boyo cared about was breakfast.

Just to be extra careful, Al took one of the strips out of the crackling grease and split it with a knife: not a trace of pink. If there was a death he feared more than the snake-in-the-mailbox, it was murder by undercooked poultry. Of all the ways he could kill himself, that one seemed the dumbest, so he always made sure to practice kitchen safety. That meant a lot of dry, rubbery chicken in his guts, but after a couple of tallboys, he didn't mind so much. He tossed a stale tortilla onto a skillet, letting it get crisp, covered it in pre-shredded cheese. By the time the cheese had turned into a melted slab of orange goo, he'd rewarded the cat for its temerity with a meaty strip. A little purloined Taco Bell Fire sauce finished off his own breakfast feast, so Al wrapped everything up in a paper towel, planted himself in front of the Hillbilly Bigfoot-ghost show, and ate.

Two bites in, the show transitioned into something called *Ghost Quest*, and Al nearly choked on his fat-and-protein wrap. There was Faux-hawk in all his high-def Technicolor glory, overly-dramatic exposition spilling from his face like simple syrup from a gravy boat. Boyo sidled up to Al, rubbing his head against his bare leg in what most people mistake for a sign of affection, but which in truth marked Al with the cat's scent in a less obnoxious way than spraying him with urine would; the man had fed him, which was enough to make him tell the other strays to back the fuck off, as this human was taken.

"Well Boyo," Al said, munching his not-quite-a-burrito. If Faux-hawk knew about ghosts, maybe he also knew about ghostpunching, which was something that currently topped his list of things to be interested in.

"Guess I know what I'm doing today."

Chapter Five: Tertiary Like Sunday Morning

Cyclops, Sunday Morning

Lilith scribbled something in her notepad, her new silver pen ping-ponging the light served up by the bulb overhead. She couldn't remember where she'd picked it up, but it wrote really well and her hand-writing was actually legible when she used it, which was odd. Its weight balanced perfectly, and even though she couldn't read the inscription on the barrel, she liked the way it looked in her hand. Even better, ever since she'd had it, her tips had almost doubled, and she always seemed to be on time.

The last bit had been especially helpful today, what with the owner showing up at the Cyclops after the night she'd had. It would have been dumb not to expect him to drop by after the other night's row, but the inevitability of the owner's presence did nothing to soften its actuality. The second he'd walked through the door, Charlene went pale and distant, following him down into the cellar like a grade-school troublemaker on her way to the principal's office. That's why Lilith found herself behind the bar instead of out on the floor, letting the dishwater cool off before she tackled the few glasses that needed washing, scratching away at her notepad with her new lucky pen.

It wasn't that they were scared of the owner or anything like that; it's just that he was creepy as fuck. He had this air of intimidating calm about him like you would do anything within your power to keep from disappointing him. Not upsetting or angering him, mind you, as, for as long as she'd known him, Lilith had never seen him angry or even heard him raise his voice. And she was positive she didn't want to.

Like most Sunday afternoons, this one saw the Cyclops mostly empty. The only customers were Marshall, the skinny guy with the blonde afro, and his buddy Wade, the one in the oversized hoodie and rocking a dreadlocked beard that reached to his belt. Lilith had heard they were some kind of underworld guys, but they were always polite to her and kept to themselves, and she just couldn't see it. Plus, they came in every Sunday with a box of boutique donuts and shared them around, along with a pair of colossal milkshakes, into which they emptied a bottle of Jack Daniels over the course of a couple of hours.

"Lilianne," the owner said, emerging from the kitchen with all the commotion of a wraith rising from the grave. Even looking straight at him, Lilith could never really quite tell what he looked like; he just had one of those faces so unremarkable as to defy description. He also refused to call her by anything but the rather pedestrian name she'd been born with, and she wasn't about to correct him. "I'd like a beer."

"Hey, guy who owns the Cyclops," Marshall said, his voice a stony monotone. He opened the box of donuts and held it out for the Cyclops's owner. Beside him, Wade spooned bourbon, milk, and ice-cream into the inky recesses of his hood. "Have a boutique donut."

"Marshall," the owner said, taking a seat a stool away. He peered into the box, and, after some indecision, pulled out a long, thick éclair wrapped in bacon and drenched in maple cream. Lilith set a pint of Rogue in front of him. "No, give that to Wade. For a treat so rare and wonderful as this, I'd like something from the special fridge. Something... Quebecois. Get me a magnum of Maudite, and three small glasses. Marshall, Wade, and I will share, as they have shared with me."

See?

Creepy, weird, off-putting, but not quite scary.

Lilith did as she'd been told. Once she split the bottle three ways and set the glasses down, the owner gave her a look she couldn't quite interpret. Then he smiled. She'd never seen him eat, or drink, or smile. "And for you, Lilianne. I don't think it will impair you too much."

Lilith smiled back, poured the rest of the magnum into a fourth glass. She kinda liked this version of the owner, who raised his beer and the monster donut. From the latter, he took a man-sized bite, the rich sweet cream filling jizzing onto his face. He passed the pastry to Marshall, who followed suit and held it out for Wade to sample. The maple-bacon miscreation of a breakfast confection disappeared into his hood. Wade left behind the smallest of morsels, which he held out for Lilith.

"I'm gluten intolerant," she said, hands held up in deference. She wasn't, though; she just wasn't sure where Wade had been. "And, you know, vegetarian."

In response, Wade stripped the last bit of bacon, tossed it into his hood. She didn't know how, but Wade had mastered the art of the shadowy hood, and seeing his pure white smile light up beneath his dim blue eyes had the effect of making Lilith more uncomfortable than she enjoyed.

"Please, Lilianne," the owner said. "When someone offers you a donut, you eat the donut."

Lilith sheepishly acquiesced, taking the last piece of fried dough into her mouth. Instantly, her eyes got as big as headlights on a Mack truck, a sugary electricity lancing from lips to toes and back to scalp. If you asked her right then, she might have traded every boy and girl (except Neil de Grasse Tyson and Dame Judy Dench, because they were untouchable) on earth for that donut.

"See, it's good," the owner said.

"Yeah," Lilith said, breathless, showering in the sizzling afterglow.

"Now, as we have eaten, so shall we drink," the owner said. "To the Sun, for all its bold impetuosity."

"To the moon," Marshall said. He held up his glass, mirroring the owner. "For its brazen mockery of the day."

Wade followed. "To the sky at dusk and dawn, when the sun and moon flee from one another."

Six eyes turned to Lilith, who had no idea what to say but didn't want to mess things up. Suddenly flustered, she scanned the bar for a way out, her eyes landing on her notepad. She didn't remember writing them, but her scribbles had gathered themselves into letters and words, so she read them out loud.

"To each of us, alone in day and dark, and the things that pass unseen between us," she said.

The owner nodded his approval, and the three men drained their glasses. Lilith was quick to follow, the thick, powerful

Quebecois wheat beer easing down her throat to drown her insides.

With a satisfied belch, the owner stood. He noticed Lilith's shiny silver pen, picked it up for an appreciative examination. "That's a nice pen." He focused his gaze on Lilith's green eyes, fixing her in place. "Keep hold of that and don't lose it, Lilianne. Something like that, it could write all sorts of wonders."

Lilith nodded slowly, tucked the pen into her apron. Either the Maudite or the strangeness of their shared bread and beer had apparently hit her hard because her head was swimming a bit and she felt flushed.

The owner turned to Marshall and Wade. "Now boys," he said, "that thing the other night.

"You had nothing to do with it, I'm sure."

"If we were involved," Marshall said.

"You'd know," Wade said.

"I would, indeed," the owner said. He bowed to each of them in turn, just the slightest show of respect. He then smoothed a twenty on the bar for Lilith and left the Cyclops without another word.

After a moment, Lilith looked to the boys, a bit overwhelmed. They finished their milkshakes and stood. Each of them left another twenty, Marshall's as crisply smooth as the day it was minted, Wade's looking like it had been smuggled into prison the hard way.

Marshall gave a little two-fingered salute, snapped on a pair of shades. "Seeya, sweets."

Wade slipped his hands into the pockets on the front of his hoodie. "Be good, little girl."

Stopping short, Marshall grabbed a napkin and laid it on the bar. He regarded the box in his hands and, after some deliberation, withdrew a fat, unadorned cruller, set it with care on the napkin.

"For Charlene."

They took the rest of their boutique donuts with them, the chime of the bell hanging above the door ringing at their passing.

No sooner had they gone did Charlene emerge from the kitchen, looking tired and unkempt. Lilith perked up, the last few minutes of weird slipping through her mind like neglected children through the welfare system.

"You look less than happy, Cherry Lane," Lilith said, bright-eyed and bushy-tailed because that's what she figured Charlene needed. "Want a donut?"

Charlene did indeed want a donut. Charlene always wanted a donut, but Jake the DJ wouldn't approve. He wanted her fit and lithe as she'd been at twenty-three, a goal at cross purposes with the eating of donuts. But that was a fine-looking cruller sitting on the bar, and Jake the DJ wasn't around.

"Oh my fucking Christmas," Charlene said, shuddering as she bit into the rare treat. Fireworks and sex, wrapped in a crispy doughy chrysalis.

"That good, huh?" Lilith said. She never felt as good as she did when she saw Charlene happy and hadn't seen her happy like this since that time she and Al had flown to Austin because her sister had an extra couple of tickets to see Billy Idol at Stubb's. *That was what, five years ago?*

"Yeah," Charlene said. "Where'd you get this, and why do we not have more?" She scarfed the rest of the donut and got a little sad that it was gone, but not nearly as sad as she was glad to have eaten it.

"Marshall left it, specifically for you."

"The guy with the blonde afro?"

Lilith nodded, and Charlene wrinkled her nose a tad, but anyone who delivered a cruller like that couldn't be all bad. "Hey, did the owner say anything to you before he left?"

"Not really," Lilith said. She was sure he'd said something, but couldn't quite put her finger on what it was. She'd remember if it was important, but for now, she just let it go like she let go of the image of his face every time he left the room. "He mad about the brawl?"

"Nope," Charlene said. She took a seat on a stool, ignoring the suds-stained glasses. She sipped absently from a mostly empty milkshake, tasted bourbon, then gulped it down to completely empty. This uncharacteristic scavenging she punctuated with an equally uncharacteristic burp, and Lilith couldn't help but laugh. Charlene just rolled her eyes and stuck out her tongue. "Hey, better out than in."

"You realize you just drank Wade's leftovers, right? What's up, la Chara?"

"Nothing, it's just," Charlene wavered, trying to piece together what she and the owner had been talking about. She couldn't make the puzzle look like the puppy on the box, but the ears and tail stood out. "It's just that he didn't seem to care about the cops or damage or anything. Just... he wanted to know about that Dax Vagance guy."

"That guy's too good-looking to be such a tool," Lilith said, clearing the bar. She wondered briefly why there were three twenties stuffed into her apron, then realized that she'd make her rent a week early if she could keep them there. The pleasant realization of fiscal solvency, however momentary, gave rise to a perky little pursing of her lips, which in turn gave way to an over-ripening of said fruits and an instantaneous blossoming of her eyes into grapefruit-sized approximations of exclamation points. "OH-EM-muthafukkin-GEE!"

"What?" Charlene said.

"Seriously, what kind of a tool do you have to be to get Eldon Garvey of all people so riled up?"

"Who the hell is Eldon Garvey?"

"Skinny black guy, glasses, Harry Potter fetish?"

"You mean, Alton, the little dude who's always puppy-dogging around Al?"

Lilith suddenly and explicitly remembered exactly what it was about Charlene that had driven her nuts ever since they were in school. Once again, she took a deep breath and tried to remind herself that Charlene wasn't an idiotic, stick-up, self-centered twat, but the only friend she hadn't ever tried to sleep with and was always in the midst of some Serious Personal Drama. As such, she was a person who deserved at least a marginal level of forgiveness. "No, I mean Eldon, the guy who you've known for years and apparently never bothered to learn his name."

"Oh," Charlene said, right before forgetting to remind herself that Alton wasn't Alton's name. "What was that all about, anyway?"

"Damned if I know. One second, he and his bros were interviewing the Ghost Geeks for that Ghost Fest show or whatever, the next it was like Springer up in here. *Eldon* completely freaked out. Thought he was gonna punch Dax Vagance right in his shapely man-rack."

"You know they hate it when you call them that."

"That's what Al calls them."

"You do everything Al does?" Charlene said, snapping because she didn't want to hear any goddamned more about Al.

Lilith had to think about that one. Upon reflection, she decided that *yes*, she did do everything Al did, with the possible exception of mooning over Charlene. It was probably best if she kept that bit to herself, though, so she just said, "Does Al sit or stand when he pees?"

"I assume he stands," Charlene said, annoyed that Lilith would just assume she'd know any better than anyone else. She'd had to deal with this kind of passive-aggressive crap for years, everyone always prompting and hinting and talking behind her back about how she should stop playing around and be with Al. Dammit, there were reasons she didn't want to be with him, not the least of which being that, no matter what anyone thought, *he had never asked*. "Unless he's passed out drunk, which I guess leaves him upright like thirty percent of the time."

"Then, I guess I don't do everything Al does," Lilith said. She hadn't intended to upset Charlene, but seeing the red rash of exasperation creep across her face like frost on a winter window was turning out to be kinda fun. One more quip and she might get to see the famous *Charlene's Pissed Face*, and Sunday afternoons were always dull. "I heard Jake the DJ was back in town; can't wait till he shows up at my door rolling faces at six AM in the morning."

The rash became a full-blown crimson contagion, that winter window shattering at the points of icy daggers hurled from Charlene's eyes. "Go on a break, Lilith."

"No, I'm good," Lilith said. To emphasize how good she was, she spread her palms on the bar, arched her back, and had herself a good long stretch. "And don't you have inventory? I mean, I could do it, but you'd have to recheck everything anyway, so why not just skip a step?"

Charlene wasn't a violent person. She generally avoided confrontation whenever possible, and most of the time, she considered Lilith a friend. But right now, she wanted to punch her in the face with about the same level of desire a man just finishing up a dime in a state prison wants to find a whorehouse. Instead, she shook her head, held up her hands in defeat, and walked away, disappearing into the kitchen.

So what if they'd totally just failed the Bechdel test? Lilith had scored a rare win, she'd wrested control of the admittedly empty bar, and she'd learned that Charlene probably hadn't known and didn't like the fact that Jake the DJ liked to drop by her place for a morning booty call after a gig. All in all, these were good things, even if she did feel pretty crappy about it once the initial rush wore off. Because sometimes girls are like that.

"Oh well," Lilith said, flipping through her notepad. She'd been scribbling in it all afternoon, but all the words were just chicken-scratch now. Still, she couldn't help herself from digging the shiny silver pen out of her apron, setting it to the paper, and letting its smooth black ink trace aimless rivers across the page.

Chapter Six: A Grower, a Shower, and a Tower

-Verse 1-

Inside the brownstone at 1223 Grayson Avenue, Bitburg, Sunday Afternoon

Eldon tore his eyes away from the ancient tome, the spell of its spidery Latin tracings and unspoken arcana broken by a sound altogether foreign to this sacred place. He cast a ferocious gaze about the shadowy breadth of his sanctuary, daring all intruders to meet his fiery eyes, be they worldly foe or tormentor from beyond.

The sound, an insistent rapping, the beating of an alien heart, grew louder, pounding away at the wall he'd erected between himself and the world. He stormed to his feet, ready to command the source of his disturbance to reveal itself. A stack of books as tall as a man atop his desk blocked his vision, but all at once, the progenitor of that infidel percussion revealed itself.

"Dammit, Eldon," came the muffled voice from somewhere outside his sanctum. "Open the fuck up, man."

Someone was knocking on his door. Eldon rubbed the bridge of his nose, pushing his thick glasses up on his forehead.

He glanced behind him, past the floor-to-ceiling shelves that groaned under the weight of everything from a fourth edition of the *Malleus Maleficarum* to the only complete CGC graded 9.8 run of the Claremont/Byrne *Uncanny X-Men* in existence, to the clock on the blu-ray player. The clock assured him that it was three in the afternoon, which meant that he was late, but not late enough that any of the Ghost Geeks would have noticed, let alone made the trek downtown to get him. Besides, he was driving today anyway. *So who the hell was knocking on his door?*

Knowing only one way to find out, Eldon extricated himself from his burrow, books piled taller than him on either side of his ridiculously expensive yet equally comfortable Ekornes desk chair. Careful not to disturb the entropic bundles of notes that dotted the floor like a minefield, he moved with all due alacrity to the door. He looked through the peephole, couldn't make the fish-eyed face peeping back jibe with his expectations of reality, and went to work on unlocking every other one of the seven deadbolts.

"Christ, man," said his visitor. "I'm fucking aging out here."

Eldon turned the last lock, grabbed the steel-tipped lance standing guard beside the door. With a tug, he opened the door, saw the face of the one who had disturbed his research, and let out a sigh.

"Heya Albrecht," he said. "What brings you to the Lair?"

"My feet," Al said, shoving himself inside and a sixer of Olde English into Eldon's arms. "What's with all the locks?"

This was the first time Al had seen Eldon's place since he'd helped him move in. The kid had been so excited to be out on his own and it hadn't taken a whole lot of effort on Al's part, what with Eldon's possessions at the time consisting mostly of a milk crate full of porn and a lamp, but that didn't keep Eldon from treating him like some kind of god forever afterward. Al was the only one who showed up, and he'd brought beer, so the two had christened the place and that had been enough to earn him the title of *True Friend of Eldon*, which looked even more lame on the T-Shirt than it sounds on the page. Since then, the kid had been busy filling the place with all kinds of esoteric bric-a-brac and...

"Oh my stars and garters."

Al's eyes lit up when he saw the trove on the far side of the living room. Past all the antique books, the stacks of papers, the suit of armor and crossed claymores-- swords not mines-- on the walls, a pair of immense la-z-boys flanked a seventy-or-so inch curved 3D HDTV. Under that was a meticulous array of eight or nine game consoles, one of which was an honest-to-god Sega Dreamcast.

Giddy, thoughts of ghosts and punching them precipitously expelled from his list of interesting things, Al gave Eldon a hopeful, almost desperate plea with his eyes.

Eldon beamed.

"Go ahead," he said, feigning annoyance. He took the sixer into the kitchen, pleased as punch at Al's reaction to his gaming set-up. He'd put a metric shit-ton of work into it; about time someone saw it.

Al couldn't help it, he squeed, plopping himself into the left-handed chair, its seat smooth and unblemished in comparison to the ass-shaped contours of its partner. He snatched up the bulky white controller and hit the power button. To his disbelieving delight, the start-up screen for the most perfect fighting game hummed to life.

"Soul Calibur... TWO!" the screen said.

"I know you did not just enter my dojo," Eldon said, sliding his ass into its customary spot before passing Al one of the tallboys.

"Your dojo?" Al said, donning a wicked mask of deadly intent. He popped the top, Eldon followed suit, and it was, officially and mercilessly, *on*. "Son, I was Mitsurugi-ing motherfuckers when you were still getting boners from the Pink Power Ranger. Now, FIGHT!"

Mitsurugi faced off against Voldo in a brutal reckoning years in the making. After Eldon had thoroughly trounced Al in two straight perfect victories, he dropped his controller like a battle-rapper who just schooled a buster.

"Who's house?" Eldon said.

"Eldon's house," Al said, grudgingly.

Eldon sipped his malt liquor, not quite enjoying it but not wanting to offend. He had a bottle of eighteen-year-old scotch in the kitchen, but Al had brought the OE, so he was going to drink the OE.

Something occurred to Al. Two things, actually.

"I thought Ess-Cee Two only came out on X-Box," he said because one of the things that had occurred to him was the fact that *Soul Calibur II* had only come out on the X-Box.

Eldon smirked like he knew something Al didn't. Because he knew something Al didn't, which was awesome.

"It did," Eldon said, growing more enamored of his malt liquor with every sip because that's how malt liquor works.

"Then how do you have it for Dreamcast?"

"Magic."

After what happened the other night, Al rolled with it.

The other thing was the conspicuous splendor of Eldon's home, which, once you got past the mess, played Parker Bros.' classic dice-based game of word-finding with Al's mind.

"What do you even do for a job, man? You got like, Doctor Strange's Sanctum fucking Sanctorum in here."

"That reminds me," Eldon said, standing up. He traded his can for a tablet connected to the arm of his chair, tapped and swiped a few times. "Gotta check on the girls."

"You got girls in here, too?" Al said, inwardly berating himself for not having been back to Eldon's since that first night.

Eldon made a final swipe on the touchscreen and set the tablet down. "Not girls; *the* girls."

With a smooth, lubricated action, one of Eldon's bookshelves sank back into the wall and slid behind the others, revealing a metal door that could have withstood a naval bombardment. Eldon waved him on, so Al followed him through the door and down a spiral stair into the biggest goddamned grow room he'd ever seen.

The stairs were like something out of *Dungeons & Dragons*, all hewn stone and ancient symbols carved right into the rock. The glyphs glowed with a faint blue light, and traces of bioluminescent moss almost buzzed with living energy. But the trappings of the Underdark had exactly shit on what awaited them in the chamber at the bottom of the flight.

At least fifty plants, none of them shorter than him and every one thriving in a verdant hydroponic womb, greeted the pair as Eldon flicked on the lights. Those were just the ones Al could see; the room was cavernous, the vastness of the place still mostly lost in darkness.

"Girls," Eldon said. "This is Albrecht Drue, a True Friend of Eldon and inveterate barroom brawler. Al, these are my girls."

"Holy shit, Eldon," Al said. "You grow pot?"

"I grow cannabis indica, which I supply to only the finest pot stores in Colorado and Washington, the United States government, and some guy named Wade."

"Well shit, that explains the locks," Al said.

Eldon moved like a bumblebee from plant to plant, pruning, cultivating, whispering to each one words Al couldn't quite make out. He couldn't shake the feeling that there were other things moving around just outside the buttery pools of the grow lamps, but a dude who can punch a ghost straight to hell or wherever didn't have to worry about the oogetty-boogetties lurking just outside his vision.

Eldon talked over his shoulder, completely focused on his charges. "Well, those are mostly to keep the stuff upstairs safe. You know, I once came home and found a guy trying to pick them? Seriously, he'd go through the whole line, work his magic on each one, and then get all pissed when he realized he'd locked half of them instead of unlocking them. Finally, he got so frustrated he just gave up and left."

"Neato."

"So, not that I don't like having one of my best friends show up unannounced on a Sunday afternoon, but why are you here, anyway?" Eldon said, finally satisfied with the state of the girls.

He boxed up a few of the freshly-trimmed buds in Tupperware and set them aside on a sleek metal table covered in scales and other paraphernalia.

"Oh, that's right," Al said, suddenly remembering why he'd dragged himself out of the house today. "You know that dude with the faux-hawk from the other night?"

"Dax Vagance?" Eldon said.

"Yeah, the ghost-quester prick," Al said. "Lilith said you were hanging out with him, and I kinda need to meet his ass."

Eldon cracked up a little. "Didn't you punch him in the face the other night?"

"Who can tell? I punch a lot of people in the face." That was true; Al did punch a lot of people in the face.

"Well, I doubt he'd want to see you, considering the last thing he said on the subject was, 'If I ever see that long-haired dipfuck again, I'm going to shove my lawyer so far up his ass he'll be crapping out *Law & Order* scripts.'"

"He said that?" Al said, actually fairly impressed by what he hoped was a metaphor.

"Those were his exact words," Eldon said, his fingers making their usual search through his pockets, finally closing around the keys that never seemed to stay in the pocket he'd put them in. "Why do you want to meet him so bad, anyway?"

Al thought about revealing his recent ghost-punching escapade but wasn't quite ready to make himself look like a crazy drunk. He could handle looking like a drunk, but the crazy part might be a little too much for right now.

"Just figured he might know something about ghosts and all," Al said, following Eldon into the dark. Every few yards, they passed under a sensor that turned on a light a few paces ahead and extinguished the one behind.

"You do realize that *I* know more about ghosts than that hack ever will," Eldon said, a bit miffed. They came to another door and another stone spiral.

"Christ, I thought he was y'all's idol and shit," Al said.

The stair opened into Bitburg's subterranean tunnel system, Eldon following a few memorized twists and turns to another anachronistic high-tech door, which he opened by scanning his eye over a bio-sensor. *When the hell had Eldon become a damn super-hero? He had a goddamn castle/library secret base with his own weed-cave and--*

Ho. Lee. SHIT.

A Ghost-Geeks-Mobile.

Eldon blushed, proud but just a little embarrassed by his conspicuous show of wealth. He held the door open and motioned Al into the hangar-like garage beyond, "I sell A LOT of marijuana."

This was just too goddamned much. The room full of priceless books, Al could believe. If he'd been told Eldon would have a functional Dreamcast already queued to SCII, he might have wanted proof, but he wouldn't have been surprised. The grow-room had been pushing it, but this?

At the head of a small fleet that Al didn't even bother to acknowledge was a pristine midnight-black, fully chromed sixty-eight Ford Fairlane fastback with blood-red doe-leather seats and an airbrushed ivory phantom on the hood. The license plate read, 'BSSBTCHS,' and a pair of fuzzy twelve-sided dice hung from the rearview.

Had Eldon been secretly awesome this whole time?

"He kinda was," Eldon said, thoroughly content to let Al drool near his baby, but wary enough of him getting any slobber on her that he stalked him with a cashmere chamois just in case. "Until I realized he's a charlatan and doesn't know anything about real ghosts. You know that lunatic and his idiot sidekicks are actually going up to Cardinal's Crest without even a vial of holy water or a blessed hammer to keep the spirits at bay?"

"Is that bad?" Al said, stroking the hood of the Fairlane; Eldon intercepted him, buffing the fingerprints away with the chamois before they had a chance to mar the finish.

"It's like walking into Fallujah without a helmet," Eldon said, snorting his derision.

Al took the hint and stepped back from the car, still marveling at its two tons of bestial American sexuality.

"What's the big deal about the Crest?" Al said, pretty sure he'd woken up there once but maybe getting it confused with someplace else.

Exasperation wrapped a garrote around Eldon's throat, reddening his face as he tried to explain this for the second time in two days. "Or like-- look. I get that a layman like you wouldn't understand. What we do-- the BSS and every other weekend paranormal investigation club-- is investigate bumps in the night. We go record EVPs and cold spots and look for shadow figures, and we maybe come up with some cool bit of 'evidence' we can post online for all the other guys just like us. If we're lucky, we get to witness some once-in-a-lifetime bit of poltergeist stuff. Then we go have a few beers and talk about what we're gonna do next. Dax Vagance does the same thing, only he does it on TV.

"The thing is, the Crest isn't just some haunted house. That place is evil, man, like Old Testament Lovecraft capital-E-Vil. People have been whispering about it around here since before there even was a Bitburg. You know, when the British came through here during the revolution, they could have held the entire valley with a couple of guns, if they could have taken the Crest. Only they couldn't, and the redcoats they sent up there were slaughtered to a man. They said it was Indians, but the Indians knew better than to go anywhere near it. Because Indians aren't fucking stupid."

Al raised an eyebrow at Eldon, who suddenly turned sheepish. Still, it was obvious there'd be no stopping the kid until he'd finished his history lesson. "Sorry about the language, but it's warranted. You know, the Catholics sent a team of exorcists up there back in the seventies, and *they* came back. They came back alright, one of them, anyway, insane with his tongue cut out."

"So," Al said, fiddling with a set of mechanic's tools. "Someone like me shouldn't go to the Crest? I mean, without a vial of holy water and a blessed hammer."

Eldon took the wrench out of Al's hands and set it back in its place atop the red Snap-On chest. "No, you shouldn't go to Cardinal's Crest. Not even with holy water and a hammer. Maybe you could go, if you had a gun that fired the ghosts of General George S. Patton and Mikhail Kalashnikov, each of them armed with miniguns that shoot silver bullets and hellfire."

"They make those?"

"No, that's my point. People just don't fucking go there."

"Noted," Al said.

Eldon checked his watch. "Crap. Al, I really appreciate you dropping by, but I've gotta get going. You want a ride home?"

"I'd take a ride to the gallows in that steel goddess," Al said, not even slightly exaggerating.

"Cool! Your place is on the way to the investigation anyway; just have to stop off and pick up Eleanor and Grigsby before I drop you off." Eldon entered his ride with reverence, and Al did the same. The leather buckets were like dipping his ass in warm scarlet chocolate.

"You guys doing an investigation tonight?" Al said.

Eldon inserted the key into the ignition, the Fairlane roaring to life like the Kraken getting ready for release. "Oh yeah. There's a lady up on Founders' Row who says she's been plagued by all the usual stuff, so we're gonna check it out."

He keyed a custom panel between the seats, and the garage door rumbled up behind them.

The BSS wasn't *Ghost Quest*, but Eldon wasn't a gelled-up douchebro, and if he knew what he was talking about, those might be good things. Maybe he'd been selling the Ghost Geeks short all along.

"Screw it," Al said. "I'll tag along. Cool?"

It was Eldon who squeed this time, but quietly. "Awesome. And Dave probably won't be too much of a jerk about it, either."

"What are you on about?" Al said, his most reassuring smile plastered on his face. "Dave loves me."

-2-

"What in the name of fuck is he doing here?" Dave said, pulling Eldon away from the rest of the Ghost Geeks. Before they'd even arrived on-site, Al had gotten Grigsby and Eleanor fairly well-lit on a bottle of Schnapps they'd scored along the way, and they were already endangering the mission with their decidedly unprofessional antics.

"Relax," Eldon said. "Al's just taken a sudden interest in the paranormal is all, and he wanted to see what we do. He promised he'd be on his best behavior, and I doubt he's gonna start a fight with Mrs. Barringer."

Dave bit his lip, thoroughly unconvinced that Al wasn't above punching a septuagenarian if she looked at him funny. "Fine, but he's your baggage. Keep him at base camp and keep him quiet."

"Sure thing, Sarge," Eldon said. Dave liked it when people called him Sarge, even though he'd been discharged years ago under thoroughly unpleasant circumstances.

Dave swirled a finger in the air, then whistled for the Ghost Geeks to saddle up. They gathered around Dave's black Humvee, Eleanor and Grigsby prodding each other to calm down and shape up for the pre-game. Al hung back from the group, taking in the sight.

Barringer Manor looked like a goddamned haunted house alright, a sagging Victorian at the center of an overgrown lawn complete with wilted myrtles and a wrought-iron fence way the hell out in the middle of the woods. At least it looked like it was way the hell out on the woods; all the aging mansions of

Founders' Row did. The Row drew a green oasis between Jennings Heights and the more civilized dangers of the Money District, a place where old families and old secrets could stay out of sight of the public and still keep an eye on the people who existed only to serve them.

The sun had slunk below the trees, an appropriate autumn dusk sweeping across the New England wood. Al didn't see any ghosts, though, and didn't feel anything either, which he found a bit perturbing; *shouldn't ghostpunchery have come with some kind of sixth sense or something?*

"Alright," Dave said, addressing his troops.

Grigsby had an old-school TV camera on his shoulder, aiming it like a rocket launcher at Dave. He gave the Sarge a quick thumbs up.

"Lyric, Cletus, thanks for coming early to get the cameras set up, appreciate that. We've got base camp set up downstairs. This is a big place, four stories and a basement, so we'll be platooning between each. I want EVPs taken at regular intervals, and keep the chatter to a minimum. We're not going to have much in the way of outside interference thanks to the protected nature of the location, so anything we get on tape is a possible piece of evidence. Any questions?"

Al couldn't resist. He raised his hand; Dave nodded at him with an air of aggravation. "Oh look, our guest has a question."

"Are we gonna see some action, Sarge, or is this just another bug-hunt?" Al said.

"Stow it, Hudson," Dave said, catching Al off-guard. Of course, Dave had seen *Aliens*; *why the hell else would he have joined the Marines?* "Now Mrs. Barringer reports activity everywhere in the house: creaking steps, shadow-figures, the whole bit. She's been having these experiences for years, but just recently, it's gotten to be too much.

"Anyways, this is gonna be a good one, guys, I can feel it. Squad ready? OOH-RAH."

The group filed through the front gate, following the remains of a stone path to the door, Al taking up the rear, and getting his rear pinched by a gleeful Eleanor on the way. The Oldest Woman in America met them at the door.

"Oh, I'm so glad you're here," she said. Her voice was like the rustle of dry leaves blown across frozen grass, brittle and sharp.

"Welcome to Barringer Manor," she said as they filed past her into the receiving room. She put a hand on Al's shoulder as he went by, so he smiled at her. She didn't return the smile, but wizened her eyes at him and scurried towards Dave.

There was something about the old bird that bugged Al. She looked at him like she knew him, like she knew something about him he didn't want her to.

The inside of Barringer Manor was just as foreboding as the out, its furnishings original to the place and armored in the dust of age. Oil portraits of past residents long interred in the family plots out back glared down from every angle, the whole manse done up in lace and threadbare velvet. Everywhere, in the form of leering crucifixes and austere angels, hung the trappings of militant Christianity. Al had no problem with religion, regardless of what form it took or what hats its practitioners wore; he just couldn't stand the in-your-face ubiquity of the trite, obnoxious iconography that came along with someone who wanted to make sure you knew exactly which God they thought made them better than you. The posturing and preaching was a great way to hide all the things they didn't want you to see.

The basecamp Dave and the others had erected in the dining room stuck out like an unwelcome time-traveler, banks of computer monitors and laptops congregated on a couple of folding tables. Vines of cable ran from the tables to generators outside and from room to room. Dave and Mrs. Barringer huddled together in animated conversation, the latter occasionally taking a worried peek at Al. Whatever the former said, it seemed to allay her fears, but Dave shot Al a baleful glare anyway before gathering the Geeks for some last-minute notes.

Al turned away, keeping his hands in his pockets. Absently, he poked his head around a corner into the room opposite the camp and got his first minor surprise of the evening. There was a kid in there, sitting in silence, watching a behemoth old console TV in the grey-scale darkness. "Kid" might be underselling it; he was probably sixteen or seventeen and as fat as a Jennings Heights blunt. He must have felt Al looking at him because he turned his head back and nodded in his general direction before going back to his show.

Fuckin weirdo; how was he supposed to truly appreciate the comedic genius of Sanford and Son *with the sound turned off?* He must have wanted to not disturb the old lady, but sometimes respectful deference has to take a back seat to art.

"Come on, noob," Cletus said, pulling Al towards the dining room and basecamp. Usually taciturn at best, Cletus had an air about him of absolute unwillingness to put up with Al's shit. "You're with me tonight."

The rest of the Ghost Geeks broke their formation with military precision. Al had to admit that if he'd been the one to invite a bunch of strangers into his home to suss out the root of its haunting, he'd want them looking all practiced in their matching sweatshirts and abundant gear, too. It gave them an air of officiality. Their kit backed them up, with each supernatural soldier brandishing all kinds of EMF meters, digital recorders, video cameras, and whatnots. The Bitburg Supernatural Squad had a well-earned reputation, hundreds of social media followers, and the no-nonsense demeanor rarely seen among the rubes who ended up as filler on shows like *Ghost Quest*. They were pros, and it showed.

"What do we do now?" Al said, settling into the chair next to Cletus, who just kept standing, arms crossed over his chest.

"Watch for ghosts," Cletus said. Though 'loquacious' wouldn't have described him well, Cletus wasn't an idiot. He was like a tree, or a standing stone, monolithic and silent, but aware of everything around him. Al watched his focus shift from screen to screen, simultaneously absorbing the images from the dozen or so cameras scattered around the back-bowed mansion. Cletus had done this a bunch of times before, and it was obvious that he wasn't going to miss a thing.

Al stopped watching the watchman and started watching what the watchman was watching. Except for the command center, everything was dark, seen through the greenish haze of night-vision cameras. Al had to wonder if Eldon realized just how much of his money Dave had spent on their gear; from the looks of things, these guys were better equipped than any of the crews on TV. Of course, none of that shit held a candle to Al's eyes, what with them having, you know, actually seen not just *A* ghost, but many ghosts.

The Geeks had all broken up into pairs and started sweeping the house, floor by floor, room by room. They kinda looked like ghosts from the future themselves, their night-vision goggles like little pairs of neon will-o-wisps cavorting in the gloom.

Grigsby and Eleanor went up in the attic, setting their gear for an EVP session, where they basically asked dumb questions into the dark and hoped to find some garbled response on their recorders when they played them back the next day. They worked in efficient silence, a pair of resurrection men digging up a grave.

"They seem like a good pair," Al said.

"They are," Cletus said. "Now quiet. Can't have you spoiling the evidence."

Eldon wasn't concentrating on what he was supposed to be doing, what with the amount of time his eyes spent stuck to Lyric's ass. She was fiddling with some piece of high-tech magic, prattle-whispering about the poor lingering spirits as she did. Every once in a while she'd ask Eldon something directly, and he'd say something that added a ruddy glow to his spectral face.

"Aww, look at that," Al said. "Eldon's got a Lyric-boner." Cletus shushed him, then stifled himself because Eldon's Lyric-boner was in danger of poking the poor girl every time she stopped moving.

Sarissa, as always, hung at Dave's side, her arms spread slightly, palms turned toward the floor. She didn't bother with the goggles and kept her eyes closed; her nose pointed at the ceiling. At regular intervals, she spoke, and her words almost always began with "I sense..." or "There is a presence..." and Dave swallowed that shit like it was ice cream.

"For the love of fuck," Al said, rolling his eyes and pushing away from the table. This time, Cletus smacked him in the head, and Al got the message. He tented his forearms in front of the monitors, set his chin on his knuckles, and tried very hard to study the images that crawled across them.

It wasn't much more than fifteen minutes later that the team got their first real spook of the night. Coincidentally, it was about five minutes before that when Al gave the fuck up on this perdition of tedium and stood up, just out of Cletus's reach.

"Smokin'," Al said.

Cletus's blank granite face didn't change from its normal menace, but it didn't have to for Al to know that the big man wanted to strangle him right about then. He didn't know much about the guy, other than he had a mug like one of those heads on Easter Island and a body like Solomon Grundy. Al imagined that Cletus had never been and would never be picked on.

"Outside," Cletus said.

Al held up Peace Hands, headed for the doorway. He passed the room where the fat kid was tuned in to *Sanford and Son*, the black and white snicker-snack of decades-old television goodness dancing on the walls like spastics jitterbugging.

Something struck Al, or Al's thought-box anyway, as he stepped outside, Lucky already clenched in the corner of his mouth, Zippo at the ready. He lit up, well aware that Dave wouldn't have left a single room uncovered by his own personal Big Brother setup, but almost as certain he hadn't seen the fat kid on any of the monitors. He smoked the cigarette quickly, and not all the way to the butt, before flicking the burning end into the grass and racing back inside, fire safety be damned.

He stuck his head through the doorway. The kid-- more than a little annoyed-- shifted on his couch, glaring at him. Al smiled like a cartoon character caught stealing cookies and wiggled the fingers on one hand, then shot into the command center, where Cletus made his lack of amusement apparent. Al, undeterred, half shoved him out of the way, studied every camera view with academic intent.

"Al," Cletus said, shifting his head away from Al's invading posterior. "What the-- "

"Quiet," Al said. Cletus's eyes widened, and a bit of red fleshed-out his pallid cheeks.

He was right. The kid wasn't on the monitors, even though his room, his dormant TV, and his couch were. Nobody could see him but Al, and he had a pretty good idea what that meant.

"Sorry, big guy," Al said. He made a full-body gesture of surrender, sliding away from the reddening man-giant before he popped a vessel. "Think I left something outside."

Cletus let him go, shaking away the rouge on his face and returning to his post. "Idiot."

-3-

Al sidled into the fat kid's room, all kinds of quiet friendly rolling off him in waves.

Nope, not here to punch ya, certainly not. I'm a buddy, really.

Nonchalant as a pickpocket in a room full of baggy pants, he plopped down next to the fat kid. He suppressed a cough as a cloud of dust mushroomed around him.

"How ya doin?" he said.

The kid stared at the intruder, more surprised than anything. He grunted.

"Quiet," he said. His voice, a wispy growl, made the curtains flutter for the first time in years. "Watchin' *Sanford and Son*."

"Cool," Al said. He flashed a used-car salesman's Shit-Eating-Grin (SEG), settled in, and pointed his peepers at what he knew, and could see if he thought hard enough, was a blank screen; in the presence of the ghost, time overlapped and puddled around itself, giving Al a glimpse into the interminable world inhabited by the lingering phantom.

The kid grudgingly shifted enough of its bulk that Al had room for himself on the couch. Still irritated, ghost-boy huffed and grumbled in a way that Al swore made the whole house shake.

-4-

Al was right.

Up in the attic, Grigsby jumped about three feet in the air.

True to her nature, or just her age, maybe, Eleanor only sat up a little straighter.

"You heard that," Grigsby said once he'd landed.

"With the ears God gave me," Eleanor said.

They spread the word over the radio, shivering the spines of every Ghost Geek in the house, none of whom had missed Barringer Manor's localized earthquake.

-5-

Sidelike, Al eyed the fat kid, who seemed far more interested in the show than in the intruder. The two of them were sitting together in an overlap where the Dead world mingled with the Living one, and as far as he knew, Al was the only one who knew it.

In the *Now* where the kid sat, he was in the bedroom of every 1980s parent's wet dream-- football trophies on the shelf, a framed picture of Jenny McGoodgirl, all bangs and big hair, front and center atop the monolithic TV, with plenty of All-American knick-knacks decorating the cheery dream. Al's *Now*, by comparison, was pretty much the same, just buried under thirty-odd years' worth of dust. The only real difference was that a memorial portrait of 'Our Beloved Son, Conacher Dietrich Barringer, Always and Forever,' had replaced Jenny's sophomore yearbook photo atop the TV.

The ghost kid didn't resemble the one in the picture much. Al gave him credit: if he'd been a fifteen-year-old Poeper Heights girl sitting behind him in English Comp, the Conacher from the photo wouldn't have had to do much to make her panties burst into flame. Still, the kid's eyes were the same, and that was enough to make Al recognize him.

"Jesus, Connie," Al said. He tried to reconcile the two images-- the star athlete in the picture and the misshapen flesh-sack on the couch-- and failed epically. "What the fuck happened to you?"

Conacher's ghastly profile rotated until its empty, coal-brick eye sockets fixed on Al. In a slow-expanding meld, the sockets grew, the bridge between them splitting at the middle, peeling back until only a single black circle remained. The black disc bulged, flattened, quivered itself into a round-cornered square. Shiny, glassy, glistening grey melted and dripped from the upper edge until a TV screen just like the one in front of them replaced the empty black.

Al couldn't take his eyes off Conacher's television-set head. The screen clicked, hummed, and blasted out its images.

-6-

"Holy crap," Dave said, somewhere in the bowels of Barringer Manor. "Did you— "

His breath left him before he could finish. Sarissa's arms constricted him and damn near carried them both to the ground.

The house shuddered again, suddenly festooned with silver fireflies that wriggled and danced like fireworks in the musty air.

-7-

Al watched an image of Conacher on the screen that had replaced the kid's face: lithe and magnificent, he balanced a twenty-foot pole beside him as he sprinted down a stadium track. The cheering was insane; this was an Olympic track and field trial, after all. Loudest among the fans, audible even over the hundred thousand other voices, were proud Papa Barringer and the Misses, and barely-pregnant Jenny almost Barringer, her engagement ring lording over all the lesser fiancées.

Conacher, oblivious, ran like a robber from a cop, or better yet, a war-dog toward a trembling yeoman. He wasn't engaged in athletics or anything as trivial as sport; his pole was a lance, he was a shining knight, and he was going to drive that lance through a dragon's heart. He would kill the beast, or it would kill him. He was lightning-raining Arclight napalm, hell on wheels, 18-year-old American muscle pointed at something that sure as fuck wasn't going to be able to withstand it.

Conacher drove his lance, found his mark, and lofted himself into the air. He wasn't a pole-vaulter any more.

Now he was a V2 rocket, London in his sights.

The pole bent, sprung, snapped. And the rocket exploded halfway across the Channel.

The scene jump-cuts and there's Conacher, lying in bed in this room.

Everything's the same, only there's not much Conacher below the waist. There's just the TV and Conacher watching it. In the now, the dead kid's head shows a montage where at first a dozen bodies wander in and out on fast-forward, well-wishers mourning the loss while ignoring the kid. Jenny, Mom, and Dad are most prominent. Then those bodies dwindle to a handful. There's no Jenny any more. Then there's no Dad. Then there's only mom, bringing breakfast, lunch, dinner. Mom's still there, bringing mid-morning, mid-afternoon, and midnight snacks. She's bringing beer and whiskey. All the while, Conacher's body is ballooning, but Mom's still there, cleaning his garbage and his body.

Conacher's Mother is his world for so many years. She sings to him, feeds him, tells him over and over that she will keep him safe. She lets no one in, and never once lets him out. She and the TV are all he knows, and somehow, he's happy. The outside world had no place for a broken little boy, but Mother would always be there to make sure he was happy and loved. With all his heart, Conacher believes and loves her.

Then Mom disappears. The shit piles up. The piss soaks in. Aspirations, vomiting, filth. All he can do is scream, howl, call for help that never comes. But he doesn't die crying out; he dies sputtering whatever filth has filled his lungs. The impassive TV watches from its corner, never judging, never crying. Dead eyes behold the ineffable wonders of broadcast television until there is nothing else.

Jump-cut again, and there's no Conacher. The room is clean, tidy, the presence of the corpulent half-man completely erased. Everything is just as it had been when he had been a rising star and not a fallen one. Mom and Dad are accepting the respects of nearly everyone in town, and Conacher's old coach Mulkey presents the Barringers with a beautiful memorial portrait taken from the photo the people from *Sports Illustrated* used in their

Young Hopefuls '84 issue. Mrs. Barringer has kept the shameful secret of what her son became, and she's free to live again.

Only she's not free, and neither is the boy. He's still there, watching the TV, waiting for his mother to come in and tell him everything's alright.

The screen goes blank, the image drawing into a horizontal line, the line collapsing into a glimmering pixel, the pixel disappearing, and nothing replacing the lost light.

"That fucking sucks, man," Al said, after a second. No sense in putting a shine on a piece of shit; the old lady had smothered her son with her care and her negligence both, and it was as fucked up a way to die as Al could imagine. "Your moms was a fuckin' nutbush, and she shoulda done better by you."

For the third time, Conacher Barringer's ghost shook with contempt, and the house where he lived and died shook with him.

-8-

Lyric fell into his arms, and for the briefest instant, Eldon felt what a parent must feel the first time it holds its child. Or, more accurately, the gizmo she was holding exploded in her hands and flung Lyric across the room, Eldon caught her, and he only had a second to savor his Lyric-boner before every electronic device in the house exploded in a chain reaction of vengeful fire.

-9-

The couch vibrated under Al, dust and years rumbling, putrid water on the boil. He tried to get out of the way, but the ghost moved with speed like Conacher had possessed in life, flinging him into the vacuum-tube bunker of wood and glass and distraction that had served as the incubator for the thing he had become.

The ghost rose enraged, its TV-screen head screaming awake, a shapeless, amorphous mantle whipping about beneath its Trinitron dome. Its howls, broadcast in stereophonic sound, shattered windows, exploded electronics. The engorged body flapped wide, unfurled, edges of its shroud-like surface whipping in a frenzied wind of its own creation. Conacher became an electric banshee, the wail it unleashed enough to drown out a hurricane.

Al pulled himself out of the remains of the TV cabinet, wiping blood off his mouth with the back of his hand.

"Alright, tubby," he said, dropping into the same stance he'd used back in his fighting days, pulling his hood halfway over his skull. It's not that he wanted to hurt the dead kid, or that he was pissed about getting chucked into a TV and wrecking up his clothes. He just figured that if he could hit him hard enough, those doors to the afterlife would pop up, and wherever Conacher ended up had to be better than this.

"It's ghostpunchin' time."

-10-

In her bedroom, sipping tea and flipping through the plastic pages of a photo album, Lady Barringer watched everything as it happened, and she understood. On the closed-circuit monitor, she could see Albrecht Drue getting tossed around her baby's room, and it filled her with warmth to know that there was someone who would finally see the torment she had suffered for so long.

She'd tried to show Connie he was still loved. Conacher didn't need to know that Jenny had chosen to kill herself instead of just aborting the cripple's child like a sensible person would have. Even when Mr. Barringer refused to look at the boy, had his fling with the secretary and disappeared, she had, like a good Christian martyr, stayed behind to care for her son and never burdened him with the knowledge of her hardship. She'd tried to keep him happy, keep him fed; after all, what else could the wretched mound of filth do but eat and drink? But he was so ungrateful, always wanting to go outside or be helped to the window or to have a telephone so he could call the doctors. *What do doctors even know, anyhow? And what could a boy so fat and helpless do in the outside world? It was just better for him not to be bothered, to let his mother do all the worrying.* And when she'd suffered him long enough, she would take her little vacations, a couple of days here and there to herself. It was only right that she had some respite from caring for the profane thing her bright boy had become.

Honestly, it was God's mercy on her that the boy had died while she was away. She'd met a man, stayed away a little longer than usual. How was she supposed to know Connie would get sick? Besides, everything changed for the better when he finally gave up and returned to The Lord. Mr. Barringer came back from his strumpet, and all of Bitburg society made a point of welcoming both of them back with open arms. Mayor Steen even said a few nice words at the memorial service. Mrs. Barringer knew that it was God's will to take him away, His blessing for her suffering at the boy's side.

And now, God had sent an angel to bring her to heaven in reward for her good works. An angel in a black leather jacket who smelled of liquor and tobacco smoke and could see the privation she endured. She knew what he was; there was no hiding God's touch on him.

She set down her tea and focused on the photos, her fingertips tracing an image of the son she had loved in the prime of his youth.

-11-

The Ghost Geeks assembled, shouting and blundering about in the dark of the command center, not that anyone could hear anyone else over the wailing. After the third foundation-cracking rumble, a gale seemed to spring from the very ground itself, whistling a hateful hymn through every board and balustrade. Cletus kept his head, retrieved most of the hard drives, led the crew to the front door, and broke it down.

With the house's outer seal broken, Barringer Manor began to scream, the force of its screeching powerful enough to toss Dave, Grigsby, and all the rest out on the lawn like litter before a street sweeper.

"Going back for the old lady," Cletus said, barely audible above the clamor. Through brute strength alone, he managed to keep his feet.

"Coming with you," Eleanor said. The lusty old broad was gone from her, replaced by a calm, forceful pillar of not-brooking-any-bullshit.

Cletus knew better than to argue.

"Me too," Grigsby said. Cletus stared him down, and, having at least made the effort, Grigsby let it go without even a trace of guilt.

Eldon hauled a rattled Lyric out to the lawn, where Dave broke away from Sarissa long enough to help them to the cars. Sarissa was bawling her eyes out over the 'lamentations of the damned' or some other pseudo-Biblical bullshit to the point of hysterics. She made such a fuss, in fact, that a scorched and disgusted Lyric had no choice but to slap a bitch.

"What?" Lyric said when she realized everyone was taking a time-out from the panic to stare at her. "I can fucking slap a bitch what needs to be slapped. Poop."

Apparently, Lyric was the one to call when a bitch needed slapping.

"Waitasec," Eldon said, shielding Lyric from the wind vomited forth by the manor. "Where's Al?"

"Motherfucker!" Dave bellowed, eyes bulging and face red. He may have hated the guy, but he wasn't about to leave him behind.

Sarissa reached for Dave as he shot back to the house, but didn't follow.

-12-

Banshee Conacher ceased its frantic crashing about, lowered its tone, the keen becoming a rumble that shook the room. The dust clouds stirred up by the thrashing spirit mixed with a rain of plaster from the crackling ceiling. The roar forced Al back; he dug in his heels and clenched his fists.

"Loudmouth," Al said. He could feel the heat rising in his hands, like popcorn a minute and a half in the microwave. Conacher may have been a good kid once, but the years of torture and neglect, the weeks it took to choke to death on his own shit-- that kid was gone, and all that remained was the rage that kept him tethered to this horrible place. "Lemme shut it for ya."

The blast-furnace sound stopped for just an instant; Al threw himself forward, ready to swing. A blade of noise so low he couldn't hear it ripped through his skull, dropping him. His blind punch glanced off the banshee.

It was enough to stop the sound, Conacher swirling to the ceiling in confusion. Al's hand glowed bright with the ghostfire.

"Don't worry, kid," Al said. The bassy brica-thwack flash-bulbs under his skin reached a crescendo; the popcorn finished popping. "Your mama's gonna get it, too. I've seen what she did."

That must have bothered him for some reason, because Conacher dove straight at Al, a pale mass of indignation built around a red-flickering television, its siren blaring so loud and vorpal-sharp it shredded the ears of all who heard it.

Al put everything he had into one haymaker and threw it, yelling like the last man facing down a charging horde.

"GhoooooooooOOOOOOOoooOST PUNCH!"

There is a silence so deep, so painfully vast, that it can drive a man insane. Anyone who's spent time in a sensory deprivation tank will talk about how after a few minutes, they begin to hear their own heartbeat as loud as a Mastodon concert, then the blood running through their veins like water blasting out a hose. Some will talk about hearing the Music of the Spheres-- songs sung by spirits in other dimensions-- as it filters into a silence so total it stretches across realities. Even the deaf can't understand a quiet so utter. That is the sound that fell over Barringer Manor as Al's blow connected.

There was no flash of light, no flare from Al's ghostpunching knuckles. The banshee Conacher simply was, then wasn't.

A door appeared right where the carcass of the TV sparked and smoldered. It was the bright one, the clear swimming-pool-in-sunshine one, and that made Al a little happy. Motes of eternity, bright as the glimmer in a lover's eye, coalesced between Al and the doorway.

Conacher-- his body, his young body, the one he'd had when he'd been him, returned to him-- gave Al a smile of thanks, then walked on through to the ever after. The expression on his face was confusion tinged with relief, and Al knew that neither one of them truly understood what had happened to Conacher. All they knew was that it was over and that the boy could finally leave his dingy place of dying.

Then it clicked. The reason for all the paranormality Mrs. Barringer had experienced over the years, the things that had driven her to finally call the Ghost Geeks-- it been Conacher just trying to get his mother's attention. How long had she ignored him while he was alive? How long after he had died had she let his soul atrophy before she finally decided that she had had enough, before she finally figured it was time to bury her secret forever?

The door remained a moment longer like it wanted Al to pass through, too.

"No thanks," Al said. He fought for breath, resting his hands on his knees. He had feared the glow would fade before he had a chance to mete out the other half of the justice he knew had to come, but he shouldn't have. His mitts only got brighter, began to shoot through with a spiderwebbing of black outlines and highlights. "I got an old lady to punch."

The door, if doors could, shrugged, and its beckoning flicker faded away.

Al felt each vein of black as it drew itself on his flesh. This was a different feeling than he'd felt the other night with Silky Cobra, different even than the one that gripped him just moments earlier. The fire driving him was hungry, slavering, gnawing at his insides.

The old lady had let her son die. He didn't have to go out like that; even in the dark ages of the eighties, he could have been more than just a vegetable planted in front of the TV. She'd fed him and coddled him and denied him the basic things he needed to be more than her little secret, then abandoned him. Still, Conacher had loved her until he died, never realizing that his own mother was responsible for his torment.

That shit wasn't right, and picturing Mrs. Barringer, the way she up and disappeared on Connie, kinda just pushed Al the wrong way.

He shouted, "Now where the fuck is that old cunt?"

-13-

Eleanor clung as best she could to Cletus, but there was nothing they could do. They shouldn't have come back; the sound was just too much to bear. They'd barely made it a few feet inside the house before the Banshee's low sonic bellow drove them down. She was sure they would die here, screamed to death, but hey-- at least she knew something was coming afterward; if tonight hadn't shown her full-on proof of the supernatural, nothing would. That's quite a comfort for anyone, let alone a woman her age.

She was almost disappointed when the noise cut out.

Then Cletus was hauling her up, the two of them racing to the back of the house to rescue Mrs. Barringer.

-14-

Dave burst through the remains of the front door just as Cletus was lifting Eleanor to her feet, the abrupt, relentless quietude shocking him. Then the quiet split down the middle.

"GhoooooooooOOOOOOOoooOST PUNCH!"

He must have gone deaf because Dave existed for a few seconds in a world where sound did not.

-15-

"NOW WHERE THE FUCK IS THAT OLD CUNT?"

-16-

"Such language for an angel," Mrs. Barringer said. "I'd have expected something a little more poetic."

Turns out, those were the last words the old lady spoke. Her heartbeat had been growing faster and weaker by the moment as she watched the scuffle between her son and the angel God had sent to deliver her. The shock of watching Al's pretty face twist itself into such a genuinely wrathful visage was a touch more than the old girl could take, because the gristly pump beneath her withered breast choked a bit, then kinda sputtered, then puked a last glob of blackened blood before finally giving out altogether.

She was okay with dying, really. Truthfully, she looked forward to Heaven and the rewards that awaited her. She'd known her time was coming when she stopped just noticing Conacher's presence and began to actually see him, sitting there in his room, his fat, horrific specter reminding her of how her once beautiful boy had robbed her of so much. Now, all the degradation she had endured, the humiliating burden she'd had to carry would be wiped clean by the loving hand of God. She had prayed, and God had brought her that funny little black boy and his Bitburg Supernatural Squad. That had led her to God's instrument, the Angel who would carry her soul to its final glory.

Still, there was something in the Angel's eyes that made her shiver with her last breath.

-17-

Cletus, shielding Eleanor from the drizzle of plaster and splintering rafters, crashed through the door to Mrs. Barringer's room just in time to see her breathe her last.

The stench was almost unbearable; the chamber felt as if it hadn't known sunlight or fresh air in decades. It was obvious that Mrs. Barringer had fled here some time ago and rarely if ever ventured out into the rest of the house. For a moment, Cletus imagined the sadness of the old lady's final days, shut up in this fetid oubliette, and all he could do was feel sorry for her.

He didn't know what she had done, after all, and Cletus was a pretty good guy. That's probably why, after what happened next, he never quite looked at Al the same way.

-18-

"Outta the way, Dave," Al said, and pushed past him through the foyer on his warpath from Connie Barringer's sepulcher. Stunned, Dave barely had time to get angry. He just stood, dumbfounded. Trying to understand what he'd witnessed.

Al had been bouncing around the room like a superball, his hands on fire and his eyes aflame.

Then, a shadow. A distinct but shapeless mass of utter void at the center of the maelstrom. Al's flaming fist exploding it like a flash-bang against the Kandahar sky.

And like in Kandahar, Dave paralyzed on the sidelines.

He ejected the thought from his head like a jammed round from the chamber of his M27, loaded a fresh clip bereft of his personal recriminations, took aim at the ghost and what had been done to it.

He could understand the tremors, the wind, the exploding electronics gear. All of that was possible, expected even, when dealing with a paranormal incursion of such intensity.

But, unless he'd just lost it, he'd watched a man he'd known for years punch a full-body apparition into nothingness, and he just wasn't sure what to make of it.

-19-

Al burst into Lady Barringer's nest, still shedding plaster and dirt. He startled the living shit out of Eleanor and Cletus, both of whom saw the look in his eyes and got the hell out of his way. He went straight to the bed where the old bitch still lay.

She slithered from her body, a thick ichor of ignorant cruelty clinging to her shade like a stillborn's afterbirth. A steamy cloud of befuddled incomprehension clung to the ghost, putrescent and oily as unwashed rape. The stench of it stung Al's eyes, and what he felt at the sight of Mrs. Barringer now made his initial fury pallid and weak beside it.

She didn't understand. She didn't even recognize the evil she had inflicted on her son, and likely never would. *She fucking should have.*

Dave, always the battlefield commander, came hot on Al's heels, but Cletus held him up.

Al halted, hands flaring, at the side of the bed, and bellowed, "YOU!"

-20-

It was a wicked thing, thin and bent and withered like the switch an old hag would beat the neighbor's grandchildren with. It lingered near the body, confused, growing angry. In the moments before Cletus and Eleanor burst in on her tomb, Mrs. Barringer crept into the afterlife like a carrion insect.

From the listless ether, the portal to the world that would come next began to appear, and she knew that judgment awaited beyond it. A voice from somewhere outside herself, toneless and without language, resounded in her mind. It told her in simple terms that she could go to whatever judgment awaited, or she could stay in the place where she had died until the final verdict was rendered on the world.

Mrs. Barringer's ghost saw the door, red and fuming, and made her choice. She sure as hell wasn't going through that. "You!" someone hissed beside her.

It was her angel, the man she had been so sure God had sent to bring her home. Looking on him now, she knew what he was, and he was no servant of any God she worshipped.

"He was your son! He was your son and you hid him in filth and watched him die!" Al's fists shone brighter than the headlights of an oncoming truck, flickered with grasping fingertips of ghostfire.

The shade roiled its eyes at her deliverer, a contemptuous knot tying itself on her emaciated face. She had been a fool to think this rasping, barking man was a servant of God.

"You," she said. Mrs. Barringer's voice was the vacant wheeze of an empty fire extinguisher aimed at a blaze that had no intention of being put out. "You are no angel."

Al about damn near choked on the laughter that ducked its way past his rage. "Lady, if that ain't the fuckin' truth, there isn't one."

Then he called up every ounce of violent retribution he could muster, balled it into a fist that crackled with fire that would have made Hell envious, and punched that ghost bitch right in her goddamned ghost bitch face.

In her second death, Mrs. Barringer felt a pain more raw and primal than anything she'd known in life. She shattered under the impact of a fist she never even saw coming. For a moment, she wished she'd gone through the door.

Then she simply ceased to be, lost to whatever unknown unknown lurks beyond the afterlife.

-21-

Al waited for the pieces of Mrs. Barringer to reassemble themselves and go through the door.

They didn't.

Instead, the flames inside the portal quelled, red faded to black, and the passage just winked away.

"Oh well," he said.

"Snatchrag had it coming."

-22-

Nobody shat themselves, but all three Ghost Geeks looked as if they might at any moment.

"What the hell is wrong with you guys?" Al said, puffing from the exertion of the last few minutes; cardio wasn't exactly his thing. Dave, Eleanor, and Cletus were all staring at him; more directly, they were staring at his hands. His glowing, pulsating, flame-flicking hands.

"Oh that," Al said. "Ghostfire. That'll wear off in a minute. Howbout we get the fuck outta here before this whole place comes down around our ears?"

Dave moved to block Al, but Cletus pulled him back. As he passed her, Eleanor put a hand on Al's shoulder. He looked her in the eyes, her sweet, beaming eyes, and saw her smile reflecting his own.

"Al, baby," Eleanor said. Amazement and incomprehension had a knife-fight on her weathered old face, but eventually gave up their arms and let concern have the floor. "What just happened?"

Al flicked his hair over at the corpse, then at where the door had been. He wasn't sure, but he had a good idea. It's not like he heard a voice or read a memo, but he kinda got the message anyway, because he, unlike most characters who find themselves confronted with the supernatural, wasn't a moron, and chose to roll with it.

"I'm pretty sure I just punched a ghost to death."

He wasn't sure what that meant, exactly, but he spent the several seconds of silence between him and the front door enjoying on a preternatural level the fact that he had just done a thing no one had ever done before. If he could go by the sudden upswing in the need for someone who could punch a mother-fuckin' ghost, he had to figure that he could go on using his particular set of skills to monetize his aptitudes indefinitely. By the time he got to the door and looked out over the lawn at the gaping mouths and awe-fuddled expressions of those who hadn't witnessed his miraculously badass exorcism of not one but two grade-A haints from a haunted-ass Victorian mansion, Al had already figured out a job title to put on the new business cards he'd have to get printed up.

That's when it hit him: no, not some cathartic sense of accomplishment, like he'd found the secret thing that would drive him through the rest of his life and let him become the engineer of his Universal Locomotive. It wasn't a sobering acknowledgment that his shitty life had become something more than he ever expected it to be, that maybe there was something bright and wondrous and magic in this world and that he could be a part of it. It wasn't even the inkling that, if life with super ghostpunching powers kept to the same tropes as the video games and pop culture he'd grown up with, he could probably find some decent loot around here if he looked hard enough.

What hit Albrecht Drue as he walked out of the house where he'd freed the incarcerated spirit of a sad fat kid and punched the ghost of an old lady hard enough to disintegrate her soul, was a four-foot length of two-by-four swung by a US Marine Corps Sergeant who didn't take kindly to long-haired flame-fisted freaks punching little old ladies in the skull.

Chapter Eight: Fuck You, Dave

-Verse 1-

Barringer Manor, about twelve seconds after the previous chapter

Getting cracked across the back of the skull in real life is not the same as it looks in a movie. That said, the one thing about it that stays mostly the same is how fucking much it hurts.

Sergeant Dave had counted on that, seeing as how he'd intended to inflict some real bodily harm on Al. If you asked him about it after, he'd probably tell you that he'd just seen the guy kill an old lady right after he'd watched him fistfight a ghost and that he feared for the lives of his friends. In other words, he would have lied right to your damn face.

If he'd been feeling a little more honest, he might have gone on about how he'd spent his entire post-Active Duty life hunting for ghosts and come up short, only for a no-discipline-having punk civilian drunk to not just find but somehow interact with the departed his first time out in the field. If he hadn't completely lied to you, he would have gone with that story, because even though it didn't excuse his behavior, it made his motivation understandable, relatable, and maybe even forgivable.

But it still would have been a crock of shit deep enough to serve the whole platoon.

Dave went upside Al's head with a two-by-four because he'd always wanted to go upside Al's head with a two-by-four, and he figured he could get away with it, given the circumstances. He watched as Al just tried to shuffle off into the sunset like he was some kind of goddamned Wild West hero, saw a piece of board loosened by the general chaos whipped up over the last half hour, and just did what came naturally.

What he hadn't counted on was the blast of golden flame that jetted from Al's entire body in response to the blow, a whooshing bellows-blast of eldritch fire that engulfed the front lawn of Barringer Manor and scoured it clean of darkness in a single flashing burst.

The fire didn't burn, but its sudden inflammation and immediate snuffing sucked in all the air for a hundred feet around, affecting a miniature sonic boom that knocked everyone but Al right on their asses.

Al stood there, smarting, rubbing the back of his cranium through the supple leather of his hood for a minute, pretty sure that he should have suffered a traumatic head wound, and fairly certain that he hadn't.

He stared down at Dave, his eyes smoldering with quick-time lashes of that same red-gold-red strobe-light of otherworldly brilliance. The resurgent ghostfire didn't last long, and Al felt it fade away like the doomed afterglow of hooker sex. Whatever fueled him had already consumed its kindling, and in the absence of a lingering haint, there wasn't anything to keep the fire burning.

"Fuck you, Dave," Al said, then stepped over the Marine's stunned body. He was suddenly tired, not nearly as drunk as he would've preferred, and would have kept on walking down the pathway back to Eldon and that cherry Fairlane if not for the flying bear-tackle Cletus applied to him.

There wasn't any flash of supernatural flame this time, just a giant, roaring slab of human meat taking a sputtering drunk to the ground like a fat cop on a Berkeley student who probably deserved it, but not in the amount he received.

"Stay down, Al!" Cletus said, laying one thick arm across the back of his opponent's neck while he used the other to twist Al's left wrist up into the small of his back. Al squirmed and wriggled, bucked hard enough take the three-hundred-pounder a foot off the night-slick grass, but couldn't get himself free.

In the frame of Barringer Manor's front door, Eleanor watched the melee unfold through a slow-motion filter, like her mind had ordered the rest of the world to slow down while it caught up to the things she'd just witnessed. She wasn't a stranger to violence- you don't get called Auntie in Jennings Heights without having a couple of scars to show for it-- but the craziness Al had just made her a part of was enough to make her take a step back from the reality in which she'd been living up until now.

Out by the Humvee and the Ghost Geeks Mobile, Sarissa, Grigsby, and Lyric were all playing stunned bystander, not a one of them able to find the words to make sense of what they were seeing or the voice to speak them if they had. Even without having a front-row seat for Al's little impromptu pugilistic exorcism, they'd heard enough through the walls and seen enough of the undercard to get that shit had gone three ways para- of normal.

For a couple of moments, the only sound on the estate was the muffled panting that squeezed its way out from under Cletus's massive butt.

Eldon finally fractured the still-frame image that had gripped the Ghost Geeks. Unconsciously, he fingered the questionably lucky rabbit's foot in his hoodie, shouted as he snapped out of his inertia and broke into a run. "What the hell, Cletus?"

Cletus looked up, and for an instant locked eyes with the hollering streak of incomprehension charging him from across the lawn. Under normal circumstances, Eldon displayed all the visible dexterity of a newborn giraffe, but just then his stride was certain, steady, and quick enough that the big man had thrown an arm out to protect himself before he even knew what he was doing.

The little guy went flying, hit the turf hard enough to make him puke a little.

Cletus turned three shades of white and sprang to his feet without the slightest hesitation.

Which is kinda something you don't want to do when you're sitting on top of a good two-hundred-twenty pounds of angry drunk, especially when that angry drunk happens to be a dirty-fightin' Texan who's suddenly grown weary of all this shit.

Al rolled over on his back and planted the toe of his boot so far up Cletus's asshole that he tickled his prostate, and Gargantua Hayseed dropped like he'd been shot.

Al was on his feet in no time, gave Cletus a shot to the stones just so his other boot didn't feel left out, and swung around to face the spot where Dave still struggled to make words come out of his mouth.

"You might not be a ghost," Al said stomping over to Dave. The Marine scrambled back, the two-by-four still in his hand, the training he'd received in the Corps burned into his muscle memory. "But that don't mean I ain't gonna punch your ass to fuckin' hell anyway!"

Everything happened at once, and all Eldon could do was watch from the spot where he'd fallen, sucking wind and wishing there was something he could do to stop what was bound to come next.

Grigsby shot straight at the fracas, working something out of his peacoat, with Sarissa and Lyric right behind.

Eleanor struggled up from the porch, and only she and the Almighty could tell you why.

Cletus spat blood and tried to stand.

Dave swung his club at Al's head, caught him in the temple, collapsed him like a prize steer taking a bolt gun to the head.

The Marine towered over Al, who didn't do a damn thing because this wasn't a movie and he'd just taken another board to the dome.

"You piece of fuckin' trash!" Dave said, raising his bludgeon for another attack. "You loud-mouthed, alcoholic, low-life piece of shit!"

He used two hands, and even with Al's jacket absorbing some of the impact, the crunching slap of wood breaking ribs was loud enough to echo across the yard.

But it wasn't louder than the gunshot.

Dave froze, still as a burglar when the lights turn on.

"Next one's in your balls, mate," Grigsby said from behind the smoking barrel of the Beretta he hadn't pulled in years.

None of this made any sense, at least not to Eldon, who had barely gotten back some of the wind knocked out of him by Cletus's reflexive attack.

Dave threw down his board, scowling, seething. Grigsby relaxed slightly but didn't lower the weapon.

This should have been the happiest moment of Eldon's life-- hell, it should have been the same for everyone in the Bitburg Supernatural Squad; they'd all just been part of a major supernatural event, and even though he hadn't directly seen what happened after he'd escaped the house, he knew it had to have been something amazing. But his best friends in the world were trying to kill each other and he didn't even have the breath to ask why.

Sarissa caught up to Grigsby, lunged at the gun in his hand. She didn't have the skill to take it away, but she weighed more than the Department of Health would have recommended, and that was enough to at least knock him aside.

Grigsby reacted so quickly you'd have thought he was some kind of secret ninja. He just felt that two-and-a-half-bucks' weight of insufferable self-absorption break the surface tension of his personal awareness bubble and switched on his automatic defense system or something; one second, Sarissa was flailing at his shootin' hand, the next she was spun around and three centimeters shy of getting a pistol-whip to the bridge of her nose.

If whatever reflex that made Grigsby go all Jason Bourne on the Ghost Geeks' resident psychic hadn't also made him stop just short of smashing her face in, there might have been a reason for Dave to take umbrage. But Grigsby did stop just short of rearranging Sarissa's face because he wasn't the fucking psycho people who weren't Al imagined him to be. He even held up his hands and let the pistol spin into a submissive grip, to show that he wasn't up for any further violence.

Eldon watched Dave snatch up his club and turn it on Grigsby, and he still doesn't understand why Dave wouldn't just let it go; hell, he never really understood why Dave had bushwhacked Al in the first place.

He did understand that Dave wasn't going to make it across the two or three yards between them before Grigsby could bring the pistol to bear on him, and after that, there'd be no coming back from what happened after.

[Now, if you're the kind who thinks this story does just fine with Albrecht Drue as the only goddamned conduit for otherworldly forces, then skip the next four or so paragraphs, because they're gonna piss you off. But if you do that, it's only gonna keep you mired in the reality where only little miracles can happen, and the world at large is still bound to more or less be as unsweetened a glass of iced tea as you were ever forced to drink.]

The truth is, Al didn't have much swing with the way reality worked; he was just a random fucker who got shown a little part of a larger world. As it happens, that's how most folks get to see any of it.

But there are some guys who work for their insight. Most of them never see the payoff, but sometimes it just so happens that one of them does.

Eldon closed his hand around the rabbit's foot he'd sewn into his hoodie. He focused his chi or anima or whatever else you want to call it because that's what all the knowledge a smart guy whose abundant free time had been devoted whole-hog to discovering everything there was to know about the occult, the paranormal, and the magical underpinnings of the universe told him he was supposed to do. In a way he never had before, he felt the living, rampant energy spill from his body into the little totem. He didn't stop to think about what he had to do; he just played his part in the circuit. Because he'd made it just for that purpose regardless of what he allowed himself to believe out loud, he let the insignificant little fetish gather and focus the wild free energy around him.

Back at the Cyclops, he'd almost spoken the words of a spell, only to be cut off by the arrival of a coked-up Network sleaze. He'd carved glyphs of protection into the stairwell that led from his home to the arboretum underneath, chiseling the stone just the way an eleventh-century druid had described, but never really had cause to believe they'd do anything but look cool. He'd even chanted incantations over his plants to make them grow stronger after spending weeks tracking down just the right nuanced pronunciations of words human beings weren't meant to pronounce. Eldon had crafted the rabbit's foot just as the ancient spellbook in his home library prescribed. All of these things he'd done because he'd really, truly, desperately believed there was real magic in the world, but he'd never been a hundred percent on whether or not any of it was more than him just screwing around, and he'd never allowed himself to commit to using his knowledge with the full force of his faith that it would work.

But now, he'd just seen some amazing things happen, his friends were about to maybe kill each other, and his sharp brain remembered every spell, hex, curse, and invocation he'd found over the course of a life spent searching for them. He didn't have time to question what was real and what wasn't.

"Just stop!" he said. He said some other shit, too, a whole bunch of syllables in the tongue of the Elder gods and the Old Ones who had been here long before the first dead guy had given up the first ghost.

The Ghost Geeks and Al, pretty much as one, stopped what they were doing and stared at the little guy in the hoodie and the Harry Potter glasses.

Eldon stood there, elation throwing down with shock on the canvas of his features, with disbelief sneaking into the ring with a steel chair ready to smash him over the back of the head.

"Stop it, guys," Eldon said. His voice wasn't much more than a whisper, his face just a Rorschach of imploring command. "Just stop it and go home and we can figure all this shit out later."

Al, his face uglier than normal but mostly intact, couldn't get any further than up to his knees, but still managed to get in a line, because that's how he rolled. "The fuck, Eldon? You havin' some kinda goddamned apoplexy over there or you just get your dick caught in your zipper?"

It might have been magic. It might have been the way Eldon had cut through everyone's momentary insanity by leaping around and screaming nonsense in tongues. Either way, the air of violence blew itself away as suddenly as the hurricane had died out the instant Conacher Barringer's corrupted soul had departed this plane of existence.

Dave dropped his two-by-four.

Grigsby pocketed his gun.

Eldon let go of whatever effluvial ribbon of liquid infinity had empowered him, let it flow back to where he'd diverted it from. Then he thought long and hard about how a preposition is sometimes the best way to end a sentence because that's how Eldon's overactive brain rolls.

Grigsby hauled his beat-to-fuck buddy to his feet, keeping a daring eye on the others; Cletus and Sarissa were all about making sure a seething Dave didn't get himself in any more trouble.

Like a pair of wan stars orbiting a black hole-- fragile lights ready to wink out at the slightest ripple of violence-- Eleanor and Lyric slid around the baleful center of gravity until they converged at Eldon's side.

"Again I say," Al said. Again. "Fuck you, Dave."

Sarissa had her pudgy fingers all over the Marine, cooing and soothing and pleading after his health and fawning over whether or not he was okay; he shrugged her off and contented himself with staring razorblades at Al.

"This ain't over, drunky," he said. "Soon as I get home, I'm callin' the cops."

"Call 'em right the fuck now," Al said. He jerked free of Grigsby, even though the damage to his middle would have been enough to put a sober man on injured reserve for a month.

He may not have been as drunk as he'd like, but Al was drunk enough to dust up his knuckles one more time if it meant punching the smug off Dave's face.

Her arms wrapped tight around a girl she'd known since one was in halter tops and the other diapers, Eleanor let Lyric hide in the warm haven of her surprisingly perky old boobs, mainly because she didn't have any words to challenge a warm set of tits for comfort and consolation. Auntie Eleanor didn't know what to make of these kids she called friends; she'd just-- they'd all just, Lord help 'em-- come face to face with absolute proof of the terrible, beautiful world that existed just outside their basic perceptions, and here they were, reminding her of the ugliest parts of that old ugly world.

Maybe it had something to do with them all being so young. But Eleanor had been around a long time, done a lot of things to keep her time going, and as humblingly glorious as it was to see that something was waiting after death, it was nearly as terrifying to know that there might be someone waiting for her explanations on the other side.

Cletus moved to back up Dave, just as ready to go as Al was; you don't shrug off a bruised prostate, ever.

Al blew him a kiss and said, "Fuck you, too, Cletus. Fuck you in Dave's ass."

Once again, it was Eldon who got between them.

"Dave, just go home," he said. "Al, get in the car."

Eldon looked like a winter-stripped tree in the path of opposing storm fronts. He felt like he might blow diarrhea right out his mouth, but nobody saw that; if anything, his inability to squeeze any more words out of his mouth lent him a silent kind of authority.

If Dave had bothered to say what was on his mind, he might have saved a whole lot of the shit that went down over the next few months. But he didn't ask how Al had done what he'd done. He didn't even ask why he thought he'd been given such a gift. All Dave did was lead Cletus and Sarissa over to the Humvee, usher them in, and start it up without another word.

"Eleanor?" Cletus said, leaning out the window. He was back to being an ambulatory Easter Island Moai, laconic as the house behind them. "Lyric?"

Auntie Eleanor squeezed Lyric tight, reclaiming sole possession of her boobs. She wanted to say something to Al as she passed by, but nothing would come. She knew he hadn't killed the old lady, but she also knew he'd done something, and what he'd done was maybe a lot worse. She did kiss Eldon good-bye, though, then clambered into the back of the truck.

The pretty little girl who never had anything much to say watched her go, enjoyed a little tennis match between Cletus's blank expression and the look of bewilderment dancing on Eldon's face. Finally, she waved to the big man, looked the kid in the eye, and said, "Fuck those guys."

Once they'd gone, Al stopped posturing and collapsed.

"Fuck me with a borrowed dick," Al said. He was hurt, and even though he knew Dave had never liked him, it wasn't just from the broken bones or the oozing rip in the side of his face. "Least I never hit nobody with a goddamn piece of floor."

He stomped over to the Ghost Geeks Mobile, every step reminding him that he was getting less drunk by the moment. He got in the car, and let the luxurious embrace of the heated seat and the doe-leather upholstery get to work on what promised to be an excruciating reminder of his first night as a paranormal investigator once he got all the way sober.

That stray bit of reasoning scared him more than anything he'd had to face so far. With the last of anything he'd call strength, he wriggled around until he could reach the back seat, and by the time he found the mostly-expended bottle of

Schnapps, Grigsby had already climbed in and snatched it out of his grasp.

"You fake-Scottish fancy horse-fucker," Al said, not yet ready to turn back around and give up on his prize. "I may be beat to fuck, and I may be about to lose my gaht-damn mind, but if you don't make with the Schnapps, I swear to god I will see you in Hell before I forgive you."

Grigsby drained the bottle and tossed it out the window, looked Al right in the eye. "You were saying something?"

Before Al could see whether or not he had one more punch left in him, Lyric plunked herself down beside the ginger prick in the back seat, the sudden addition of her weight shifting the car just enough that Al had no choice but to spin back to the front.

"Ouch," he said, enunciating to keep from bawling.

Eldon plopped down next to Al, his head full of questions and his heart full of achy excitement. His eyes, though, were full of a grown man about to cry.

"Ahhh," Eldon said, his regular sheen of helpful exuberance smearing across his face. He poked a finger into the console between the seats. The top of the console retracted, revealed a glowing, frosty chamber of pure delight. Raised by oiled gears that might as well have been angel wings, a slightly chilled, unopened bottle of Fighting Cock bourbon ascended into the cabin.

"Eldon," Al said, finally letting a tear roll down his face. "I don't want you to get the wrong ideas, but I think I might love you."

-2-

Al watched Eldon and Lyric on the steps of her Industrial Age apartment building, the pair of them looking like a couple of high-schoolers waiting for the other one to make the first move on a good-night kiss. He was really pulling for the kid, but in the end, Eldon just stepped awkwardly off the stoop and damn near broke his neck. The girl retreated inside, and, contrary to every gem of experience Al had gleaned from thirty-odd years on a world where nice guys never get the girl, Eldon bounded back to his Fairlane like he'd just gotten news the doctor had meant 'candy' instead of 'cancer.'

Getting rid of Grigsby had been a proper, manly affair, one which did not challenge Al's constructs of how a guy was supposed to behave in any way.

"Home, my good sir?" Eldon had said once they'd gotten out of Founder's Row and started their long detour around Jennings Heights. Cardinal's Crest loomed above them like a gargoyle halfway through a strenuous dump, but staring at it gave Al a crux on which the whiskey-spins and pain-nausea could rotate. Grigsby didn't have a spare fuck to give about the moon-hued skyline or the bawdy lights of the asphalt/neon river that carried them away from Barringer Manor, while Lyric and Eldon couldn't take their eyes off the damned rearview mirror long enough to see anything but the other's staring back at them. So Al was left to appreciate the darkness of the night and the barren slumber of the Quiet City from his lonely seat up front.

Grigsby chuffed. "If by home you mean the only place I can wash away the PG-13 sexuality dripping off you two with a proper deluge of triple-x titties and potential STD transference, then by all means: let us to the *Gentleman Wanker*."

Grigsby voice-navigated the backstreets and boulevards with a surety that both pre-dated and eclipsed the bleeding-edge custom GPS Eldon had installed in the GGM, and without having to stop or double back even once, led them straight to the most storied and least hygienic nudey-bar/strip-club/den-of-iniquity in Bitburg.

That is if you didn't count the whorehouse under Saint Magdalene's, but that was a different kind of place altogether.

That ginger prick had reached in, scabbed a shot out of Al's bottle knowing full well that he couldn't stop him thanks to the busted ribs, then drummed his hands on the roof before bidding them adieu with a bow and a flourish.

"I'd ask if y'all wanted to come, but since I most definitely do and I don't see you three as anything but a right fuckin' impediment to that, kindly fuck off and I'll ring you the next time I want to see the goddamned veil between life and death whipped back for a tic."

That was how manly, whiskey-drinkin', ghost-punchin', bender-goin' men said good-night, and Al could have done well without having to see Eldon and Lyric make goo-goo eyes at each other for the half-hour it took her to remember how to get home from that particular bad part of a bad town.

Back then, Lyric didn't know one bad part from another, and her learning the difference was one of the few things Al would come to regret.

She'd offered to let Eldon take Al home first-- and anyone with half a goddamned brain or two-thirds of a ball-sack could have seen how she was angling for the chance to invite him in when they did get to her stop-- but the kid wasn't having any of it. He played he like didn't get the hint; at least Al hoped to God, the Devil, and John Bonham that he was playing because he feared for the little guy if he couldn't read the invitation written on her smile. But Eldon had questions and assumed Al had answers and wasn't a damn thing in the world he wanted more than that.

So when they finally did get Lyric home to her wide, tree-lined boulevard and its rows of townhouses where the only thing more secret than who the husband was fucking was which parent was fucking the kids up more, Al had looked Eldon in the eye while Lyric scrambled unaided out of the back, grabbed him by the collar, and laid it down.

"That girl," Al said. "She's just been through some shit. You give her as long as she wants to take, then maybe we can talk."

Of course, that had been a good twenty minutes ago, Al was running out of booze again, and it looked like his topple down the stoop had jogged something Eldon desperately wanted to say that would keep the conversation going for another half hour.

Sick of this shit as he was, Al laid on the horn, scaring the everloving shit out of everyone on Scathian Blvd. with a hundred-fifty decibel *Wilhelm Scream* instead of a more traditional but infinitely less awesome automobile horn. It served its purpose, set off a few car alarms just for fun, and brought Eldon back to the car.

You'd swear Eldon's goofy-ass grin was too big to fit in the front seat, but he managed to squeeze it all inside, even if it did make room by driving out Al's stubborn aura of gloom.

With just the two of them left, Al knew it was time to give in to the squirrel of curiosity Eldon had been struggling to keep caged, but that didn't mean he had to encourage it. He killed the stinging in his face with a slug of Kentucky Fission, lit up a Lucky Strike with swollen fingers and the Zippo he'd been carrying around for the last decade or so.

Eldon waited as patiently as he could for Al to take his first puff, the euphoria of the last few minutes losing its fight with the voracious inquisitiveness that normally occupied his mind. When he finally decided to acknowledge his true friend, Al shoved that squirrel of curiosity into a plastic bag and pulled the drawstrings tight.

"We gotta go back," he said, blowing smoke out the window because he wasn't a complete savage.

Eldon hid his irritation underneath the seat, right alongside the bag with the squirrel. He cut a little hole in the plastic so it could breathe, promising to let it out as soon as it was safe.

Eldon put the Fairlane in gear, pulled out into the street. "Any particular reason?"

"Loot," Al said.

"Loot?" Eldon said, sliding three tons of steed out into the concrete night.

"I defeated the boss mob," Al said. The pain in his side wouldn't go away and had begun to resist the efforts of the rapidly diminishing whiskey to soothe it. "Means I get to loot her lair. It's the only way that makes sense."

He didn't necessarily agree, but Eldon wasn't ready to give up on learning whatever Al had to teach him just yet, so he turned onto Rampart, kept Cardinal's Crest in front of him, and headed back to where he was pretty sure he'd cast his first real magic spell.

-3-

The old lady was right where the Ghost Geeks had left her, a testament to Dave's failure to make good on his threat of calling the cops. Or maybe he had; Bitburg's finest were just as likely to have gotten the call and transferred both it and jurisdiction over to the Row's private security. Either way, Barringer Manor remained just as they had left it.

It stayed that way for exactly no seconds once Al got back inside. As soon as they got through the entry, he started wrecking up the joint like it had been talking shit about his mom. Everything that looked like it might hide a safe or a secret staircase leading to a treasure hoard got upended within the first ten minutes. After that, Al started emptying drawers, knocking over knick-knacks, and clearing bookshelves like a crackhead on the first night of a house-sitting gig.

Eldon let him have at it; he should have maybe felt a little guilty over the indelicate nature of their search, but if what Al had told him was true, old Lady Barringer deserved to have her house wrecked. Besides, he was pretty sure he couldn't have stopped his big Texan friend if he'd tried.

"She was an evil dried up cunt of a monster asshole," Al had said on the way out of Lyric's gentrified outpost at the corner of Rampart and Scathian. "She murdered her kid and she died of natural causes and that's all there is to it."

"And you just punched her soul straight to Hell?" Eldon said. As deft and inquisitive as Eldon's mind was, he had a hard time accepting the matter-of-fact nature of Al's adult-onset superpowers. "Because you can do that."

"Nope," Al said. "I punched her into oblivion."

"Right," Eldon said. "No red door for her. No blue door, either."

"Nope."

Eldon had chewed on that all the way to Founder's Row, where it struck him how odd it was for one of the oldest, richest parts of town to be so utterly free of visible security measures.

"Take it from a guy who learned it the hard way," Al said. "Place like this doesn't need walls or gates. Place like this has eyes everywhere, and those eyes belong to things with sharp teeth."

He had to work on his foreboding metaphors, but Eldon got the idea. He didn't have to know that Al had been playing with what his sense of personal branding insisted he call his *ghost-eyes* ever since he'd had to figure out how to occupy himself for the twenty minutes spent waiting for him to not get a good-night kiss from the fair maiden Lyric; Al could see the ghastly things lurking in the shadows between the stately manses and the ancient urban palaces, and all it took was looking. He'd seen the world around Connie Barringer the way his ghost saw it, and once he added up the obvious and rolled with it, it wasn't any kind of trouble at all. Because, as it turned out, ghosts were fucking everywhere.

In a way, Eldon could see them, too. He didn't see the phantoms or hear the chittering specters, but he felt the void they marked in the living energy of the world. He'd felt that omnipresent mystic electricity flow through him into the rabbit's foot totem; he'd felt it change and return to the world through his friends. All he had to do was feel for the parts where the living

magic wasn't, and the presence-- if not the forms-- of the dark-
ling sentries revealed itself.

"Mother of fuck-shitting whores!" Al said, the sound-- if
not the fury-- somewhat deadened by the walls between them.
It was just the start of a truly epic litany of filth that fed and
expanded upon itself as Al intensified his search through the old
lady's personal quarters.

Eldon continued to hang back, not quite sold on the idea
that just because the ghost of a seventies-era pimp/stereotype
had been guarding a secret treasure chest, every lingering spirit
had a similar cache of loot just waiting to be claimed by whoever
punched it to the next stage of existence.

As Al rattled on down the hall, inventing more expletive
gerunds than the English language should have allowed,
Eldon drifted through the wind-ravaged house, exercising
his nascent awareness of the larger world. In the room where
Conacher had died, he could feel the emptiness that lingered.
From the part of the house where Al continued to redress the
absence of words like "whore-diddling," "twat-chewing," and
"rumpus-raping," he could almost taste the bitter traces of
shame.

But it was the front chamber where Cletus had set up basecamp for their investigation where he felt the most nothing he
could imagine. The arcane-- because at that point, there wasn't
any reason to quantify anything outside of a mystical linguistics
set, as far as Eldon was concerned-- pulse that had destroyed
most everything of an electronic nature did one hell of a number on the gear they'd left behind, and Cletus had made off
with whatever hard drives that hadn't been obviously beyond

salvaging, but there was something about the remaining cairn of plastic and fiberglass that practically screamed at him.

Against all the laws of expectation and all reasonable concepts of hope, Eldon found a blinking LED amongst the rubble of tens of thousands of dollars' worth of high-end audio and video recording apparatus. Like a fish gasping for air in the wet shards of its bowl, the little green light demanded acknowledgment, and Eldon gave it. He followed the cord to the handheld Go-Pro Cletus had been wearing while he watched the monitors.

Eldon picked up the camera, stepped back for a few high-speed minutes. An image caught his eye, so he let the thing play. As he did, a smile etched itself on his lips.

"Nothing!" Al said, exasperated beyond reckoning, almost to the point that he didn't have the energy to kick the shit out of the table and send anything that might have been saved flying across the room. "Not a gaht-damn, goat-fellating bit of loot in the whole taint-smoking house!"

Eldon didn't have a good reason not to show Al the footage of his battle against the Electric Banshee. The ghost didn't show up on digital, but anyone who wanted to doubt its veracity as proof of the paranormal would have had to figure out how they'd created such a stunning special effects reel on a damn Go-Pro. Still, Eldon kept it to himself, and the only justification for doing so was the niggling idea that if Al got a hold of this, he'd keep it to himself, and Eldon would never have a chance to see what other secrets it might be keeping.

Either that, or he just felt like screwing with his buddy, and it's hard for a loot-ninja not to ninja loot.

They didn't talk much on the ride back, not until they pulled up in front of the shithole Al called home. All Eldon got the one time he pried was something about "the goddamned Universal Locomotive jumping its tracks," and anything else was lost in a short nap brought on by chugging the last of the whiskey. Whatever harried Al's dreams made itself apparent on his face, but that final squeal of the Fairlane's brakes must have scared it off.

When he got out of the car, he shook something out of himself that Eldon hadn't expected to see: a real, genuine, honest smile.

"Thanks, kid," Al said. "I mean, for the ride." There was more to it than that, but neither of them had time to get into it. "Just one thing I want to know from your side, though."

Eldon couldn't imagine what that would be, at least not until Al reminded him. "Ask away, kemosabe."

"How'd you get everyone to knock it off back at the house? I figured Grigs would have blown Dave's damn head off, but you got him to back off. How?"

Eldon just grinned and pushed his Harry Potter glasses up on his nose.

"Magic," he said.

Al didn't argue. "Neato."

Eldon drove off and spent the rest of the night watching the video of his best friend, Albrecht Drue, punching a ghost into the afterlife, and trying to figure out what he could do to make sure he was there when it happened again.

Because if Eldon knew Al, there was damn sure gonna be a next time.

-4-

For his part, Al spent a good chunk of the rest of the night pray-
ing to the Porcelain God, because once Eldon dropped him off,
he tore into his emergency booze like a goddamned Tasmanian
Devil on a henhouse. To say he got drunk would be akin to saying a fish got wet, then not qualifying your statement. Al drank
enough goddamned whiskey to completely forget every damn
thing he'd ever known about France, logarithms, and anything
he might have done in the time between getting dumped at his
shithole and whatever day it was he finally ran out of booze.

It was another week of puking, howling, and damn near
dying before he even thought about sticking his head out the
door, his only companions being that stray cat and the mailbox
snake who still refused to reveal the reason for its presence.
There were times during that week when he would have been
happy to die, times he refused to eat because he just didn't want
to deal with waking up again.

No one came banging on his door to see what was wrong.
No one heard him retching and came running to his rescue.
All he could do was suffer in his sweating solitude and wait to
either die or get so goddamned bored of lying around in his filth
that he had no choice but to get up and see what was left of the
world outside his little oubliette.

When he did finally stitch up enough humanity to venture
outside, his first stop was his mailbox, because responsibili-
ties, man. He didn't remember the number because he didn't
have to; his was the only box on the wall that still locked, and
most of the others didn't even have doors. Nobody else lived in

the shitty building where he'd died a thousand blood-poisoned deaths, which made it easy to tell who anything waiting inside the unlocked door was meant for.

Among the other, flatter crap that awaited him, a compact white box demanded immediate attention. Not having the strength to fend off such demands, Al tore it open, vaguely remembering that he'd ordered some shit online at the very start of his bender.

He got the box open, pulled out one of a few hundred two-inch by three-inch white paper rectangles. The stock was heavy enough to be expensive, and the embossed type on the printed side read clear and bold. It declared an e-mail address and a phone number, along with his name and a job-title in black *courier new* type. A red slogan underneath in a deliberately contrasting sans-serif that-- because Al wasn't a complete dick-- wasn't *Helvetica*, gave it that funny 3-D effect, which was way more than Al's empty stomach should have had to deal with just then.

It read,

Albrecht Drue, ghostpuncher.
I punch ghosts,
right in their goddamned ghost faces.

Al slapped the business card against the back of his hand a few times, acknowledged that it could use something-- like maybe a cool logo of a fiery fist smashing some fool ghost in the head-- in the way of some visual pizzazz, but that it'd do for now.

Never one to question the shit he came up with when he was fucked out of his goddamned mind on whiskey, supernatural fisticuffs, and the acquisition of loot, he figured he might as well start small and see if he couldn't make a go of things.

After all, he was unforgivably sober at the moment, booze wasn't free, and no matter how much he might have wished it otherwise, he had some miles to go before his Universal Locomotive pulled into its last stop.

Framing Device Two: Still Pip

Cardinal's Crest, right about the same time as what just happened at Barringer Manor

Pip was bored. As a matter of fact, he was motherfucking bored. Scratch that.

Pip had passed boredom a long time ago, left ennui and tedium behind like they were old, not particularly memorable ex-girlfriends, and barreled headlong past monotony with the unenthused sighs of a neophyte jogger realizing that yes, he probably could go another mile, but what was the fucking point?

After that, madness entertained him for a bit, what with the whole wailing and gnashing of teeth being fun enough ways to pass the time, but all the affectations of insanity proved tiresome. His heart just wasn't in it. He missed his wife, and that longing was easily enough twisted into an implacable rage at her death. So he'd set about locking himself in an eternal battle with that damned jailor of his, but even that lost its edge after a few decades; there were just so many times they could murder one another before it got old, and, even worse, it kept him thinking about a love he knew he would never know again. You'd think he and the Witchfinder might have developed something like a friendship after a while, but apparently, mister high-and-mighty Servant of God couldn't lower himself to find amicable companionship with a servitor of the Beast-- his words, not Pip's-- so the Witchfinder's spectral self just flitted about the keep snuffing the life from everything it saw. Pip found himself left to his own devices, which meant he had the run of the house and the keep, but after a couple of hundred years, there just wasn't shit to do.

In life, Pip had enjoyed nothing more than a good screw, some fine spirits, tasty foods, and interesting conversation. Well, the solitude denied him two of those, and his unnatural state the others. Probably a good thing about the latter; all the comestibles had disappeared centuries ago, and he'd spent a good ten years drinking every last drop of whiskey, wine, and whatever else he could find, with the resultant hangover something he absolutely did not want to go through again. He didn't need to eat, he wasn't thirsty, really, but god damn if he couldn't use a fucking drink right about now.

Even the books in his vast library hadn't taken much more than a hundred years to get through, which was good, because most of them had long ago turned to dust. It was in one of these, some unnamed Kabbalic scripture guarded against time by spells far stronger even than the ones keeping him bound to the Crest, that Pip had learned the art of astral projection. At first, he thought he'd be able to free himself from his dungeon, but all he could do was go out and watch, like some deranged pervert, as the world went about its natural progression towards modernity, then come back to his body and have a good long wank. Still, it kept him up on current events, and once they'd been invented he could always find a movie to watch; the Cinerama over in Bitburg had probably kept him as close to sanity as could be hoped.

Yet no amount of masturbation or movie watching could ever replace actual fucking or just getting out of the house and doing something every once in a while.

So, when it's said that Pip was bored, sitting there in the loge above his library, there should be no misunderstanding just how utterly, inconsolably, unremittingly bereft of anything interesting he felt at that particular moment.

The moment in question being the same one when Dax Vagance et al. started unloading their SUVs in the courtyard of his beloved Cardinal's Crest. A twisty pink smirk unraveled across his lips; a little bird of joy fluttered in his unbeating heart: he knew these idiots from TV. Whatever else, this at least promised a momentary distraction. Quite effortlessly, Pip let his cosmic essence-- he wasn't sure whether or not he still had a soul-- slurp out of his body and drift outside to watch the show.

*   *   *

Age hadn't done shit to the Crest, except for maybe making it look even meaner. Before, there had been light and life, the stink and aroma of baking bread and burning garbage. Now the vines crept up the red-brick walls, creepers vining their way through the gardens, etc. etc. and all that. As the sun slunk behind its far walls, it drew a shroud over the Bitburg's long-serving sentinel. The thing was, before the Witchfinder came, Cardinal's Crest had been a home and a haven for over a hundred people, regardless of it being a fortress. It had been host to parties and feasts, births and wakes. It had breathed.

Now, it was a grave.

*   *   *

Dax jumped out of the lead SUV, absolutely pumped-- *PUMPED, BRO!* -- to finally be here, at Cardinal's *Freakin* Crest. He bounced up and down like a boxer before a fight, even threw some punches for good effect. This was going to be a monster of a Gravewalk-- a term he'd coined, by the way, even though no one ever gave him credit-- and he wanted to make sure the guys knew it. He knew they looked to him for leadership, guidance, and even though they wouldn't admit it, pussy, but that was another thing altogether.

"Cardinal's *frikkin'* Crest, bro!" he said, shouting. The sound couldn't have been more out of place than a Klansman in line for a portapotty at the Million Man March. If he disturbed anything, it didn't show it; being that there was nothing to disturb. "Herman, let's get some establishing shots, okay? Make sure you get a nice panorama of the main keep and another of the house itself. Then I want a sweeping shot of the- oh, shit, bro."

Dax's fellow investigator, JT, and Herman the equipment tech were a little slower in their egress and a lot less showy in their enthusiasm, having spent the night before hooking up with some of the local color while Dax finalized his notes for the investigation.

"That's Benny's job, Dax," Herman said, digging crud out of his eyes with his middle knuckle. Dax was an okay guy, but his gusto put him somewhere between yapping puppies and irate husbands on the list of things Herman wanted to see right when he woke up.

The second SUV had, by this point, belched out the aforementioned Benny, along with Marianna, the cute redhead intern who just plain was not going to let Dax fuck her, no matter how hard he tried. This particular afternoon, Benny looked a little like Woody Allen on a cocktail of steroids and crack, dressed in an expensive but unaltered grey suit and constantly dipping a nail into a fresh pot of coke. He was a producer, their main liaison to *The* Producers, the guys who ran the whole show behind the show: if he wanted to bang bumps in front of God and everybody, that was his business. Benny and Marianna already had their gear slung over their shoulders, ready to bust out another of Dax's 'Gravewalks' and grab themselves another paycheck.

JT, after adjusting the parking brake, turning the wheels away from any potential danger, and ensuring that absolutely nothing was left awry, was last to let his feet hit the ground, the other end of him completely unaware that in doing everything just right he'd locked the keys inside, still stuck in the ignition.

"Alright, boss," JT said, not even slightly sarcastic. Dax was, after all, his boss, and if it wasn't for him, JT might still be stuck at a real job. "Let's get... wow."

The little cluster of Ghostquesters stopped dead in their tracks, gathered around Dax to try and comprehend exactly what it was he was pointing at. On the far side of the quad, tucked under an eave between the house and the keep, huddled a tangle of oddly well-preserved automobiles. As they crept their way over, they made out a Volkswagen bus, a circa 1950 Renfield Special hearse, even a 1970s police-model Crown Vic. Deeper in the shadows, even older conveyances had been tucked away: horse-drawn buggies; a couple of artillery pieces; even a Civil War-era ambulance. They might have been parked here yesterday, for all the wear on them; there was no overgrowth, no vermin, nothing at all to rot them.

"Yeeh-ha, bro!" Dax said, his face a Pollock of elation spangled with joy. "Herman, get--"

"On it, bro," Herman said, shouldering his camera and framing Dax with the vehicles. A little mouse, Marianna padded over and hooked up Dax's mic; whatever else they were, the *Ghost Quest* crew were veteran professionals, and this was something that needed to be recorded before the initial shock wore off.

Dax tested his mic, shooed Marianna away. With a deep breath, he summoned up his Serious Investigative Gravitas, then waved for Herman to start the camera.

"Cardinal's Crest," Dax said, hitting both Cs as hard as he could. "Like a spectral Gargoyle, it watches over the city of Bitburg, just like it has for the last four hundred years.

"They say that since the night just after the Revolutionary War when it was consumed by an unexplained conflagration, no one who has ever set foot on these haunted grounds has ever returned. Well, we can testify to that now— "

Dax swept an arm over the cars, a magician's reveal. "The last known expeditions to brave the rusting iron gates of Cardinal's Crest either walked home or never left and are still here, waiting to tell their stories."

*　　*　　*

Pip's astral-self chuckled. He remembered some of those guys; the last ones were a bunch of Catholics looking to gobble up his home for some kind of monastery bullshit. He'd had a nice long giggle over what the Witchfinder's shade had done with them. His normal cruelty inspired to new heights by bitterness over his imprisonment and his god abandoning him, Pip would wager.

If Dax Vagance thought the lost cars impressive, wait until he found what was left of the drivers.

*   *   *

"Great open, Dax," Benny said. "Why don't you all check your gear while Marianna and I set up base camp?"

"Forget that," Dax said. "I want to go in right away, get a preliminary scout-through before we set a single camera down. JT, on me; Herman, keep the directional mic running."

Dax strode towards the looming maw of the house's main door, propelled by something he hadn't felt in a long time. They'd been under the gun of producing a weekly show for so long that they could, and often did, make the most mundane place imaginable seem like it served as host to Satan himself, but this was different. This was what it was like before the show, before the fame, back when it was just him and JT sneaking around abandoned buildings looking for something the living world couldn't offer.

"Boss," JT said, struggling to keep up. "K2's going nuts."

Sure enough, the handheld meter they used to measure potential paranormal energy had *Spinal Tap*ped and let out an almost frightened buzz.

*　　*　　*

The K2 surprised Pip a little bit by actually detecting him, and he couldn't resist playing with it for a sec. This elicited a flurry of commentary from the crew, and he wasn't sure, but Dax might have cum in his pants. *This was going to be fun!* Astral Pip bled his way back to his body; there was a lot more he could do to screw with these guys from there.

Back to himself, Pip flew from the Library to the grand rose window overlooking the courtyard. Halfway there, he stumbled, the sword poking through his heart having caught on a corner of stonework; he'd been trying to pull the damned thing out for hundreds of years, but it just wouldn't budge. He ignored the blade, reached out with his mind, and took hold of the iron gates outside, four centuries' corrosion offering no challenge at all as he swung them shut with a thought. He'd had time enough to learn all sorts of neat things his mind could do and practiced them daily just to pass the time.

*   *   *

The K2 dropped to almost nothing all at once, and the group let out a collective gasp. The gasp turned into a shriek at the sound of the gates clanging shut a few dozen yards behind them.

"That did not just happen," Marianna said, pale and cold. She'd taken this job because she wanted to work in TV, not because she believed in ghosts or any of that stuff. Two years of running around the country and making scaredyface at every little bump and clang hadn't changed any of that, and she wasn't at all prepared to change it herself.

"Yes it did, bro!" Dax said, bouncing around like a pogo stick on crack. "But did we get it on tape?"

"Sorry," Herman said. "I missed the gates, but I sure as shit got that."

Four sets of eyes traced a line from Herman's camera to the rose window, and four sets of eyes could not blink away what they saw. There was a man standing there, or at least the shadow of one, and it was watching them.

Dax Grabbed Herman's camera and shoved his face into the lens.

"We haven't even stepped inside the main building yet, and already Cardinal's Crest is treating us to a paranormal display unlike any we have ever seen. The iron gates behind us--" Dax swung Herman and the camera over to show them-- "just slammed shut BY THEMSELVES, and there, in this unedited footage-" Dax swung his equipment tech and his equipment back to catch the figure in the window- "you can plainly see a man watching us. Is this some living, breathing soul, a homeless man perhaps, or is it something from beyond?

"Find out as we delve into the heart of death itself when we Gravewalk into the legendary fortress of Cardinal's Crest. This... is *Ghost Quest*."

A few long steps towards the house later, Dax realized that he was by himself. Annoyed, he spun on his crew, not a one of whom had budged an inch. Herman stood dumbfounded, camera hanging limp at his side, staring at the man in the window.

"Come on, guys! This is it, let's go! Benny, Marianna, grab your gear and let's get inside before he gets away!"

JT crept forward. "Dax, what if that's some crazy psycho? I mean, it's not like we had to get a permit to go in. There could be someone, anyone living in there."

Dax had a soothing rejoinder ready, but Marianna squashed it. "And what if it's not? What if it really is some sort of ghost, or worse?"

To Dax's shock, Benny was the one to step up and step in, tearing himself away from the pack to stand at Dax's side. "Exactly. What if it's not? What if, after all the bullshit cases we've had to go through, we actually found what we were looking for? This is *Ghost Quest*, people; not Ghost Jerkoff." Snort.

Way to go, Benny.

"He's one hundred percent right, bros," Dax said. "A long time ago, I saw something, and when I told you about it you believed in me, and we've been searching for it together ever since. Let's not lose focus now."

"Besides," Benny said, whipping a 9mm Glock out of his waistband, "If it *is* psycho-killer bums, well, we can deal with all the psycho-killer bums that are dumb enough to come after us."

Dax pleaded with his eyes; his whole body clenched tight. JT shook his head in acquiescence; the fact that Herman had already re-shouldered his camera told Dax all he needed to know. Marianna, visibly shaken, cleared her throat.

"Fine," she said. "But I want to be in this one. Part of the team, not just the girl in the background, off-camera."

"Done, you're in. Welcome to the team," Dax said. "Now, let's Gravewalk!"

*   *   *

Pip pressed his palms together in front of his chest, clapped them from the wrist, and bobbed back and forth on his heels like a schoolgirl waiting for her birthday cake. There'd been a time where the coming slaughter would have disgusted him, but three hundred years alone had done away with that part of his psyche. As the *Ghost Quest* crew humped their gear into his home, all he could think about was how much he wished he had some popcorn... and, to a lesser extent, how much he wished he knew what popcorn tasted like.

*   *   *

For the first time in decades, the grand doors opened on the great hall of Cardinal's Crest's main keep, a thin, reckless stiletto of daylight shivving the derelict black. Because it knew better, the light retreated almost as soon as it pierced the darkness, scurrying away like a kid who stepped in on his parents having sex. The sun set on Dax Vagance and his crew, leaving them to the mercy of the lifeless fortress.

"Go ahead and switch on the night-vision," Dax said, leading the way. His enthusiasm, though not even slightly diminished, tempered itself with wariness. The air here was stale, still, stunted; the bricks and stones held their breath. "Benny, Marianna, let's rig some lights and find a spot to set up base camp."

No one else spoke; whatever dread Dax felt, they felt more strongly, and no amount of speechifyin' was going to allay their fear. Herman couldn't keep the camera steady, and JT was having trouble making his feet carry him any deeper into the endless single shadow their world had become. Still, they all fanned out and jumped into the routine they'd come to know so well.

Guided only by the light of the camcorder he used to supplement Herman's footage, Dax hadn't taken ten steps before he tripped on something dry and brittle. He panned the lens down, then jumped back.

"Holy shit," he said, breathing hard. Staring up at him from the faded carpet, limned in the grey-green sheen of unnatural electronic sight, was the face of a man, forever frozen in a scream that hadn't stopped until after he'd died. Dax swept the camcorder across the floor, broken shapes suddenly apparent all around him.

Marianna, focused on her work instead of her trembling fingers, managed to get a lantern plugged into the generator. It was a good lantern; the kind cavers use to keep themselves safe and sane a thousand feet underground; she'd picked it herself. That was the kind of crap they'd been having her do for years, going off and picking up all the stupid inconsequential junk they couldn't do without. But now, she was going to be part of the show. She'd have her name in the credits right there next to Dax and Herman and JT, and the last few years of her life would finally have been worth something. She stood up, a bright bulb of pride managing to outshine her trepidation, then flipped the generator on. A strumming rumble preceded the light, and light preceded the terror.

They all saw it at the same time, illuminated in a single stroke by Marianna's fancy lantern: it wasn't just that no one who dared the Crest ever came back; they never even got past the entrance. The pillowy hedonism of Pip's home served now as the plush floor of a charnel house, a hundred or more bodies scattered about like toys after a tantrum. Dax stood in a cluster of slaughtered clergymen, their robes still intact. The corpses betrayed no sign of what had killed them, but the wracking agony death sculpted upon them hinted at horrors beyond imagining. These shattered priests were just one of a dozen clutches of the dead, tidy bundles of mummified bone and sinew representing three hundred years of failed attempts to breach this chamber.

Watching from his hidden roost, Pip couldn't resist. Like a puppeteer twitching life into his marionettes, he twiddled his fingers toward the bishop whose rest Dax had disturbed.

One by one they rose, herky-jerk stop-motion caricatures of living men, the dozens and dozens of trespassers murdered over the centuries. The effect on the Ghostquesters was immediate and totally satisfactory to Pip's sensibilities, as they just freaked right the fuck out.

"Zombies!" Benny shouted, whipping out that Glock like a Crip in Compton. "Headshots! Headshots!"

The crack-crack-crack ratta-tat-tat of Benny's pistol rang in the ears and drowned out the cries of Dax's crew; it would have been an impressive display of bravado in the face of terror if he'd have hit anything. Anything besides Herman's camera, anyway.

The exploding camera pretty much meant the end of Herman, the equipment tech. He hit the ground hard, Pip's puppets falling on him in a dogpile. They didn't eat him or anything, what with them being animate corpses and not ghouls, but the weight and the shock were enough to pin the tech to the stony floor.

Dax froze, staring into the empty eye sockets of the priest at his feet as it tried to claw its way up his leg. JT flew to his boss's side, swatting at the monsters with his camcorder. Benny kept firing, emptied one clip, and managed to reload before he finally managed to blow the head clean off a guy who looked like he'd stepped out of a Civil War reenactment. Marianna never even got a chance to get clear of the generator before someone went and spoiled Pip's fun.

"ENOUGH."

The voice was sandpaper and the sea crashing against a floundered ship, and with it came a swirling wind that scattered the not-quite-zombies pell-mell like an angry loser flipping a

Monopoly board. Gripped by the will of whatever new malefic entity had stolen over the hall, Marianna's lantern exploded. Fire jetted as high as the ceiling, carpeted the rafters, threw cruel illumination over the little mouse of a PA. Much as they had almost three hundred years ago, the flames guttered together in a single finger of heat and hate that traced the cord back to the gas-powered generator. The engine ignited, and suddenly Marianna no longer cared about having her name in the credits, or anything but the fact that she was being burnt alive.

With nothing left to light it but the sputtering torch that had been a pretty little production assistant who was never going to let Dax Vagance fuck her, the darkness of Cardinal's Crest rushed in again, engulfing the hall and the doomed souls inside it.

Dax felt a scimitar wind slash by him, heard the last gurgled pleas of his fellow investigator, JT. Benny lit the place up with another few rounds of nine-milli futility, only to have his existence replaced by a sound not unlike the one made when a frat boy crushes a beer can against his skull. When Marianna buckled into a slow twitching red ember, he knew that whatever they had found would have him next, and he very much disliked the notion that he was going to die on one of his Gravewalks, and no one would even get it on film. He felt an icy fist wrap around him, grip him from toes to nose, and he dared whatever it was to do its worst.

Now, it can't be overstated just how much of a douchebag Dax Vagance was. The fauxhawk, the black jeans fastidiously matched and paired with black Ed Hardy T-shirts, and the basic assumption that he was smarter, better looking, and more in-tune with the universe than anyone else in the room were all admissible evidence. And the tattoos. It's not that tattoos make one a douche; in fact, most tattoos are pretty cool. But when you come complete with barbed-wire on both arms, the LA Raiders logo between your shoulder blades, Kanji characters that may or may not translate as "Dumbass Whiteboy" down your spine, and forearm sleeves misquoting seven or eight trite Bible verses, that's a pretty good sign you may, in fact, be a douche. Dax had all of these inky bits and one other that didn't fit the mold.

When he'd signed on to do *Ghost Quest*, the Producers put a few quirky provisions in the contract. No smoking, no marrying, no paranormal research outside the purview of the show; these seemed pretty standard at the time. The one that felt a little less so was the tat they had him put on his chest. It didn't look much like anything, and it wasn't words. Just a bunch of weird symbols he couldn't translate. They'd also had their own corporate tattooist inscribe it, and the inks he'd used had left Dax feverish and itching for days afterward. Still, when it was finished, it looked pretty boss. Thanks to the admittedly odd contract stipulations and that free tat, he had nearly unlimited resources with which to pursue his dream of finding proof of the supernatural and showing it to the world. As much as he might have been a douchebag, a true, genuine quest for truth drove Dax Vagance, and that's not something that can be overstated, either.

So as the hand of oblivion wrapped round his creaking body, Dax reached down inside himself and tried to grab hold of whatever it was that had been driving him all these years. Much to his surprise, he found it, and when he did, he cried out in a pain as pure as water drawn from a sun-stroked glacier.

The symbols on his chest began to wriggle and crawl, worms made of acid etching his skin. Unidentifiable scrawl snapped and twisted into a recognizable emblem of the occult, glowing with a pearly brilliance that lit the room as clearly as a full moon lights the midnight desert.

Dax looked into the eyes of the thing that had killed his crew and meant to kill him. What he saw was not fit for man to see, and as the specter fled, hissing and singed by the snowy light blazing off Dax's tattoo, so fled Dax's mind. He collapsed to his knees, blank, as the arcane glow receded. Then, like a wounded animal, Dax bolted from the great hall of Cardinal's Crest, disappearing into the indifferent night.

Pip watched him go, not altogether disappointed by the show, yet entirely un-blownaway. He'd wanted to play with his corpsepuppets a little more, maybe get the Ghostquest crew to pop off some witty one-liners, but the damn Witchfinder had to step in and ruin it all. Still, the burning girl was fun, and the guy with the gun had at least made a go of it.

Come to think of it, this had been one of the more entertaining instances of morons trying to get into the Crest. One of them had even survived. True, he'd probably go nuts, but who knew what might come of someone making it out alive?

"Possibilities, possibilities, possibilities," Pip said, picking his way across the floor. Something caught his attention, and to his delight, he found Herman, un-shot beneath the wreckage of the camera, still alive and struggling to extricate himself from the pile of corpses. Pip reached down and flung the largest body away, freeing just enough of Herman that he could breathe freely and see clearly. Well, see clearly if it wasn't so bloody dark. Pip snapped his fingers, summoning a diamond of flame that he held out so as to remedy that particular inconvenience.

"Look at you, my good man. Way to not be dead. And you might ask, what do you win for not being dead?"

Herman had given up on being terrified. He just wanted to get this over with; he'd seen enough horror movies to know that he'd been spared just long enough so that the monster could have his dramatic exit. Truth be told, he'd never really considered himself a main character in the play that had been his life, just a foil for Dax, a guy to fill out the shot. Not quite a sidekick, not quite a comrade. Just a Redshirt, really. Just now, he couldn't even think of his own backstory.

Herman didn't hear whatever Pip said next, just saw the fiery diamond stretch and flow like glass in the forge, then pour itself down his throat. It wasn't that bad, really; felt like really high-proof booze, all the way down to his belly. It didn't take long for him to die, and by the time he did, Pip had decided that, while not absolutely blown away by what the day had finally turned up, he was most assuredly no longer bored.

That night, the few who happened to look up at Cardinal's Crest, knowing full well that something was looking back, felt an even deeper shudder of fear than they normally would. Because the thing that had always been watching them in silence had now begun to laugh.

THE END

Acknowledgments

First, I'd like to thank my publisher, editor, and ardent supporter Charlie Franco, because he saw something over a hundred literary agents and even a few members of the Montag Press Collective didn't. I'm not quite at the point where I'd say "fuck those guys, I got me a Charlie Franco!" but, you know.

Gotta thank the Old Man because he made sure I had a hole to write in and a window to throw it out when I was done. The rest of the fam can ride on that because even when they gave up on me, it wasn't permanent.

There's an army of friends, acquaintances, blood-sworn foes, crushes, and ladies out there who might recognize little bits of themselves in the pages of this book; well, at least the ones who can read and aren't in the midst of a lingering dirt nap. Let's just say that I appreciate all that you did to help make me who I am on my way to finding a place that was worth writing from ... and for giving me the inner fortitude to end a sentence with a preposition when the situation calls for it.

Vigo Constantin of Seattle gets his own nod because if he reads this and doesn't, I ain't gonna like the response.

Most though, and forever, I gotta thank my wife, Harmoni deMae Miller. She said that this is all gonna work out just the way I wanted and she's been at least half right so far; hell, she even promised that my beloved Caps would eventually win the Cup, and we see how that worked out. She also gave me my Bubbagir, little miss Babylon Amadeus Miller, who won't be allowed to read any of this for another fifteen or so years, but without whom I wouldn't have made it through the last two-and-a-half.

So that's them thanked. Now I'ma thank everyone who bought, stole, or borrowed a copy of *Albrecht Drue, ghostpuncher.*, because I want you to demand the rest of the books. I got me some shit to do, and it's gonna take some paper, so y'all get on that.

Last, I gotta thank Mr. Albrecht Drue himself. He kicked his way into my world when there wasn't anything else in it and shows no sign of leaving any time soon. If he hadn't, I dunno what might've been, but the world's better for it.

Paul Daniel Miller was born in Austin, Texas just before shit there turned Weird with a capital W. The son of an Artillery Officer with a Ph.D. and a San Angelo Librarian, he was pretty much doomed to be both forever fighting and too damn smart to know how dumb he was.

Paul's formative years were spent all over the United States and he considers himself to be, for good or ill, an American in the classic sense: an enlightened criminal who never misses a chance to either help a body out or to tell someone to go fuck themselves. Details beyond that are pretty scarce, but it can be said that he spent his twenties trying to find himself, his thirties getting over himself, and whatever comes after trying to get himself paid.

Alabama's stuck with him now. He lives there with a wife, Harmoni deMae, who deserves better, a cat named Banshee who needs to calm tee-eff down, and a daughter, Babylon Amadeus, who's never gonna know the guy who wrote the books is the same one who changes her diapers.

As ever, if you'd like a word with the man, send some bourbon along first.

Made in the USA
Columbia, SC
18 May 2024

35416134R00174